The
UNSTOPPABLE
Letty Pegg

BLOOMSBURY EDUCATION
Bloomsbury Publishing Plc
50 Bedford Square, London, WC1B 3DP, UK

BLOOMSBURY, BLOOMSBURY EDUCATION and the Diana logo are trademarks of
Bloomsbury Publishing Plc

First published in Great Britain 2020 by Bloomsbury Publishing Plc
Text copyright © Iszi Lawrence, 2020
Illustrations copyright © Helena Perez Garcia, 2020

A catalogue record for this book is available from the British Library

ISBN: PB: 978-1-4729-6247-8; ePDF: 978-1-4729-6248-5; ePub: 978-1-4729-6245-4

2 4 6 8 10 9 7 5 3 1 (paperback)

Typeset by Newgen KnowledgeWorks Pvt. Ltd., Chennai, India
Printed and bound by CPI Group (UK) Ltd, Croydon, CR0 4YY

To find out more about our authors and books visit www.bloomsbury.com
and sign up for our newsletters

The UNSTOPPABLE Letty Pegg

ISZI LAWRENCE

BLOOMSBURY EDUCATION

LONDON OXFORD NEW YORK NEW DELHI SYDNEY

To Naomi Paxton (it is all your fault)
With thanks to everyone at The Jiu Jitsu Foundation

第一章

ICHI

Lettice Pegg didn't care if it was weird to put marmalade in porridge. It was just as sweet as jam and it looked more summery. She needed to feel summery. It was gloomy outside, with rain pattering on the window. Every day this week it had rained. She'd made a note of it in her policeman's notebook – a gift from her father, who was a constable. If it was still raining tomorrow, Friday, that would be an all-time record. A twelve-day streak.

Lettice was sitting at the kitchen table, watching her father eat his toast. They shared a teapot and marmalade. Florence Pegg, Lettice's mother, was playing the piano in the living room: playing a jolly tune that made the weather seem less bleak. Lettice knew her mother would be quietly humming the song to herself at the same time, still in her nightclothes and Lettice's father's dressing gown. They might not be wealthy, but they were the only family in the building who had a piano. It belonged to Lettice's grandmother who, despite threatening to take it back, had so far let them keep it. Probably because neither the piano nor her grandmother's servants would survive the journey down three flights of stairs. Besides, her gandmother already had plenty of pianos, and houses to put them in. And leaving it in their small London flat was a constant reminder to Lettice's father that he was of a lower class and had never learned to play as a child.

A glob of marmalade was clinging on to the end of her father's moustache and made tiny circles as he chewed. It went faster and faster in time with the piano. Lettice winced as the glob detached, and flew high through the air... Little did she know that the very next day, she would be flung, like that marmalade, rotating vertically in mid-air. Although she would be propelled off a little woman's back, not her father's moustache, and she would land in a massive pile of horse dung... not on top of the butter dish.

Whatever her father was reading in the newspaper was agitating him. His eyebrows dropped so far they

2

looked like they they were trying to climb down his nose. He caught her staring.

'Eat up,' he said.

'What are you reading?'

Jack Pegg looked over his shoulder towards the hallway that led to the living room. 'Some news that will upset your mother.'

Every bit of news upset Lettice's mother. Mrs Pegg was a suffragette and being upset by the news was her favourite hobby. Every headline gave her a burst of fresh outrage, making her bound out of the front door powered by righteous anger. She'd return hours later clutching plans to craft, rosettes to make, letters to write, banners to sew. Recently her big idea had been to get a telephone. And a badge press. Both things Mr Pegg had put his foot down about.

'Eat up, Lettice. School isn't fun on an empty belly.' He got up from the table with his second slice of toast still half-eaten in his hand.

School wasn't fun anyway, Lettice thought as she watched her father march into the hallway to put on the rest of his police uniform. He liked to look in the mirror while he did this. To make sure his buttons were just so. The maid, Tilly, had polished his boots a second time that morning. Mr Pegg was a particular man who would also polish them himself in the evenings after patrol.

It was a silly thing for either of them to do, Lettice thought idly. The information her father could get from talking to shoe shiners in the street would help his investigations. The boys who did shoe shining hardly ever turned up for school. They knew all the goings-on.

'Line up!' Lettice's father barked and Lettice set down her spoon next to her empty bowl and ran into the hallway. She liked this game. Her father stood by the front door in his full uniform, helmet under his arm, winter cape hanging from his shoulders. He looked so tall and scary – nasty people would be terrified of him, Lettice thought. It made her feel proud.

'Chop, chop!'

Lettice stood at the end of the line of coat hooks, back straight, eyes forward, heels and toes together, arms straight by her side. Her father started at the furthest coat hook, pretending to inspect the coats as if they were on parade. He looked each one up and down before nodding and moving on. Finally he got to Lettice.

'Aha, a new recruit!' he said. 'Name?'

'Lettice Pegg,' she said.

'Age?'

'Eleven and a half, sir.'

He bent over to look at her closely. 'Clean shoes, neat clothes... clean face. Brushed hair. Excellent. But I'm afraid I can't let you join. Do you know why?'

She knew why, but it was not the reason she gave. 'I'm too short, sir!'

'Indeed you are,' her father said, standing up and reaching into his top pocket. 'You need to grow to six foot to be a policeman.'

'And be a boy too, sir?'

'Do not answer back,' he said automatically.

'Sorry, sir.' Lettice looked straight ahead again.

'You need feeding in order to grow.' Her father handed her some coins from his top pocket. 'To school with you! Wait for Tilly. She'll be downstairs no doubt.'

He kissed the top of Lettice's head. She put on her hat and coat and he opened the door to let her out. The landing was ice-cold, but she skipped happily down the stairs.

Sure enough, Tilly was in the lobby, holding a duster and looking bored. She was only a few years older than Lettice and, despite a strict upbringing in the workhouse, she was very casual about her job as a maid.

'Raining out,' she said as Lettice bounced past her.

'You don't need to come with me. I'll walk with Eleanor.'

Tilly shrugged, and went back to picking at her duster.

It was only a short distance to school. The pavement was already filled with children heading that way. Mothers and maids bustled their charges against the businessmen and tradesmen marching briskly in the opposite direction. Groups of children walked together, the boys making crowing noises that Lettice could just about make out over the gusts of wind. A horse buggy trotted by a hansom cab, which was stopping to pick up a couple who were heading towards Westminster. A motorised van tried to turn around, causing a group of gentlemen on the other side of the road to wave their briefcases at the driver in frustration.

Lettice stood on the front step of the flats and scanned the children heading for her school. She immediately recognised Mabel's bright red coat and paused to avoid her, stepping back into the doorway. The last thing she wanted was everyone to see her arrive at school with the strangest girl in the class. Mabel never talked about normal things, just the weird books she read, or the insects she trapped or how much she enjoyed maths. She wouldn't shut up about them until she was satisfied that whoever she was speaking to was equally enthusiastic. Hard to do if the subject was woodlice.

Fortunately, Mabel didn't spot her; she was talking to one of her tight-lipped maids. Tilly's uniform was just a black dress and grubby white pinny, but this maid had little crests sewn on her cape and looked much grander.

There was a mix of children at Lettice's school. It was north of the river, and the intake included those who'd later go to private school, as well as children from less well-to-do streets like the one her friend Eleanor lived on. Lettice looked further down the pavement towards the noise of crowing boys and spotted Eleanor with her brother, Sam, turning the corner. Once Mabel had safely gone past, Lettice ran to meet them.

'All right, Lettice?' Sam was tall, and despite being a year younger than the girls he was already bigger than they were. His frame wasn't exactly beefy though. His limbs poked out of his clothing. His knees were the widest part of his legs and stuck out below his tatty shorts, shining a ruddy pink. Every twenty steps or so, he stopped to pull up his socks. Eleanor wasn't as skinny although it was hard to tell under her coat. Unlike her brother's, her sleeves reached her wrists.

'Good morning,' Lettice greeted them. Despite the drizzle, Sam beamed down at her. She was concerned about the grin on his face. 'Have you had some good news?'

Sam smiled knowingly. 'Mr Metcalfe said he was taking over your lessons.'

'Don't listen to him. He's having us on,' Eleanor warned.

'That's what he said yesterday,' Sam insisted.

'Liar,' Eleanor scoffed. 'Why would Mr Metcalfe take over the girls' lessons? And why would he tell *you* about it?'

'Miss Ward wasn't there yesterday, or on Tuesday,' Lettice pointed out. She was worried about the absence of her teacher. 'That's why we had to join Miss Troxel's class.'

'Exactly,' Sam said. 'Word is she's been sacked. Which means we get Parsons, and Metcalfe is taking over teaching you girls. I'm dead happy.'

'Why was Miss Ward sacked?' Lettice asked, but her question was interrupted.

'Why can't *we* get Parsons?' said Eleanor, outraged.

Mr Metcalfe was the worst teacher in the school. He took prayers on Wednesdays in the hall. Anyone he disliked would be made to stand up and face the wall for the whole assembly. He used the dunce's cap and cane more than anyone else. Parsons was wet by comparison. Lettice had never been taught by Mr Parsons, but she'd seen him walk around the boys' playground ignoring the punching and swearing. Mr Metcalfe, by contrast, marched about looking cross all the time. The only occasion Lettice had ever seen him smile was when he was talking to Miss Troxell, who took the infants. She never smiled back at him.

'I heard Metcalfe made a boy stand on one leg all lesson, and when the boy got cramp, he beat him,' said Sam.

'That never happened,' said Eleanor.

'He took Evan's lunch money too; made him eat out of the slops for a week.'

'Oh, that reminds me,' Lettice said, and took out her lunch money. 'Here.'

'You sure?' Eleanor smiled and took the penny from her. 'Thanks, posho.'

'Don't call me posh!' Lettice hissed. She checked to see none of the other kids were close by.

'What about last winter when he refused to light the fires?' continued Sam.

'There was a coal shortage!' Eleanor protested.

'The heaters downstairs were fine,' said Sam.

'So you think the infants and girls should have gone cold?' Eleanor asked.

'You have petticoats and boots. We have shorts. And stupid socks.' Sam pulled his sock up again. 'There was plenty of coal. He's just mean. Hates children. You'll see.'

'Won't. Because he's teaching YOU, not us,' Eleanor said stubbornly.

But Eleanor was wrong.

第二章

NI

When the girls reached their classroom, Mr Metcalfe was there: standing upright, away from the teacher's desk, silencing their nattering with a stern look as they entered, their eyes wide at the sight of the cane in his hand.

They scuttled to their usual places like mice to their hidey-holes.

Mabel was already sitting neatly at her desk at the front. Her black plaited hair and clean face were made more annoying by her expression of eagerness. She was as oblivious to the danger they were all in as she was to everyone's hatred of her.

Lettice followed Eleanor to their desks and slotted in behind her.

'Quiet,' Mr Metcalfe said to the silent room. 'I need two monitors. One to fill the ink, the other to check the fire. Two lads did it this morning as no one here had bothered.'

'Miss Ward usually lights the fire, sir.' Mabel's hand had shot up as she spoke. Thirty-nine pairs of eyes darted between Mabel and their teacher.

How did she do it? Lettice couldn't imagine just talking up like that. It had taken her several goes to speak to Miss Ward, and that was after a month of lessons. She had no problem with family, or kids her own age, but she hung behind her mother in shops. Her biggest fear was anywhere she didn't know everyone.

She could never interrupt a teacher the way Mabel had just done.

But if Mr Metcalfe had been about to punish Mabel he was soon distracted. Alice, two seats down from Lettice, chimed in, 'Miriam… Newman is the inkwell monitor.'

There was a murmur of agreement.

'SILENCE!' Mr Metcalfe walked over to Alice. His eyes were shining. He whipped out his cane and standing some distance from her pointed it at parts of her body. 'Dirty shoes. Tatty collar. And your hair is tangled. Show me your hands!'

Alice, her face nearly as red as her hair, uncrossed her arms and showed him her hands. Lettice wasn't sure what Alice was expecting: maybe a comment on the state of her sleeves, or to be told that her hands were grubby too. Instead, Mr Metcalfe struck Alice on both hands with the cane.

There was a gasp as everyone in the room jumped at the noise.

'NO ONE,' he barked, turning his back on the class and marching to the front of the room, 'CARES what you have to say!'

Alice sat down, trembling in shock. She hadn't uttered a yelp but Lettice wasn't sure how long that would last. Next to her, Angela looked outraged at this assault on her friend and was glaring at Mr Metcalfe like she meant him injury.

'I don't care what Miss Ward did. I don't care how things were done before. Your opinions do not matter. I am here to instruct you to use what little minds you have to keep you out of the gutter. No one attending this school is going to end up working in a factory or married to a layabout.' He looked straight at Alice.

'Name?'

'Carter, sir.'

'A lesson for you all,' Mr Metcalfe said as he marched behind the teacher's desk. 'Children are to be seen and not heard. Understand?'

The class was silent, scared it was a trick question.

'Understand?!'

'Yes, sir!' they answered.

Mr Metcalfe sat at his desk and inspected the register. 'I see you have all written a great many essays on literature, natural history and archeology,' he scoffed. 'Did Miss Ward realise she was teaching girls?'

Lettice wondered whether this was a question they needed to answer.

'Your maths is up to standard. Apparently. We will see. You –' he pointed at Miriam on the front row – 'seven times nine.'

'Seven times nine is… sixty-three?'

'You aren't sure?'

'No, I…'

'You,' he pointed. 'The fat one. Eight times twelve.'

Joan frowned. 'Eight times twelve is ninety-six.'

'Good. You.'

Lettice flinched. His cane was pointed at her. The back of her neck got all prickly. She couldn't remember anything. She felt sick.

'Three times six.'

She didn't know. She didn't know the answer. Three times five was fifteen, she knew that. Why didn't he ask that? Fifteen, add three…

'Eighteen,' she gasped. She looked at her feet. Her stomach was clenched. She felt dizzy.

'Nine times eleven.'

That was easy, nine times ten was ninety, just add nine…

'N-n-n-n… ninety-nine,' she stammered, still unable to talk properly.

'N-n-n-n-no!' he mocked her.

'But she's right!' said Angela defiantly from across the classroom.

Lettice felt a smidgen of happiness that Angela was sticking up for her. Angela usually laughed at her for one reason or another.

The feeling didn't last long. Mr Metcalfe walked up to Angela's desk.

'What did I say about answering back?' he demanded.

Angela instantly shut her mouth and hid her hands under her desk. Mr Metcalfe turned to Lettice. 'You do not know multiplication by heart. You're calculating the answers in your head. This is slow and inefficient and opens you up to possible failure. These girls know the numbers by rote. They have become instinctive. As one. Class! Four times four?'

'Four times four is sixteen,' everyone chanted.

Mr Metcalfe pointed his cane in Lettice's face. 'Women's reasoning is often faulty, but their memory is *nearly* on par with that of a man. In future, when you're purchasing items for your children, you will have enough calculation going on and not knowing your multiplications will only vex you further. What is your name, girl?'

Lettice couldn't speak.

'Pegg.' Eleanor jumped in. 'Her name is Lettice Pegg.'

Mr Metcalfe didn't speak to Lettice any more, but wrote something in the register. They were made to recite their times tables and, since it seemed to be the day for memory tests, to recount all the countries that made up the Empire.

As Angela had her pronunciation of the word 'Ceylon' corrected, a boy from the floor above ran down the corridor ringing the school bell.

Lunchtime.

'Dinner money. Now.'

Eleanor stood up eagerly and waited for Lettice to get the feeling back in her foot. It was the longest

Eleanor had ever gone without any form of distraction. Usually they would pass notes, sometimes a game of hangman, or see how far they could flick a spitball. They could never quite reach Mabel, so they'd aim for the crack in the high ceiling instead. Miss Ward wasn't as observant as Mr Metcalfe. He had even shouted at Miriam for scratching her head. Today, they'd sat so still the numbness had developed into pins and needles, and both girls giggled as Lettice hobbled to the end of the dinner queue. Eleanor tucked in behind her.

Angela handed her money to Mr Metcalfe, gazing at him with perfect disdain. Angela was very good at hate. It made her beautiful face pointed and scary. She could flip between welcoming and spiteful in a heartbeat. One moment she liked you, the next she was telling everyone you were an idiot. Sometimes it was because you had things she didn't, like a new coat or winter boots. Other times it was because you didn't have what she had. Like roller skates.

Being denied roller skates by her parents last summer had hindered all the progress Lettice had made at making friends with Angela and Alice. They had skated down the length of the playground, doing jumps and spins. All the children had applauded. It didn't seem to matter that Angela and Alice weren't from well-to-do

families, they were so carefree, confident and pretty…
everyone wanted to be like them. Lettice certainly did.
She was so very plain by comparison and so timid when
talking to adults.

If only she could make friends as easily as her
mother could.

Lettice handed her tuppence to Mr Metcalfe. He
took it and checked her name.

'Cabbage, wasn't it?'

She didn't correct him.

'Hold on…' He was looking at the register. 'Says
here you have first-class luncheon. I should have
thruppence. You only gave me two pennies. Where's
the other one?'

Lettice paused. She looked over to see Angela was
listening at the door.

She licked her lips and stammered, 'I… I always
have the second-class dinner, sir.'

This was true. Angela started whispering to Alice in
the doorway, curious about the hold-up.

'You can conduct your clucking outside!' Mr
Metcalfe informed them. He waited till they had left
the room. All of a sudden the air grew serious. 'Where
is the missing penny?'

'I have it,' Eleanor said.

Mr Metcalfe whipped round. He'd barely noticed the mousy girl until now. 'Why do you have it?'

'She gives it me every day, sir.'

'She gives it *to* me,' he corrected. 'Why? Are you blackmailing her?'

'N-n-no, sir!' Lettice stammered, her cheeks now tingling more than her leg. She wanted to explain that Eleanor didn't have the money for a big meal and she didn't get breakfast. By giving her a penny, she could make sure they'd both get a second-class meal and sit together. But she was nervous and could barely speak.

'Why give her the penny then? Do you consider her a charity?'

Eleanor interrupted again. 'Hardly anyone gets the first-class dinners; this way we get to sit at the same table and…'

Lettice wanted to say that this way they didn't get picked on. If you fitted in, you were less of a target. The first-class dinner table was right next to the teachers' table, on a platform in the school canteen. So few people had first-class dinners that there was only one table for the girls, and you had to sit with all the younger children – and Joan… and Mabel. You couldn't talk openly sitting there because the teachers could hear. Not that you'd *want* to talk to Joan or Mabel. Not unless you wanted everyone in the school to look at you and point.

There were several girls' second-class tables and a few third-class tables too. It was much easier to slot into those and be part of the crowd, even if only Eleanor and Miriam would ever talk to you.

'However noble you think you're being, giving money to the poor, the money is not yours to give away.' Mr Metcalfe narrowed his eyes. 'You're a thief.'

'Lettice ain't no thief! Her pa gave it her... to her,' said Eleanor, choosing her words carefully.

'Her father wishes her to have a hearty lunch. She is the property of her father and therefore doesn't have a choice in the matter. That was not *her* money to fritter on an imagined good cause.' Mr Metcalfe swished his cane. 'Neither of you will be having lunch today. Make sure you return all the money to your father.'

He slid the two pennies towards Lettice and both girls left the classroom. Lettice was bursting with indignation. The injustice of it!

'He says my father wants me to have a hearty lunch, then stops me getting any!' she raged as she hurried alongside Eleanor outside the dining hall. They were as close to the wall as possible, trying to stay out of the rain.

'At least you had breakfast. I'm starved,' Eleanor huffed.

'Sam's right. He is cruel,' agreed Lettice.

'You still got those pennies?' Eleanor looked hopeful.

'Yeah but…' Lettice was concerned. If Mr Metcalfe told her father what she had been doing all these months, giving away his money…

'You gonna give it back like what he said? Cos we could get us some grub after school.'

Lettice frowned. 'If my parents find out I didn't have lunch and I don't have the money either…'

'But you *will* have had lunch… just a late lunch and not a school lunch,' reasoned Eleanor.

'What happened with Metcalfe? Why did he keep you back?' Angela and Alice had rounded the corner.

'You weren't at lunch,' Alice said in an accusatory manner.

'No,' said Eleanor. 'Metcalfe wouldn't let us.'

'Why?'

Lettice panicked. Angela mustn't know that she was supposed to have the thruppenny lunch. It was only posh girls like Mabel who did.

'You know how Eleanor and I…' Lettice corrected herself, 'Me and Ellie have the tuppenny meal?'

'Yeah.'

'Well, Miss Ward has it written wrong. So Metcalfe thinks I have a first-class lunch and Ellie has a third-class,' Lettice lied. 'He was accusing Ellie of stealing a penny from me. Stupid.'

'He's mad,' agreed Alice. She was still holding her hands funny.

'Yeah.' Lettice could tell Angela didn't quite believe the story, but she was more interested in finding new ways to hate Metcalfe. 'Miss Ward better be back soon.'

'Where is she?' Alice asked

'Not sure...' Angela frowned.

'Sam said she was sacked,' Lettice said with a conspiratorial whisper.

'What for?' Angela asked, leaning closer.

'Could be anything. You seen the leash they keep teachers on?' Alice scoffed.

'We're gonna get some food after school anyway,' Eleanor said, bristling a little at her brother getting credit for this gossip and wanting to change the subject.

'We could buy him some butcher's bones and take Metcalfe for walkies,' Lettice said.

Everyone giggled.

'They don't keep the male teachers on a leash, they've hardly got no rules,' Alice grumbled. 'I've seen Troxell's rulebook they gave her. She's not allowed out of her house after eight at night and she can't travel anywhere with a fella who isn't her father or her brother.'

'That's normal isn… ain't it?' Lettice asked.

'How's she supposed to find an 'usband?' Angela responded.

'If she gets married she'll get sacked. That's in the rules too,' Alice said.

'So it makes sense to make it hard for teachers to marry,' Lettice concluded.

'Parsons is married,' Eleanor said.

'Is he?' Lettice looked surprised. 'I've never seen his wife.'

'Who do you think that woman was with him at Easter and the nativity and stuff?'

'That's his wife?' Lettice was shocked. 'I thought that was his brother!'

The girls cackled. Lettice grinned from ear to ear. She was doing very well at making friends today.

'The point is,' Angela said, 'you can't marry and have a job, not unless you're dirt poor.'

Eleanor stopped smiling. Her mother worked. Lettice noticed this and tried to change the subject.

'Poor Miss Troxell. Doomed to solitude,' she said, then, noticing the confused faces, 'She'll be a spinster forever.'

'Unless Mr Metcalfe has all his wishes granted,' Alice said.

The girls laughed again.

'I'm glad we skipped lunch!' Eleanor said. 'The thought of marrying Metcalfe… I'd be sick!'

'We'll get some food later, right?' Lettice said, hoping to invite Angela and Alice along with them.

'I hear the pies down Romney Road are to die for,' said a shrill little voice behind them. It was Mabel. She beamed at them. 'It's near Letty's flat.'

'My name is Lettice,' Lettice snapped. She didn't want anyone calling her Letty, not after last year when Angela had called her Toiletty and everyone had laughed.

Mabel's big brown eyes and stupid round cheeks didn't hide the slight trepidation in her voice. 'I know where we could go.'

'We weren't inviting you,' said Angela with a sneer.

Mabel weathered the rejection very well, ignoring the other girls and looking directly at Lettice. 'It's a good place. I have some money too.'

Angela and Alice exchanged glances. This was awful, thought Lettice. It was the first time Angela and Alice had approached Eleanor and Lettice. Almost like they wanted to be friends. And now Mabel was ruining everything. Smiling like an idiot. Offering to take them out. Like they were friends. She wanted her to just go away. But Mabel wasn't going anywhere.

'They serve this amazing vegetarian pie,' she continued ignoring the glares of all four girls.

'We don't like curry.' The words were out of Lettice's mouth before she could help it. Eleanor let out a cackle. Alice and Angela were grinning too. Mabel opened her mouth and shut it again.

Rumours circulated about Mabel's parents. She looked nothing like them. *Nothing* like them. Mabel was a lot younger than her three brothers. They were all fair-haired and blue-eyed. Mabel was different. Everyone knew Mabel was adopted. Except Mabel. She seemed oblivious to her dusky skin, her jet-black hair. Miriam thought she could be Jewish like she was, and so hated her for not admitting it. Eleanor at one point said she might be Spanish. Lettice, though, was convinced Mabel was Indian. Her posh voice was like the one Lettice had to put on when she visited her grandmother. Mabel was a fake.

Tears were welling up in Mabel's eyes. 'I don't like c-curry e-either.'

'You must eat a lot to know that,' Angela said, but Mabel had already turned away and fled.

Lettice felt a pang of regret. She hadn't needed to do that. A 'no, go away' would have sufficed. A terrible guilt pricked deep in her chest. It wasn't the fact that she'd been rude to Mabel, she had meant to be. It was how she'd done it. Lettice knew it wasn't Mabel's fault that she was Indian or adopted, so picking on her for it was wrong. But that wasn't the core of the bad feeling that made Lettice feel a little sick. Lettice was hit with the horrid thought that what she'd said meant she thought being Indian was bad. And being adopted was bad. Of course she didn't think that. Not for a second!

Lettice wanted to apologise immediately. But she couldn't. Mabel had gone and the girls were still giggling. Lettice tried to shoo away the guilt in her stomach. It was Mabel's fault. She tried so hard, but it just made her look desperate. And Lettice seemed to be her main target. For some reason Mabel had latched on to her, like a stray puppy... Not a week went by without Mabel reaching out to Lettice and Lettice ignoring her. Lettice didn't hate Mabel, even though she told herself she did. She was just scared of being associated with her. Lettice didn't want to appear strange. She just wanted to fit in.

'That was brilliant!' Eleanor smiled. 'You should be on stage with that wit!'

'She should know better,' Angela said. 'Just 'cos she has money doesn't mean we have to be friends with her.'

'Why does she like you so much?' asked Alice.

Lettice shook her head in disbelief. 'I don't know…'

The girls spent the rest of the lunch break huddled out of the rain, talking about what they would do when they left school. This was a common topic as they would all be twelve next year. By law you had to be fourteen to leave school, but it wasn't uncommon to work part-time from twelve, or leave school altogether.

Angela was going to marry, of course. As soon as possible. She wasn't going to wait till her twenties. Lettice didn't believe her story about a roguish Irish gypsy fiancé, but Angela was insistent it was true, and she was a bit too scary to question.

Alice was going to be a maid for the hotel her parents already worked in. She wasn't too pleased with this as a prospect and hoped to find a husband soon. Eleanor was certain she would get a job in a shop, one of the new ones. There was no way she would be a maid. She'd even stay living at home for a few more years if it meant she could save up some money.

She wanted to work in the jeweller's. You meet all sorts selling jewels. When a rich young man came in to get an engagement ring, she'd get him to give *her* the ring instead of his intended. Then they'd travel to America in style and knowing all the British colonies in order wouldn't matter because the Americans hated the

British, and the new king. Lettice wasn't sure Eleanor was confident enough to snare a bachelor, even an imaginary one, and worried for the imaginary fiancée he left behind. She worried even more for her friend if she wanted to marry a bounder like that.

'Well, it's better than being a maid,' Eleanor said in a huff. 'Why, what will you do, Lettice?'

'The way you handled Mabel, perhaps you should get on stage as a comedy turn,' suggested Alice.

'I wouldn't dare!' Lettice chuckled, blushing slightly at the compliment but feeling guilty all the same.

'We're off to the music hall tomorrow,' Angela announced.

'Oh wow,' said Eleanor. 'With your parents?'

'My eldest brother goes,' Angela said. 'He takes us. But I think we're going to the Aquarium not the Canterbury tomorrow. We're a bit bored of George Leybourne to be honest. Do you want to come?'

Lettice had never wanted anything more in her life. 'Yes please!'

'Don't you even care who's on?' Alice snorted.

'Isn't it usually the Great Vance at the Aquarium?' said Eleanor.

'Tomorrow it's Little Tich, Harry Tate and Hetty King. So it will be well good. Get changed quick after school and we'll meet you both back at the gates at five o'clock.'

***

The afternoon lessons were a bit better. Mr Metcalfe instructed them to carry on with their embroidery. Little did he know they weren't supposed to be embroidering. They had been darning, an altogether more mundane task. Lettice enjoyed embroidery, creating patterns that looked like flowers and keeping each stitch the correct size. The result was so neat a machine could have done it. Eleanor was more of a wild interpretation sort. Her flowers resembled her family – all growing at different rates, some stretched out, others short and round.

Lettice missed flowers and the sweetness of summer. She spent her summers with her grandmother in her country house. There were stables and horses. And big trees she wasn't allowed to climb but did anyway. There wasn't much green in London. Everything was cobblestones, red brick and wrought iron, washed grey in the rain. Gardens were closed off behind iron gates and, once the trees had emptied their leaves, the soot and the mud seemed to cover anything remaining that wasn't already grey.

The final bell rang, and the boys marched past the girls' classroom on their way home. The girls silently filed out, each bobbing a curtsy at the picture of the king as they left. Stupidly, it was the wrong king. He had died in the summer but Miss Ward hadn't changed the portrait to the new king. Tilly of course wasn't there to collect Lettice – it wasn't a duty their maid stuck to very often – so she walked home with Eleanor and Sam, stopping to buy them all lunch at the sweet shop. Sam insisted on wine gums, which he thought contained wine but actually tasted quite bland. Eleanor got marshmallows and shared Lettice's sugar mice. Excitedly, they made plans for Friday evening.

Plans that would be wrecked the moment Lettice got home.

第三章

SAN

'Eat your spuds…' Lettice's father said.

'Potatoes,' Lettice's mother told him. And when he looked annoyed, she apologised. 'Sorry, darling, correcting language is a habit battered into me by my governess. A stupid remnant of a privileged childhood.'

'My old man would all 'em taters,' Mr Pegg grunted.

'It's a pity he never met my mother – can you imagine?' She started laughing.

Lettice had been surprised to find her mother at home when she got back. She'd only just finished the bag of sugar mice and hastily hid the wrappers in the trunk in her room. She wasn't sure if it was the sweets that had made her feel a bit sick or the fact that her mother had done the cooking.

Mr Pegg had returned from work in a sombre mood. He'd come straight home (not via the pub), which hadn't pleased him. Lettice's mother was in quite a spirited mood. She was happily explaining how she had been to a meeting that afternoon, that the government had been bad again and that she and her friends were planning a big march the following day.

This news made her husband sigh deeply.

'What's with the long face?' Mrs Pegg asked.

'I've got some news too… some good and some bad. Mostly bad.' Mr Pegg sighed. 'I'm afraid you'll have to skip your protest tomorrow, Florry.'

'What?!' Lettice's mother looked furious. 'I can't! I've promised to go.'

'We're going to Brighton.'

'You can go to Brighton. I'm not stopping you.'

'We're going see your mother. I telegrammed her this afternoon. She'll be expecting us at nine this evening.'

'You hate my mother!'

'That's not true.'

'She hates you too.'

Mr Pegg tried to reason with his wife. 'You've been on and on at me to try and get along with her, and now I'm making an effort.'

'Why now, suddenly?'

Mr Pegg piled food into his mouth so he couldn't answer.

Lettice took the opportunity to ask, 'Are we going to Grandma's tonight?'

'No,' said her mother.

'Yes.' said her father.

'You can't miss work,' Lettice's mother protested.

'I've taken a family day,' Lettice's father said. 'A long weekend. It will be nice. The sea air will do us all some good.'

'You should have discussed it with me first before you made plans!' Lettice's mother said crossly.

'Weekend?' Lettice felt a slight pang of doom. 'Does that mean I'm going to miss school tomorrow? And I can't see my friends in the evening? We were going to the music hall…'

'Quiet!' her father barked. He gathered himself and tried humour to placate Lettice's mother. 'You have time to write to your friends and let them know your terrible husband is finally taking your advice and building bridges with your equally terrible mother.'

'I've been on at you since Christmas! And now, on the eve of a really important protest, you take me away! Why tonight?'

Mr Pegg looked at his wife. 'Just coincidence.'

Lettice saw her father's ears growing pink. He was lying.

'I refuse,' Mrs Pegg snapped. Lettice admired her mother's pluck. She was hoping she would win out. Lettice couldn't miss the chance of going to the music hall with Angela and Alice. This was her one shot at having them as friends.

'You cannot refuse.' Lettice's father crunched on his potatoes. 'You are my wife.'

'Are you going to force me? In handcuffs?'

'That won't be necessary.' He smiled. 'Your mother is expecting you. You know better than to mess with her.'

Checkmate.

Lettice got up from the table. She needed to pack her overnight bag.

It was a short cab ride to Victoria train station. Lettice sat between her sulking parents, her things in a little brown suitcase on her lap. The rain beat down as she was rocked from side to side. Her father was reading the evening paper, which had got soaked as they'd left the building. He held it up to the lamp in an effort to make out the scattered words on the wet paper. Lettice's mother was busy reading a lengthy letter from one of her clubs, tutting every now and then. Lettice didn't have anything to read. She focused instead on not being sick as the cab lurched over the uneven cobbles.

Victoria station looked marvellous in the winter. On entering it they were met by billows of steam. The whole station was a cloud trap. The cold air met the hot engines and mingled with the breath of hundreds of travelling businessmen in thick wet overcoats. Men in flat caps also moved through the crowds in their workmen's clothing. Lettice caught sight of the occasional woman. Their damp furs sparkled when they walked under lamps. They were all accompanied by husbands or maids. The floor rang with footsteps and the chink of canes; umbrellas flapped shut; the notice board clicked over, applauding each cascading change as trains departed. The man at a newspaper stand provided the only distinct human voice – otherwise, all Lettice could hear was fractions of shouted conversations over the angry hiss from the nearby engines.

As each train threatened to leave, the roar grew impossibly loud against the scuffle of footsteps around them. Lettice shut her eyes, imagining she was in a dragon's lair. The clicking, clacking and clanging of the trains became reptilian scales, and the umbrellas and movements of tightly packed bodies were like leathery wings beating as the beast roared and hissed sulphurous steam. Suddenly she felt something on her left shoulder.

'Get away from her!' The fear in Florence Pegg's voice was palpable.

Lettice opened her eyes. Her father was advancing, looking above her head at something behind her. His nostrils flared over his moustache and his eyes widened under the brim of his hat. He stepped forward. His face was growing redder, like he was about to explode. To Lettice's horror he reached over her to strike. She slipped out of the way, literally, her feet finding it hard to grip on the wet floor. She felt something tug on her hair and when she turned she saw her father punch a man in the nose. He had been standing right behind her. Like a spider lowering itself on a silent line, he had been creeping closer, breathing her in.

People gasped and the man held his face, a trickle of red blood leaking through his fingers.

'It's all right; I'm a policeman,' her father yelled over the crowd. 'This blaggard had his filthy mitts on my daughter!'

The crowd murmured and the men who had moved forward stepped back. Two women shouted, 'Shame on you,' to the man on the floor. Lettice shrank slightly as the eyes of the crowd looked suspiciously at her too.

'How was I meant to know she was yours?' Lettice could only just make out the man's shouts as the engines continued to hiss. 'She had her hair down. I was only feeling it!'

'She is eleven years old.'

'I thought she was alone.' The man got up and took a hanky that was offered. 'Honest, guv, I didn't know she was yours.'

Lettice felt affronted. It was *her* hair he had touched. Why wasn't *she* getting the apology?

'I should arrest you for perversion.' Lettice's father squared up to the man and he ducked away.

'I never touched her: just her hair!'

Lettice was shocked at the expression on her father's face when he looked at her. She had thought he would be worried, would want to comfort her. Instead it looked like she was next in line to be punched. His expression didn't change when he addressed her mother.

'Get her out of here.'

Lettice couldn't make out what her mother said, as another engine had started up. Either way, both her parents were acting like she'd done something wrong. She'd been so far away in her dragon dream that she'd not noticed the man starting to play with a lock of hair that poked out from under her hat. Her father took her by the arm and marched her towards the train.

It was possibly for this reason that Lettice and her mother went to sit in a green compartment marked 'ladies only' while her father went to sit with the men further down the carriage. Lettice's mother took their luggage and placed it in the rack above their heads.

'What do I always tell you? Make sure you keep your hair under your hat,' she said crossly. 'There are strange men in this world and you don't want their attention.'

'Yes, Mama,' Lettice said, fixing her hat as best she could. There was no hair coming out of it now.

'Don't be one of those girls who like attention,' her mother said.

'I didn't do anything. What was I supposed to have done differently?'

'You can stop answering back for a start,' Florence Pegg said, and that was the end of their conversation. Lettice felt more confused than ever.

***

The train pulled into Brighton station after what felt like hours of icy silence. Lettice had to clasp her gloved hands over her ears as the train screeched to a halt. She followed her mother closely, clutching her suitcase in front of her. As they made it to the cab line, they found her father in the queue.

'Bit of a line,' he finally said, breaking the silence. 'Let's walk!'

Lettice's mother looked up at him. 'No.'

The women in front of them in the queue turned and looked, with raised eyebrows. Lettice moved away from her parents, trying to ignore their public bickering.

'It's not raining…' Mr Pegg persisted.

'We are *not* walking.' Florry glared.

More people were staring. Mrs Pegg was talking to her husband like he was her footman. It wasn't that they were airing their laundry in public; it was the difference in their accents that was embarrassing. Everyone thought them uncivil.

'You want us to show up at my mother's house like a gang of vagrants?' Mrs Pegg asked.

'The thought had crossed my mind.' Mr Pegg smiled to himself.

'I thought we were here so that you could bury the hatchet?'

Lettice wished her mother would be quiet and do what her father wanted. She didn't like the idea of walking in the cold either. Her toes were already frozen in her boots. But she would rather walk all the way back to London than have everyone gawping at them. The ladies ahead of them had made it into a cab now. Lettice thought she heard them laughing about the bossy Pank and 'her wife' as they shut the door. Lettice couldn't even look at her mother. Mrs Pankhurst was the leader of the suffragettes and people who didn't like her called her followers Panks. Lettice's mother *was* a bossy Pank. And Mr Pegg didn't tell her to be quiet. Lettice couldn't look at either of them.

When they finally got in a cab, the conversation had dwindled to how they all looked. Lettice's mother was fussing over Lettice's clothing, and getting her to readjust her hat. It wasn't the smoothest of rides; Brighton was very hilly, and making oneself presentable while bouncing around a moving carriage in the dark wasn't easy. If anything, Lettice was looking more and more bedraggled and her mother's anxiety increased the closer they got to the town houses on the beachfront.

'You're to be polite,' Florry said for the sixth time as they rang the doorbell.

'Yes, Mama,' Lettice answered, reaching to readjust her hat which had been jammed on far too far down her head so it was squeezing her eyebrows.

Her hand was slapped away by her mother as the door opened. They were instantly bathed in the brightest light.

'James!'

'Mrs Pegg. Mr Pegg. Welcome.' James the butler answered the door with formality.

'It is so good to see you. Can you take these?'

'Of course, madam. May I introduce you to Sarah; she's the new maid here. Sarah, take their coats and seat them in the drawing room.'

'Yes, sir.'

The entrance of her grandmother's town house was similar to the lobby of Lettice's entire block of flats. Except it was nicer. And bigger. Instead of a plain entryway with pigeonholes for the post, here paintings of horses and flowers hung high on the striped wallpapered walls. The tiled floor was covered with a rich red rug that led to some glass doors. Sarah showed them through. The drawing room was heavily curtained, with a large fire that crackled. Electric bulbs were dotted around the walls, their light so white they made it possible to see all the little people in the picture frames that were placed on the dark oak furniture. Lettice recognised herself as a six-year-old, a tiny blurred face sat on her mother's lap. Her father was standing behind them, barely recognisable without his moustache and his police uniform.

They all retreated to opposite corners of the large room: Lettice looking at the pictures on the side table, her father pacing from the window to the fire, and her mother perched uncomfortably on a chaise longue, her eyes flicking between her husband, her daughter and the door.

Sarah came in with a tray of drinks: some Scotch for Mr Pegg, a gin for Mrs Pegg, and a sweet hot chocolate for Lettice. There was another glass on the tray filled with a darker, almost black liquid.

Lettice, sipping at the steaming chocolate, felt slightly comforted. Although she could write to Eleanor to tell her she wouldn't be able to come to the music hall, she didn't want to tell her why. Most families stayed in one place and only went to the seaside for a day or two once a year. Lettice's mother travelled so often that Lettice was frequently placed in the care of her grandmother or an aunt. She didn't want Eleanor to think her even more weird.

'When I don't turn up to school they'll assume I'm sick,' she thought, 'and they'll know it isn't a deliberate snub.'

Lettice occupied herself pondering which possible non-infectious overnight disease might elicit the most sympathy from her friends. Her fantasy was interrupted by her grandmother entering the room, arms outstretched. Lettice's mother jumped up and both women came together in a big hug.

'Darling!' they both exclaimed and kissed each other on the cheek. Twice each side.

Lettice's grandmother looked a lot like Lettice's mother. She was plumper, but still lean. Her long grey hair was tied beautifully above her head. Her dress was dark green and velvet. Next to the glittering broach on her bosom, there was a simple Christian cross.

Grandmother's greeting to Lettice's father was less elaborate but not unfriendly, and when she turned to Lettice she beamed.

'Dearest creature!' She opened her arms. Lettice set down her cup and ran over.

Grandmother smelled like clean bedding and soap.

'You've grown again. Not too much, either. Good. You don't want to outgrow the pool of male suitors, rich men aren't all six foot you know.' She took a seat in a wingback chair opposite the fire. Lettice and her mother sat too, although her father stayed standing.

'I've taken to drinking port in the evenings.' Lettice's grandmother raised her glass. 'Chin, chin.'

Everyone raised their glasses. Lettice lifted her cup of hot chocolate.

'So good to see you all, even if it is rather last-minute,' she continued. 'I've barely heard from your brother since he went to India, but I suspect they must have had their child by now, God willing. That is the trouble with sons; they fledge very far from the nest.'

'Not me,' Lettice's father spoke up.

Lettice winced. She had sat silently in the corner of enough parties and functions to know that it was the host that set the subject for conversation. Her father trying to join in was like a workman walking over the carpets in his muddy boots.

Grandmother's voice became cool. 'At least you're living north of the river now and out of the slums. So, enough idle chit chat. What are you doing down here in Brighton? Chasing a prisoner on the run?'

'I wanted to clear the air,' her father replied. 'Before Christmas. Make sure we don't repeat last year.'

Last year had been a disaster. Lettice and her parents had travelled to her grandmother's country house on the morning of Christmas Eve and were on the train back home the very same day. Lettice wasn't sure what had gone wrong, as she'd been in the stables. The last glimpse she'd got of her grandfather had been of a tired old man, sat behind his desk. He'd died in the summer, just like the king.

'Everyone knows what a good man you are. You've already proven that.' Grandmother said this with a touch of sarcasm.

'I married your daughter because I love her. We met quite by chance,' Mr Pegg replied crossly. Lettice didn't understand where his response was coming from.

'You arrested her,' Grandmother scoffed.

'I was protecting her!' Mr Pegg's voice was raised now. If there was one thing Lettice knew from spending summers in her grandmother's house it was to never show emotion. Not real emotion. Talk of emotion, let alone real emotion, was very bad manners. It was not done. By letting his temper show, Mr Pegg was walking his muddy work boots over Grandma's carpet again. 'An anti-suffrage mob nicked her sign and beat her with it.'

'Dear Lord,' Grandmother whispered, almost shuddering.

Mrs Pegg took her mother's horror as concern for her well-being. 'Oh, Mama, you didn't mind me getting involved in suffrage back then.'

'I didn't see the harm in it,' the old lady agreed. 'I thought a little activity would distract you. But now you're mixing with dreadful working-class yobs. There were pictures all over the newspapers of women playing brass instruments, in trousers. Their cheeks all round and red.'

'How could you tell they were red? The paper is black and white,' Mr Pegg quipped.

'If I were caught making a racket in Hyde Park, *my* cheeks would be red.'

'I was there,' Mrs Pegg said with pride.

'I'm just relieved you let me take your *only* daughter for the summer,' she said the word 'only' pointedly. Having just one child was unusual, most of Lettice's classmates had brothers and sisters. 'Better than her marching up and down with those spinsters.'

'We could move out of the city if you let us have my inheritance,' Lettice's mother said sweetly.

'You'd never leave London if I had to drag you.'

Her mother's voice returned to a more businesslike tone. 'This is silly. We are living hand to mouth, in a flat we cannot afford, with a useless expensive maid and… the thing is… I've been offered a job…'

'No!' Grandmother interrupted. It wasn't a no of disbelief but one of resolute refusal.

'… working in the suffrage offices,' Mrs Pegg continued. 'Oh, come on, Mama, you worked for Father…'

'I was never paid,' the older woman spluttered with indignation.

'You did his books,' Mr Pegg said. 'You were the mastermind behind the company.'

The old woman looked fierce. 'You cannot work, Florence! What will I tell my friends?'

'I already volunteer there.'

'Volunteering is different. You can't actually have a job. It is too undignified.'

'We need the money,' Mrs Pegg said.

'I see now what this visit's all about.' The old woman put down her glass and hugged her shawl to her. 'I'm being blackmailed. Fine. You can have SOME of your inheritance. On condition…'

Mr Pegg hushed his wife before she had time to protest. 'What condition?'

'Firstly, no more suffrage. No meetings, campaigns, petitions. Enough is enough.'

Lettice's mother pursed her lips. Her eyes flashed at her husband's outstretched finger, held up at her to shush.

'And Lettice is to go to finishing school,' the old lady said, ignoring her daughter's disbelief and turning to Mr Pegg. 'Which means you will need a suit.'

'Me?'

'Parents are vetted, not just the children. She won't get in if her father is wearing a shabby, low-ranked uniform. Still a constable after how many years?!'

Mr Pegg grew red. 'It's not that simple.'

Lettice's grandmother turned her head towards him. 'You were in the army; you know how rank works… constable, inspector, chief inspector, commissioner… Work at it.'

Mr Pegg looked both embarrassed and furious. 'Fine.'

Grandmother's eyes narrowed. 'In the meantime we will get you a suit. My tailor will come tomorrow. He will measure you and send you something suitable. I trust you can find shoes in London.'

'Yes.'

'Black ones.'

'Yes.'

'Leather.'

'Yes.'

'Not police clodhoppers.'

Mr Pegg pouted. Sarah entered the room and replenished everyone's drinks. Mr Pegg's moustache was twitching. He was about to explode.

'I'm not a doll for you to play dress-up with,' he said through clenched teeth. 'We don't need your money!'

His wife turned on him. 'So we don't need her money when *you* have to do something, but sending your daughter away and stopping me from seeing my friends is fine?'

'Why should we jump through hoops for your inheritance?'

The old woman spoke calmly. 'Unfortunately, you aren't in a position to bite the hand that feeds you.'

'These hands feed me!' Mr Pegg shouted, holding them up. 'I've fought in wars! I patrol the streets protecting people like you from violent criminals.'

Grandmother's eyes flashed. She spoke very quietly. 'People like me? We both married into money, dear boy. At least *I* wasn't foolish enough to pretend I was still common.'

What her father said, or rather yelled, after this comment Lettice didn't hear. Sarah was beckoning to her from the doorway. Silently, she got out of her seat and crept out of the room. She followed the maid to the kitchen. On the stove a pan of milk was waiting to simmer.

'I thought you'd best be out the way.' Lettice watched Sarah turn out a large mixing bowl and, with rolled-up sleeves, knead at the dough. 'Is it true you go to a regular school, just a parish one?'

Lettice nodded.

'Diamond in the rough, huh?' The woman watched as the girl sat quietly. 'You're a quiet child, aren't you?'

The yelling upstairs got louder. The maid went to the stove and poured Lettice a mug of warm milk, before returning to the dough. Lettice liked the fact she wasn't being pressured to talk. It made her relax.

'I hate money,' Lettice whispered.

'That proves you're well-to-do!' Sarah laughed. 'My young 'uns love it.'

Lettice looked up at the ceiling. 'They're fighting about it.'

'Adults argue, and what they argue about is never really what the matter is.'

Lettice wiped her nose on her sleeve. She felt a little calmer, and was starting to like Sarah. 'What's finishing school?'

'It's where they send girls to get more elegant, to attract a better class of man.'

'Oh.'

'They learn to play instruments and get taught how to ride, dance, shoot and talk right. So you don't say nothing too interesting. They teach you how to walk too.'

'I know how to walk!'

'Ah, but can you walk with a book balanced on your head?'

'Do men like that?'

Sarah laughed. 'I don't think men know what they like.'

'I don't want to be married,' Lettice said, listening to the yelling continue.

'That'll soon change,' Sarah said knowingly. She was shaping the bread dough into rolls now. After she'd placed the last one on a large metal tray she walked over to Lettice.

'You might not like money, but take my advice: when you don't have none, you'll pine for nothin' else. I don't care how far your ma gets with getting that vote; it won't make a blind bit of difference. Money is what you need and the only way you're going to get enough for you and any little 'uns is through a good marriage to a wealthy man. Be smart. I married a poor one and he died, and now I work all hours. Don't do what me and your ma did... Oh heck.'

'It's all right, Sarah.' Lettice's mother was standing in the doorway.

'No, it ain't. I'm sorry, madam. I shouldn't be nattering to the young mistress.'

'I suspect she enjoyed it.' Lettice felt a hand squeezing her shoulder.

'It wasn't my place…'

'I don't relish the idea of anyone being put in their place.'

Sarah blinked. 'I… I best get these buns out the way.'

They ascended the stairs, Lettice following her mother, watching closely as she took out her hairpins. Florry's long chestnut hair cascaded down her back. She led her to the guest room Lettice usually stayed in. It was nice to be in familiar surroundings. Lettice flopped down on the bed.

'Can you keep a secret?' Lettice's mother dropped to her knees and rested her chin on the blanket to look her daughter in the eye. Lettice held her breath and nodded.

'I promised Papa and Grandma that I would stop going to my meetings and seeing suffragette people.'

'But you like your Whizzpoo meetings,' said Lettice.

'You can't keep calling it Whizzpoo, darling. It was sweet when you were younger, but it makes you sound uneducated now.'

'WSPU,' Lettice corrected herself. 'Is it because of the money?'

'It's in the Bible. Honour thy father and thy mother. Besides, your father will never get promoted if his superiors know his wife is a suffragette.'

'The police don't want us to have the vote?'

'Of course they do. Your father does…'

'Then why…'

'Because the politicians don't. And the politicians tell the police what to do.'

Lettice nodded. She didn't really understand why her mother was so desperate to vote for politicians who didn't like her. 'So you're not going to be a suffragette any more?'

Her mother smiled knowingly. 'That is what I told your father and grandmother…'

'Oh!' Lettice realised her mother was letting her in on a big secret. 'You mean you aren't really giving up?'

'Not right away.'

'So are you still going on the march in London tomorrow? Can I come back to London too? I could go to the music hall with Angela!'

'Not so fast!' Florry chuckled. 'I'm not going to London. I'm delivering pamphlets to a group in Hastings tomorrow. But I've told Papa and Grandma that I'm going to spend the night with Great-aunt Catherine in Lewes… It's the only excuse I can think to get away. Unfortunately both of them are insisting I take you with me. My own fault as I forgot how keen your aunt is on children. I need you to make up an excuse to stay behind.'

'Why can't I go with you?'

'It will be very boring, darling. A long train journey, then a meeting with no cake or tea. You'd have more fun staying here. I need to be on the ten-thirty train. Can I trust you?'

Lettice nodded reluctantly. Something didn't quite add up... Her mother had been so upset about coming here. Why, when she planned to go to Hastings with leaflets for a meeting? And where had she got the leaflets from? Lettice hadn't seen any. Perhaps they were in her bag? As she lay there, looking into her mother's eyes, Lettice realised she didn't care. It was sad she was going to miss the music hall and that she wasn't getting to spend the day with her mother, but she was so proud that her mother was confiding in her. Trusting her like a grown-up. Like a friend.

'You're such a good girl, Lettice. Just make up an excuse and stay with Papa. I'm counting on you.'

第四章

YON

Breakfast at Grandmother's was a much grander affair than at home. Ham, eggs, sausages… the rolls Sarah had shaped the previous evening. They sat round a large dark-wood table. Lettice resisted the temptation to pick at the doilies.

At least the atmosphere was lighter today. Everyone was making pleasant conversation about the sea air, the wet November, and whether they thought a general election would be called.

'I hope not,' Lettice's mother said. 'An election will get in the way of the bill to give women the vote.

Don't roll your eyes, Mother! It is 1910, we've been campaigning for decades!'

'You don't need to vote,' Mr Pegg teased. 'Men do what our wives want anyway.'

Lettice's mother ignored him. 'Who would you vote for, Mother?'

'Not the Liberals,' Grandmother said stiffly. 'That squiffy chap who can't grow a moustache...'

'Women are rational, eh?' Lettice's father said in an 'I told you so' manner.

'The only reason she'd vote Conservative is that the Liberals will tax her,' Lettice's mother snapped back.

'No more politics,' Grandmother reminded her. 'It will be hard enough for Jack to be considered for promotion to inspector as it is, without his wife being involved with dangerous gangs.'

'Inspector? I've got to be a sergeant first!'

'The WSPU are not a dangerous gang.'

'You spit in policemen's faces and get yourselves arrested.'

'Mrs Pankhurst agreed to a ceasefire so the consolidation bill can get passed.'

'The anarchists are much more dangerous to the peace. Much more of a threat than a gaggle of weak women,' Lettice's father chuckled to himself.

Lettice's mother was about to answer back when her grandmother interrupted. 'So, are you all going to go along to the pier?'

'I thought I would spend the morning with you, Mother,' Florry replied. 'Then meet Lettice at the station, so we can visit Aunt Catherine.'

Her mother gave Lettice a knowing look.

'I'll drop her at the station.' Lettice's father nodded.

'Just make sure you're back in time for the tailor,' Grandmother said.

'I'd best take our young constable out on the seafront. Get the soot out of her lungs...'

Lettice got up and followed him out of the house.

Brighton in the winter was a lot less pleasant and a lot less crowded than in the summer. Lettice had seen a Punch and Judy show here on the waterfront, only a few months ago, in the sizzling heat. There had been ice cream. Her summer gloves still smelled of vanilla.

Lettice's father handed her the parcel he had been carrying. 'I know you've wanted them for ages, but... if you start practising now you'll get good for next summer.'

The parcel was wrapped up in brown paper and string. It was similar to the deliveries of soap that Lettice's mother ordered from the druggists. Lettice loved the smell and she would run down to the entrance lobby just so she could press her nose to them.

This parcel barely smelled of anything, though that was hard to distinguish over the sea spray and faint tang of malt vinegar from a nearby shop. It was heavy and made a clomping noise as she set it down on a wet bench. Inside was confusing. Lettice thought for a second she was looking at some sort of medical vice or kitchen equipment. However when she saw the tiny rubber wheels she recognised her present instantly.

'Roller skates!' she squeaked. 'Oh, Papa! Thank you!'

They were tricky to put on. Each toecap needed to be tightened to the right size over her boots, and the leather straps adjusted. Once the job was done, Lettice swung her legs proudly. She'd begged her parents for roller skates. Angela and Alice had got in trouble for skating in them down the infants' corridor. She'd so wanted to join in, but had been told money was tight. Now she could go with them to skate rinks and spin around in the playground. Everyone would applaud.

However, Lettice's fantasy about owning roller skates was ruined by the reality of wearing them. She was far from a natural. Her father laughed heartily as he watched her cling to the bench, her feet sliding away from her.

'It's not funny!' she yelled.

'You look like a drunk pony!' he cackled and started to walk away.

There was only one thing for it. She would get over to the iron railings a few yards from the bench and then pull herself along the seafront. It was in her haste to reach the railings that the accident happened. It didn't look like much: a girl clinging to a bench, standing up as straight as possible, pushing herself away from it, trying to turn and reach for the railing. It was the trying to turn bit that went wrong; she stopped mid turn so she decided to take a step, but her foot immediately slipped out from under her and she fell flat on her face, arms outstretched.

Her father was still laughing when he picked her up.

'Come on now, no need for tears. Nothing's broken.' He helped her back on the bench and took the skates off for her. 'Next time we won't try on such a beastly day.'

Lettice, however, felt a bit sick. She'd thought roller skating would be fun. She hadn't realised how hard it was just to stand up. Her respect for Angela had only grown.

'You'll get better with practice,' her father said calmly, using his hanky to rub the little stones from her stinging hands.

Get better with practice... It would take a pound of chocolate for Lettice to ever put those things on her feet again. Why was she hopeless at everything?

'There we go, big brave constable!' Mr Pegg wiped the tears from her cheeks and used the string from the package to tie the roller skates together. He placed them round her neck rather like a scarf.

'Oh, blimey.' He checked his watch. 'We'd better get to the station.'

Lettice's knees hurt. She was frustrated. She hated herself for being unable to roller skate and she hated her father for laughing at her. How was she going to make friends if she couldn't skate? She'd quite forgotten her promise to her mother about staying with her father for the day. She'd forgotten her mother had said she wasn't going to take her to see Aunt Catherine and was instead going to Hastings. She'd forgotten to come up with a lie so she could stay with her father and grandmother.

Lettice only remembered all this in the cab, just as they were approaching the station.

'Oh!' she exclaimed.

'What's wrong?'

'I er... ' She couldn't think of anything; her mind was blank. 'Can't I stay with you a bit longer?'

Her father looked confused. 'I've got the tailor and your grandmother has organised an…' He sighed and mouthed the words, 'Elocution lesson. Besides, you like Aunt Catherine! It would be rude not to show up.'

'But…' Lettice started.

Her father was ignoring her, looking out of the window. 'There's another queue…'

The wait for a cab looked even longer than it did yesterday. 'Lettice, can you find your way to meet your mother at the train? I need to stay in this cab otherwise I'm going to be late.'

'By myself?!' Lettice sounded shocked.

'It's only a few yards, love. Your mother will be at the right platform. You know how to read a timetable,' he reasoned.

'But Papa.' Lettice raised her eyebrows. 'I'll be *alone*.'

She usually delighted in him treating her as a son. All this talk of joining the police when she was of age… but it meant he never saw her for what she was. She wasn't a boy. She couldn't be seen to walk alone.

'Here –' he reached into his pocket and brought out some money – 'buy your mother and yourself some digestives for the journey. I have to go. You'll be fine.'

Lettice got out of the cab, clutching her coins. The cab driver looked at her with pity as he geed the horse to move round. She watched the carriage travel past the long line and back out of the station entrance

Lettice was alone.

Curious glances were being shot at her from all angles. A woman whispered something to her companion and both shook their heads. Lettice's face grew red and her impulse was to dash back to her grandmother's house and explain that she had missed the train. But as she was about to step that way, a small man with a wispy moustache touched his hat.

'How do you do? Can I be of assistance?'

Lettice's eyes widened and she turned on her heel, walking in the opposite direction at speed, into the station. Her heart was hammering so loudly she swore everyone could hear it over the noise of the engines and peeps of the train whistles.

That was the first time in her life a strange man had addressed her. A man she hadn't been introduced to. A man she didn't know and who didn't know her family. It was scary. Never speak to strangers, particularly not without good reason – that was the rule. A couple was staring at her with disgust. She must look like a pickpocket. Boys went on their own a lot – delivery boys, paper boys, shoe shiners – girls did not. It was unseemly. Even match girls would set up in close enough proximity to each other… and the stories she had heard about them… It wasn't just matches they sold. Kisses too. Is that what people thought she was doing?

She clapped her hand over her mouth and hurried into the main part of the station, towards the ticket office. Maybe the train to Hastings was delayed; maybe her mother was still here somewhere. She found a timetable. It was printed on very thin paper, with very small letters.

Scanning the chart, her eyes wandered to weekday morning trains to London Victoria.

Friday, 11.05: Platform 3

She couldn't. It was impossible. Go to London alone? Her father thought she was travelling to Lewes with her mother and her mother thought she was with her father. She had a pocket full of money. She could go to the music hall after school. Her heart began to beat excitedly. The fear drained away. She could do it. There was no one stopping her. In her excitement, she didn't think of where she would stay the night, if Tilly was at the flat or if Eleanor would let her stay with her. She didn't think of how she would get back on Saturday.

She only saw the music hall in her mind, and making friends with Angela and Alice.

The large station clock was visible through clouds of steam caused by the ten fifty-five getting its engine going. She had time.

A group of young shoe shiners were staring at her, curiously. They must be her age and she desperately wanted to confide in them. She wanted help so badly.

'You looking for your ma?' asked one. He was tall and reminded her a little of Sam.

'Or husband?' a cheeky freckled boy grinned. They all laughed at her.

She put her nose in the air and walked into the ticket office. She was still in a panic. She stood in the queue trying to look as confident as possible.

'Can I help, miss?' The elderly man behind the ticket counter looked at her, intrigued.

Lettice somehow found her voice. 'A child return to London Victoria, please.'

'Second class?' The man looked concerned. He hadn't moved, like he wasn't prepared to sell to her. 'Just the one ticket?'

'I lost mine…' Lettice fibbed. 'My mother is waiting for me.'

This seemed to work. He moved into action, stamping and handing over a return ticket.

'The five past eleven is boarding now. Platform three…' he said, doubtfully. 'You best hurry.'

'Thank you!' Lettice smiled.

And as she turned the sight that met her eyes caused the smile to drop. She had lied to the clerk at the ticket office. Her mother wasn't waiting for her on the platform. Her mother had told her she would be on the ten thirty to Hastings. Her mother should be travelling on a train right now. So why was Florence Pegg walking through the crowd towards platform three?!

第五章

GO

Lettice didn't notice the stares from the crowd any more, or the comments about the roller skates that were still hanging around her neck. That was definitely her mother, now boarding the five past eleven train. To London!

Lettice was furious.

Why had her mother *lied* to her?

The people around Lettice seemed to vanish. She handed her ticket over for inspection and watched from the platform, outraged, as her mother climbed aboard a first-class carriage. Lettice paused. She could run up to her now. She could demand answers. Why wasn't she going to Hastings? Why had she made Lettice stay behind in Brighton? Didn't she want to spend time with her?

Lettice wanted answers now. But she also feared her mother might drag her from the train and make them both stay behind. Then she wouldn't get to go to the music hall with Angela, Alice and Eleanor. And anyway, Mother might lie again. So she'd miss the music hall just for fibs, and that was even more unfair. No. She'd find out the truth for herself, like a real policeman would.

So Lettice made her way to the second-class, ladies-only compartment. There were already five people inside. One woman gasped and moved her daughter to the side as Lettice, her face angry and red, heaved herself up the steps. They all stared at her. Lettice sat by the window nearest the door. She noticed them all shuffle away.

'Whatever's wrong with me isn't catching,' she snapped.

She didn't notice the tuts or clicks or murmur of conversation as the train left the station, just her own red face reflected in the window. At every stop, Lettice leaned out of the carriage door towards her mother's compartment to make sure she hadn't alighted. Lettice could see her fellow travellers staring at her in the reflection of the glass. Eyes were glaring, mouths pursed. They didn't like sharing their air with a moral outcast.

Lettice didn't care.

The one thing on her mind was finding out what her mother was up to. So by the time the train pulled up with a screech at Victoria station, Lettice was like a greyhound in a starting trap, bursting to get out. She jumped out of her carriage and barged past the luggage porters and suitcases. Masked by the steam and the crowds, Lettice kept out of her mother's sight as they trotted along the platform. Mrs Pegg had been joined by a gentleman and four other ladies.

Such a large group wouldn't fit in a single cab, which gave Lettice hope that she'd be able to follow them. They walked past the underground entrance and once out of the station they continued, not towards the tram as Lettice expected, or even the big red omnibus that had just pulled up. They were going on foot. And fast... Lettice struggled to follow them.

They headed towards Westminster and as they got closer, the noise of the streets changed. The thoroughfare had been closed to through traffic and there were only a few horses and a van in the street.

But it was full of people. In the distance Lettice could hear a roar of a much bigger crowd. It sounded like the wind and reminded her of the time when she passed a football match being played, only this wasn't a singular celebration or cry of dismay. It was chaos. After a couple of minutes Lettice hung back and watched her mother's group enter a building. There was a lot of commotion as women hurried in all directions. Some were limping up the steps.

'You're not going back there!' A woman tugged at her friend's sleeve.

'I am! They have to let us in or arrest us.'

'Oh goodness, Miss Lockyer!'

'I'm fine, I'm fine,' said the blonde woman called Miss Lockyer as she limped past Lettice. 'It's only a nosebleed; I'm more annoyed that the duffers squashed my hat. I'll see you back out there.'

Lettice saw her mother and the others exit the building carrying a banner. They were walking quickly and Lettice had to trot to keep up.

Lettice knew exactly what this was. Her mother was going on a march. After she'd promised everyone she wouldn't do any more campaigning for Whizzpoo! Lettice felt furious that she had not been confided in.

Her anger rose again as she chased her mother into the throng of people. She didn't notice the atmosphere growing darker.

Lettice had seen suffrage marches before: held her aunt's disapproving hand as they watched her mother parading by; waved at her father, who had been on duty protecting the marching women from the counter-protesters across the street. The counter-protesters had been a mix of prim and proper women in unfashionable hats and some grumpy men holding signs saying 'Keep families together' with pictures of crying abandoned babies. Lettice had thought them silly. Now she felt they might have had a point.

She stomped through the puddles, not caring how mucky it made her boots. She was so focused on the back of her mother's hat that she failed to notice how many counter-protesters there were lining the pavements. How many were angry leering men. Blinded by her mother's betrayal, Lettice also failed to see the vast line of policemen defending Parliament. She didn't see them jeering along with the crowd.

Lettice didn't hear the taunts, the insults, the shrieks, nor the whinny of horses. She didn't feel the occasional arm reach out and grab at her coat. Or hear the grunts as the women surrounding her were pushing up together as they neared St Stephen's Gate.

She caught up with her mother and yelled as loudly as she could, 'You're a LIAR!'

Lettice didn't have time to watch her mother turn round and look aghast, or hear her mother's horrified voice cry out over the din before she heard the hot breath of a police horse in her ear. Tiny dewdrops of moisture peppered the fine hairs around its nostrils. Time slowed. Lettice's eyes widened as she realised that the muzzle was coming straight at her, the rest of the beast not far behind. She dived out of the way, narrowly avoiding getting trampled. She barrelled straight into a policeman. She noticed his number, R21, as she clung to his cape, stopping herself from falling. He was tall and moustached like her father, only older and fatter. He grabbed her by the arm and squeezed. The pressure was intense and she thought her bone was sure to break under his gloves.

'You're hurting me!'

'A young one!' He looked her up and down. 'You should be in school. How about I teach you a lesson right now?' He raised his truncheon to beat her. With her arm raised above her head, crushed in his firm grip, Lettice was nearly on tiptoes, her entire side exposed to the beating. She wasn't sure whether to cover her ribs with her free arm or save it from injury. She kicked and twisted but he held her firm, laughing.

Lettice's mother battled past the crowd and yelled at him to let her daughter go. The policeman obliged, dropping Lettice on the cobblestones and stepping towards her mother. But instead of grabbing her by the arm, his fingers closed over her throat. Lettice registered the shock, as if she too had been grabbed.

Her mother was being lifted off the ground by her neck.

Panic hit Lettice in the chest like a kick from a horse. This man, with one arm, had plucked her mother off the ground like she was a dandelion. He paused to admire her briefly, watching happily as her face turned purple. Then suddenly bored, he threw her backwards on to the ground.

Her mother's body crunched on to the pavement. She fell heavily on her back and remained motionless. Lettice too was motionless in horror.

The police were out of control. They were lifting up the skirts of the marching women and laughing as they threw them about, joking that they liked this 'rough play'. The majority of the women were doing their best to ignore them, marching past Lettice, who was frozen, clutching her bruised forearm. She saw the marchers reach the line of policemen, who picked them up, slapped their bottoms and threw them to the ground or into the jeering crowd. Some bystanders were trying to help by pulling the suffragettes out of the way of the horses and dabbing at their fresh cuts and grazes with handkerchiefs. Others were goading each other to grope and fondle cornered women – women who were screaming or in tears, pleading with the police for help. No help came.

Lettice tried to reach her mother but another policeman pushed her backwards. This time she dug her heels in and pushed back, hitting him uselessly in the stomach. The constable shoved her aside like she was paper. She spun round to find herself once again facing R21.

'I thought I'd dealt with you.' The constable raised his arm.

But just before his truncheon came down on her, she heard a calm female voice exclaim, 'Step back!'

Lettice did as she was told, and watched as the truncheon swept past, just an inch from her nose.

'Stay there!' The small voice belonged to an even smaller woman, who darted straight for R21. Distracted by his new assailant he forgot about Lettice and grabbed the little woman by the wrist. He yanked her aside exactly as he had done to Lettice. But the little woman didn't protest… there was a wide grin on her face. To Lettice's surprise the woman wasn't trying to get away. She wouldn't let *him* let go. Her hand was firmly on top of his, so he couldn't release her arm. Then she sank her weight, causing him to stumble.

'Oi!' shouted the constable. As he lurched forward, he tried to grab the little woman with his free hand. She stepped back, holding on to his fist with all her might. She clutched it to her bosom like it was her most prized possession. Then all she seemed to do was bow towards him. This small nod caused him to bend double and fall to his knees.

'My wrist! You're breaking it!'

But she didn't stop, bending further and further, stepping back towards Lettice until he was lying on the ground entirely. His uniform began soaking up the smaller puddles.

The moment R21 was on the ground, Lettice made a move to get to her mother. There were women around Mrs Pegg's body, arguing with the police. One woman looked like Mabel. She was Indian and wearing an incredibly elegant coat. It looked to Lettice like she was casting spells, trying to wake Lettice's mother up. Lettice tried to get closer.

'Stop!' the little woman's voice sounded from a few feet behind her.

Directly in front of her mother's body, a policeman had got hold of a suffragette. He had her with one arm and when he saw Lettice he lunged for her too.

'No you don't!' The little woman ran forward, past Lettice. She kicked the policeman hard in his leg, allowing his prisoner to break free. The constable hadn't enjoyed being kicked, and spun to face Lettice and the little woman, fury scrunched into his features. To Lettice's shock, he swung his truncheon at the little woman, nearly hitting Lettice who stepped back again, losing sight of her mother. Instead of running away, the little woman darted towards the policeman, grabbing his chin and bending him backwards on to his heels. Just as he was about to step back to regain his balance, she kicked his legs out from under him. The policeman fell and landed flat on his back.

It was impossible. The woman was tiny and the policeman was huge, yet she was unharmed and holding the arm of the gasping, coughing man on the ground.

R21 had seen this happen and, dripping puddle water, he staggered to his feet, pointing with his uninjured arm at the little woman and Lettice. 'GET THEM!'

Two policemen turned and made a grab for them. But at that moment a horse came from behind the police line. It wasn't a police horse however; it was being ridden by a woman.

'Make way, you toe-rags! You filthy swine!' a plummy voice bellowed at the police, as the woman swang her crop at the officers, knocking their helmets and striking theirs faces.

Cantering past Lettice, she charged onwards into the densest part of the square. She was dragged from her saddle, overcome by numbers. Lettice saw her punch an officer in the mouth and cry out for someone to give her a revolver. The commotion slowed the advance of the police, and gave Lettice and the little woman a fraction more time.

The little women, still clinging to the arm of the fallen officer, looked at Lettice.

'How d'ya do? I'm Edith Garrud. May I suggest we run away, sharpish?' she said, and handed Lettice the truncheon.

Lettice had never seen a grown woman, even a short one, sprint before. But seeing the rows of angry men charging at them, she did as Edith suggested and turned on her heel, her skates clanging around her neck.

Lettice could hear the footsteps of the policemen behind her. They were close, and she was nearly out of breath. But she was small and could follow Edith through the lines of the jeering crowd. They ducked past elbows, feeling hands grab at them, fingers pinch. The police were held up by the crowds, unable to squeeze through as easily. But they saw when Edith made a sharp left and darted down a side street, with Lettice only a second behind.

'Out of the way!' A police whistle sounded as the policemen broke free of the crowd and were back in the open again.

Lettice thought she was going to be sick. She had run so hard her ears had popped. She felt sweaty, her chest burned and her hands, normally so cold, were begging for her to take her gloves off. However, fear clawed at her back, her heart hammered on and she was still running at full speed. She followed Edith down another side street, which led to a dead end. There was nothing there except houses and an incredibly high fence, presumably the back of some private gardens. In front of the fence was a rather full, nasty looking dustcart.

Edith had stopped just in front of the dustcart and turned to face Lettice who, in panic, was heading straight for Edith with the police only a few yards behind.

Edith breathed out, and with a clenched jaw and a look of utmost concentration, lunged towards Lettice. She ducked under her so that her shoulder hit Lettice by her hip. As Lettice toppled forward over her, Edith stood. Lettice's weight rose up with her, her feet leaving the ground. For a second she was planked perfectly across the tiny woman's shoulders but her feet continued to rise. Edith stood to full height and bounced Lettice like a spring, so that Lettice rose high in the air, cartwheeling towards the dustcart.

She landed not so much on the dustcart but in it. She'd fallen on her side, so her entire leg, arm, shoulder and hair landed squarely in the middle of the surprisingly sloppy muck. The manure was fresh, but the bits of rotting bacon rind that squelched up by her face weren't. The stench was worse because she was still panting from the chase, breathing in the smell of dung, rotting food and dead leaves.

It really was a shame. While she was lying there, trying to work out what had just happened, Lettice missed Mrs Edith Garrud dealing with a two-man attack: those poor policemen trying to arrest her. There's no evidence in the archives of an arrest that day, Black Friday, of Edith, nor of Lettice. There are some complaints from policemen of suffering sore arms, wrists, shoulders and fingers. Needless to say, whatever Edith did to those constables, they were too ashamed to report the incident... or too injured.

第六章

ROKU

'You're not damaged are you?' Edith said, as she wiped horse poo from Lettice's coat. 'That was the best *kata guruma* I've ever done. With no one there to see it.'

Lettice's heart was still hammering. The little woman continued to talk, quite nonchalantly, while she brushed dead leaves from Lettice's hat. 'That was great practice for me; I had to really bend my knees to get under you. The problem with these bobbies is they're all so tall. Too easy, see? Makes for lazy technique.'

As Edith helped her down from the cart, Lettice realised she was a pinch taller than her.

'Sorry if it was a shock.' Edith nodded her head towards the two policemen who were limping sheepishly away. 'I didn't want them using you to get in my way. Now, we'd best head off in case they get their courage back. Here.' She handed Lettice her roller skates, which, aside from the poo flecks, looked to have survived the impact. 'Let's cut through the park. You're not hurt.'

It was a statement, not a question. The truth was Lettice was sore: her neck felt tight, her elbow was bruised and her legs were wobbling, though she supposed that was from the running rather than the fall. However, Lettice took Edith's words as fact and nodded.

'I'm late for the dojo anyway,' Edith said as she strode off. 'Come on. We'll clean you up there.'

Dodo? Had she heard that right? Lettice had no idea what the little woman was talking about but followed her all the same.

No one gave Edith and Lettice a second glance as they crossed the park. It started to drizzle and Edith easily strolled under the blanket of umbrellas with Lettice in her wake. They went over the lake, trotted through the traffic at Pall Mall, and on through the quieter backstreets towards Soho. The sky was darkening.

Lettice couldn't believe what had happened. She felt light with hunger, but the thought of food made her feel ill. She was so full of emotion that she was both angry with her mother and worried about her.

She also felt guilty. It was as if it had been her own anger that had moved the policeman's arm, her own hand choking her mother. Her temper had been so strong that she'd felt like throwing her mother on the ground. It was like R21 had channelled Lettice's rage and acted on it. Guilt flooded through her. She knew deep down that it wasn't her fault... but if she hadn't shouted that her mother was a liar, she would have noticed the horse sooner and she wouldn't have barged into R21.

But why were the police attacking innocent women? Her father would never manhandle people like that. And the smile that policeman had given. Like he relished the thought of striking her. The police were supposed to be good. It was as if the world, not just Lettice, had turned upside down and landed in horse poo.

Edith skipped up some stone steps and turned to face Lettice. They were in Soho, outside a rather imposing building. Edith opened the door for her. Lettice hesitated. There were all sorts of things she should do: go back to the flat, speak to Tilly, discover what had happened to her mother, send word to her father, let Eleanor know she wasn't going to the music hall tonight. All this had happened because she wanted to go to the music hall. It didn't seem to matter any more.

'You're letting the warm air out,' Edith said.

Letticed shuffled in.

'Welcome!' said Edith theatrically. 'To the Golden Square dojo!'

There was an odd smell inside. Worn rugs covered badly patched floorboards. There were places in the ceiling where the plaster had flaked off. Half the numbers were missing from the pigeonholes, and there was a random broken chair in the corner of the hallway. It smelled... Lettice shut her eyes... like the handles of a bicycle. Rubber, and stale sweat and... a sort of damp mustiness.

Somewhere in the building she could hear a hammering noise, and it wasn't just rain on the glass. A piano was playing too. Some men came down the stairs, touched their hats, and carried on their conversation. Lettice was feeling anxious. She didn't know where she was; she was trusting a complete stranger – and all because she didn't know what to do.

'I should go,' she stammered.

Edith cocked her head. 'Don't you want to know how I managed to overcome those police constables?'

Lettice blinked.

'Were you not impressed by my dazzling abilities? My lightning speed? How I, a smidge-under-five-foot woman, fought off two armed police officers half my age?'

Lettice shrugged.

'It is because I do jiu jitsu!' announced Edith, as though she was expecting applause.

Lettice frowned. 'You do what sue?'

'I do jiu jitsu! It's an ancient Japanese martial art devised by simple peasants to protect themselves against sword-wielding samurai warriors!'

Lettice didn't know what to say. 'Are there many samurai warriors in London?'

'There are dangers everywhere, young Lettice. Robbers, thieves… even the police! Men believe they are better than us because we are "the weaker sex". They think we need their protection. But we can protect ourselves. And I am going to teach you how!'

Edith trotted up the staircase.

Lettice stood still.

'Come on,' Edith called. 'Don't be shy.'

At the top of the stairs, Edith paused and looked into a mirror. She straightened her hat, rolled her shoulders back and breathed in. She seemed to grow in height. As she opened the door she bowed deeply at the waist.

The door opened into a large room. The middle of the floor was covered with rectangular mats placed a few feet from the shabby walls. A group of nine women stood on them with bare feet. But that wasn't the only alarming thing about their appearance.

None wore hats. And they had white jackets on, tied high around their waists with sashes of various colours. Each had her hair tied up with ribbon and none wore any jewellery. It was disconcerting and impossible to tell their social standing. Some were very young, others older. Most shockingly of all, they were wearing trousers.

Trousers. Like men.

The women were positioned in pairs, staring at each other with their hands up, moving around the mats in a funny manner, almost like they were dancing. Occasionally one would dart to the side, trying to get hold of the other's sash from behind, but the other would circle round and stop them. When the door opened, a girl's voice yelled an unfamiliar word and everyone stopped what they were doing.

'*Yame*!'

The movement stopped as the same girl barked to the room. 'Face the door. Standing *rei*!'

The entire room of women turned to face Edith and Lettice and all returned Edith's bow.

'*Yosh*,' came a call, and they restarted their strange circling dances.

The girl who had shouted rushed over to Edith.

'Sensei!' she said breathlessly. 'I was worried. Did you go to the march?'

"Course not.' Edith cast a warning glance at Lettice. 'I could hear it from several streets away.'

Another grown-up who lies, thought Lettice. Edith had been there on the front line with her!

'We heard that people are getting injured,' the other woman carried on breathlessly. 'Apparently the crowd is quite nasty and the police are doing nothing to stop them!'

'They are doing worse than that,' Edith said. 'According to this poor creature that I rescued from arrest.'

The other woman's eyes looked Lettice up and down. In that moment Lettice realised how young this new girl was. Probably only Tilly's age. All those grown-up women obeying her… and it was clear from her accent she wasn't exactly upper class. Lettice was a little shocked.

'Whatever happened to her?!' asked the girl.

'She was being chased by two constables... I threw her into a dustcart before they could find her.'

Lettice frowned. Edith was telling a half truth... missing out the part that it was Edith they were chasing. Normal people would think to ask why on earth she would run from the police. If Lettice was worried that she would be asked why the police were chasing her, she needn't have been. There was only one question of interest to these strange women.

'You threw her? What throw?'

'*Kata guruma.*'

'Marvellous!' She turned cheerily to Lettice. 'Are you hurt?'

'Take her to the changing room and put her in a clean *gi*. She's in a bit of a state. Do you mind taking her through some breakfalling? Though she's a natural from the way she landed in all that mess.'

Lettice wondered what on earth breakfalling was. She felt awkward. She wanted to leave. Edith noticed her eyes dart towards the door.

'In the dojo,' Edith said, gesturing at the room, 'I am sensei. Instructor. You're a novice. You've had a shock. You need to let your brain work through all that's happened. Personally I've never been one for tea, chat and a sit-down. Give yourself something else to focus on for an hour. Do as your fellow *jitsuka* say, and afterwards we'll have a chat.'

Lettice obeyed and followed the girl into the changing room. She wasn't used to getting changed in front of anyone except her mother and Tilly. She kept her vest on under the heavy cotton jacket, and struggled to tie the sash.

'The trousers are a bit long for you,' the girl commented.

'I've never worn trousers before,' Lettice admitted.

'Not even for school plays? Shall I hang those up here?' The girl gestured to her neck.

Lettice handed her the roller skates.

'Right. I'm Isabel by the way. So, the rules.' She spoke very quickly. 'No eating, drinking or talking in the dojo. You must ask permission if you want to go on or off the mat area. If in doubt just copy us.'

They walked back into the dojo just as Edith yelled, 'Are you warm?'

The women stopped their jumping jacks. Some were looking very red in the cheeks.

'Yes, sensei,' a few wheezed half-heartedly.

'ARE YOU WARM?' Edith growled.

'YES, SENSEI!' the women on the mat responded in one voice, as loudly as they could.

'Bow on the mat and join the end of the line,' Isabel said as she bowed deeply and stepped on to the mat.

'Good. Line up!' Edith shouted.

Lettice followed Isabel. The surface of the mat was cool and slippy on her bare feet. There was a bit of give, but it was harder than she expected. She ran as fast as she could to the far corner. She looked down the line of women, who all stood up straight like palace guards, eyes facing the front. It felt oddly familiar, and much nicer to be in a line of real people than coats in her hallway.

Edith and Isabel faced them.

'*Kiba dachi*!'

Everyone, including the instructors, widened their stance, as though they were all riding invisible horses. Lettice did likewise, slightly out of time.

'*Heisoku dachi*!'

Everyone brought their left leg to their right. Toes and heels together, their hands slapping their sides as they stood up straight as pillars.

'*Seiza.*'

Everyone kneeled down. Lettice followed suit, wondering what would happen next. Edith held out her arm and a woman at the far end of the line yelled, 'Sensei ni *rei*'.

Lettice quickly copied as the entire line bowed towards the instructors. Lettice got a whiff of the mat. It smelled of wicker, of her father's walking jumper… slightly smoky from the coal fire… a bit like a grass meadow but mainly… feet. It smelled of feet. The instructors then bowed back and Edith began.

'We have a novice training with us today who managed to fall from *kata guruma* without hitting her head or breaking her shoulder. We are small in number today; there is a distinct lack of WSPU members here, so use the extra space. Seniors, find a space on the mat facing me!'

Five women, including the younger instructor, dashed to a space as fast as they could while everyone else, including Lettice, shuffled backwards out of the way. They spaced themselves out like dots on a dice. Under Edith's barks they kneeled on the floor, rolling forwards, sideways and backwards. Hitting the mat with a loud smack in near perfect unison.

It looked fun. The only time Lettice had seen people work so closely together was the changing of the guard or in the brass bands that played on the seafront in Brighton. She'd never seen women do anything like this together. She wanted to learn. She wanted a go!

Her eagerness to join petered out when she saw what they did next.

Lettice gasped audibly as the women marched forwards and without a pause, leaped and spun themselves vertically in mid-air, going right the way over their heads and landing with a massive boom on their sides, getting up immediately before another took their turn. They spun and rolled and dived over each other, running the entire length of the dojo. A few weren't very good and Edith made them to do it again and again. Red in the face, they did exactly what they were told. Each time they hit the matt Lettice winced. It looked painful. After Isabel demonstrated how to do a cartwheel backwards, Edith sent her over to teach Lettice how to forward roll.

'You must have done a roly-poly at school.'

Lettice shook her head.

'Right... for this you are going to want to roll down your arm, over your shoulder, so you roll over your opposite hip...'

Lettice spent the next twenty minutes attempting this, but her brain kept telling her she would break her arm so it kept collapsing, causing her to face plant into the mat. Unlike at school, however, there was no cane. There was no dunce's cap. True, Isabel was sounding quite irritated at times, but she wouldn't let Lettice give up. She was also understanding – reassuring Lettice that it was difficult, and to keep trying. By the time Edith had circled round to check on them, Lettice's forward rolls were nearly perfect.

After the breakfalling she joined in with wrist grabs and releases.

'Never try to outstrength a man's arm with your own,' Edith said knowingly. 'Rarely will you find a man weaker than yourself. However, no arm muscle in the world has the strength of these.'

She pointed at her hips. Lettice blushed. She'd never heard a woman talk about her body so unashamedly.

'If he grabs your arm like *uke* will do for me now…' Isabel reached over and grabbed her. Lettice thought 'uke' was a strange name for someone… 'I can take him off balance by simply pinning my arm to my side by stepping back. And look what has happened to *uke*'s balance…'

Isabel, who Edith referred to as '*uke*', and quite definitely not a 'him' was now stretched out, desperately clinging on, her weight on her toes. It reminded Lettice of what Edith had done earlier to R21.

'From here I can either just look in the mirror…' Edith turned her hand from her hip, up to her face, as if it contained a looking glass. This movement twisted her own wrist clean of Isabel's grip with minimal discomfort.

'Or if I feel like it…' Isabel grabbed her wrist again, 'I can throw him.'

It was hard for Lettice to work out what Edith had done. Her arms were a blur and Isabel's balance was broken entirely. All Edith did was take a step past her and she toppled backwards.

'Throw?'

'*Shionage*,' chanted some of the group.

'*Yoshi*,' Edith said and with a wave of her hand the women split into groups.

Isabel continued to work with Lettice, and they were joined by an older woman who had to repeatedly be told to bend her knees and keep her body braced. Lettice joined in, grabbing wrists and letting the women practise the steps. It was a strange dance with unwritten rules. You had to hold on as hard as you could, but let them work out where they needed to be. It was all done very slowly. If you were off balance it was important you didn't try and right yourself, as that caused your partner to learn the wrong technique.

'Don't worry, we won't throw you today.' said Isabel. 'Next time we'll teach you how to land safely. Then you will be thrown.'

Next time? The thought both terrified and excited Lettice in equal measure.

When Edith called an end to the session, she got everyone to demonstrate the throw. One at a time, each *jitsuka* stood in the centre of the dojo and attempted the wrist release and throw.

Edith kneeled, arms folded, with a frown etched across her face.

Finally it was Lettice's go. The entire dojo was watching. Her legs were shaky. When she bowed to Edith like the other women had, Lettice thought she might fall over from dizziness.

A word from the sensei sent Isabel lunging for Lettice's arm. She gripped it hard, exactly where policeman R21 had before, where it was most tender. Lettice's heart was beating in her ears. She felt her face go red. But somehow her feet knew what to do.

She sank, elbow pinned to her hip, and twisted her arm free. The entire time she stared fiercely at Isabel, stepping back so she was free of her, her hands up in defence, ready for the next attack. Unknown to Lettice, that instinct for self-preservation was what earned her a rare smile from the tiny sensei.

'Good. Line up!'

Once again the women scrambled to the far side of the mat and the strange stance-changing routine happened again, although this time Lettice knew what was coming and how to kneel and bow properly.

'Thank you, everyone,' Edith said sagely, her face looking much softer. 'I admire your hard work on a day full of distractions. We will be back to our usual Tuesday and Thursday classes next week. I imagine there will be ongoing suffrage meetings tonight but remember, if you can look after yourselves and protect each other, that is worth more than any vote and more powerful than any law. Sit up straight.'

Everyone sat bolt upright.

'At this point –' Edith spoke directly to Lettice – 'we jump to our feet in our best fighting stance, releasing a bloodcurdling *kiai*... which is like a shout... but instead of it being up in your chest, it is from your belly. I want you to take all your frustration and anger and fire it out of your belly towards the enemy. Isabel will demonstrate. After three... '

Isabel didn't wait. With a look that wasn't rage or happiness, but a blank disconcerting calm, she jumped to her feet. The noise... it wasn't a shriek, it was controlled and super loud.

'*DAI!*'

'One, two, three…' As one the entire room jumped up. Their fists out in front of them and their faces determined. The noise of the yell and the feet landing on the mat shook the room.

After this everyone broke into excited conversation, as the women all turned to do a little bow before leaving the matted area. They put on their slippers and shuffled into the changing room.

Lettice followed them.

Her roller skates got a few comments as she hung them back round her neck. She waited as the older women busied themselves with hairpins. She was surprised to see one of the younger women with her hands in a very fine fur muff. It looked like Lettice's grandmother's, only it was white and matched the white fur collar of the woman's elegant coat. Her hat was enormous too, with six different feathers. Tilly would be so envious.

'We're going to head to Caxton Hall, Mrs Garrud,' a woman called Miss Price said on the way out. 'Mrs Pankhurst has once again led them into nothing but trouble. If we hurry, we'll get down there and find out all the news in time for the post. Although we could take Isabel with us.'

The younger instructor, now buttoning her slightly grubby green coat, beamed hopefully. 'Oh, Mum! Can I go?'

Isabel was Edith's daughter?

Lettice thought it strange for Isabel to call her mother 'sensei' all the time.

'No!' Edith shook her head. 'I don't want her returning home alone late at night.'

'Course not. The danger the men would be in!'

Everyone laughed, and as Edith said goodbye to them, she finally turned to Lettice.

'Now. What shall we do with you?'

Lettice's eyebrows were trying to pass each other in anxiety. She whispered, 'I don't know. I think my mother is dead.'

The worry that had hidden itself away on the mat suddenly rushed back in, making her tummy churn and bubble.

Edith shook her head. 'Nonsense. She may well have been arrested, however. What is her name?'

'Mrs Florence Pegg.'

It was like Lettice had said a magic word. Edith's smile broadened as she excitedly tapped her daughter's arm. 'I knew she reminded me of someone! She's the spit! Isabel, run down the steps and get Mrs Hunt to ask after Florry Pegg.'

Isabel dutifully ran after the others.

'Your father must be worried sick.'

Lettice shook her head. 'He's with my grandmother in Brighton. He thinks we're staying overnight in Lewes with Aunt Catherine.'

'But you came to London and went to the march instead?'

Lettice thought about lying. The simplest thing would be to agree. But today of all days she hated lies. 'Mama thought I was with Papa and he thought I was with her... She promised him she wouldn't do any Whizzpoo stuff any more.'

'Whizzpoo?!' Edith repeated.

'I'm supposed to be meeting friends after school. That's why I came back. To go to the music hall. They've likely already left.' Lettice felt dismayed.

'Is there no one at home missing you?'

Lettice shook her head.

Isabel came back in the hallway. 'What? You've no brothers or sisters?'

Lettice knew that being an only child was unusual but she didn't want to get sidetracked. 'Our maid Tilly might be there. But she won't bother with the chores – she'll just go out if no one is around.'

Edith looked thoughtful. 'Then there's nothing to stop you coming home with me and Isabel.'

'But what about Mama?' Lettice was so surprised she forgot to say 'thank you'.

'She'll be looked after by… Whizzpoo.' Edith smiled. 'I like that name. Isabel and I are members of the Women's Franchise League. We are a bit less er…'

'Violent,' grinned Isabel.

'Militant,' Edith corrected. 'No one could accuse me of not liking a smidgeon of violence here and there.'

'Mum doesn't like being bossed about by the Panks.' Isabel grinned, narrowly avoiding a cuff round the ear.

Edith turned to Lettice. 'Stay with us tonight. We'll find out about your mother in the morning and hopefully have some good news to tell your father.'

Lettice wanted to wrap her arms round Edith and thank her with the largest hug she could muster. But she wasn't brought up to be so informal. Instead she stuttered a little and immediately burst into tears.

'What's wrong?'

'Why… are… you being so nice to me?' she asked between gasps. 'We are p-p-perfect strangers…'

'I can't very well put you in a cab, and fingers crossed hope your house isn't locked up,' said Edith dismissively and she walked to the door. 'Keep up!'

'It's probably because you were fun to throw.' Isabel winked at her young companion. 'She wants the opportunity to do it again.'

Lettice gulped. What was she getting herself into?

第七章

NANA

Edith and Isabel lived in Islington. Their house was one of many crammed around a square of green... or it would have been green were it not dark, cold and muddy. Litter bins were overflowing, as was the public house on the corner. Lettice trotted alongside the fast-moving Isabel, trying to see in through the steamy windows where men and women yelled at each other. A fiddle played as people clapped. Lettice, still worried for her mother, didn't feel like joining them. She didn't see how anyone could be happy.

Edith unlocked the door with a large brass key and ushered them into the hallway. From the narrow galley kitchen a man's voice boomed.

'Edith?! You seen the boot polish?'

'We've got a guest, William.'

Isabel set down her duffle bag and helped Lettice with her coat as her father came through to greet them.

'Miss Lettice Pegg. Mr William Garrud.'

Lettice smiled shyly at the bookish man leaning against the banister. He was shorter than her father, older, with thinning hair and an unimpressive moustache. Although his features gave the impression of a librarian, Lettice noticed how broad his shoulders were. He didn't stand like he looked. He stood like a dancer, confident and purposeful.

'A proper street rat this one, Edith.' He smiled. He had a slightly Welsh tinge to his accent, much like Edith.

'That was my doing I'm afraid,' Edith said walking past the stairs into the kitchen. 'I threw her into a dustcart. A full one.'

'What throw?'

'*Kata guruma*,' Lettice said. She surprised herself; usually it took her a little while to feel comfortable enough to speak with strangers.

'Well remembered!' Isabel sounded impressed.

'Go and prepare the guest room,' Mr Garrud told Isabel, 'and be down for dinner in ten minutes.'

He called to Edith in the kitchen, 'Why does your throwing her in a dustcart mean we've got to keep her?'

'It is only for tonight.' Edith popped her head out of the kitchen. 'Her mother's been arrested. Probably. Possibly.'

'You best come through then.' Mr Garrud pushed open the door to the dining room. The decor was beaten up. Scratches and dents pocked the walls as though someone had been swinging a cricket bat too close to them. Strange swords were displayed above the fireplace and there were framed pictures of men wearing those funny pyjamas. There were some newspaper clippings with headlines saying 'Suffrajitsu', also framed... Lettice's eyes however kept glancing at the black and white photos of the men fighting. She couldn't help staring as they were wearing very short shorts. You could see their muscular thighs.

It was a very strange house indeed.

The fire was lit, roaring and popping embers on to the pocked rug. Mr Garrud cleared away a collection of papers from the dining table. 'She's writing a play,' he muttered and pretended for Lettice's amusement to place the papers he had cleared into the fire. He chuckled and set them down on a shelf before seating himself at the head of the table.

'Sit, sit!' He pointed at a chair away from the fire. 'What did you think of the dojo?'

'Oh, I thought it was a very grand building,' she said truthfully.

'Could do with a lick of paint,' Mr Garrud grunted. 'Isabel, set the table and bring our guest something warm to drink.'

Isabel brought Lettice a mug of tea and set about putting the cutlery in place. Lettice warmed her hands on the large mug. On tasting it she began to feel more like herself. She also realised how hungry she was. Never before had she been so glad to see a plate of steaming kidney stew. Edith placed it in front of her and it was all she could do to stop herself from inhaling it while Isabel said grace. The stew was hot and peppery, and the bread, though a bit stale, sopped up the gravy very well.

'I should get the university to do a study on diet and physical culture,' Mr Garrud said, a chunk of kidney perched on the end of his fork. 'I'd be interested to see if the new fashion to be meat-free has an impact on endurance.'

'Do your parents eat meat?' Edith asked Lettice.

'Not when Mother cooks it.'

Edith laughed. 'I can't imagine Florry Pegg at a stove! I always assumed you had a cook and butler.'

'Our tweenie Tilly cooks quite well,' Lettice said. Tweenie was a bit of an exaggeration. Tweenie meant 'between stairs' a dogsbody position for a maid who helped out an entire staff of servants. But Tilly was their only home help. She was all they could afford and Lettice didn't want her new friends to discover that she wasn't as well-to-do as they thought. She was very much enjoying being treated like an adult and had quite found her voice. 'She plucks the dusters to feather her hat.'

There was a clattering sound from the hall. Isabel jumped up, banging her knee on the table.

'Post's here!' she said, dashing to get it.

'At last.' Edith breathed a sigh. 'They should go back to three evening posts. Waiting around for this long…'

'Get a rag from the kitchen – you got gravy on the table…' Mr Garrud huffed.

Isabel came in, clutching a handful of envelopes in one hand and a rag in the other.

'Here!' Isabel sorted through the small pile. She handed a brown envelope to her father and a letter to her mother along with two postcards. Lettice noticed her slide another postcard under the table.

'That better be gossip from your friends and not a love letter,' Mr Garrud growled, opening his own letter.

Isabel blushed red. Edith was reading and re-reading her postcard. It was crammed with tiny writing.

'Well, Lettice,' she said looking serious. 'The good news is your mother is alive.'

Lettice felt an invisible hand release its squeeze on her heart.

'The bad news is she has been arrested,' continued Edith, 'with… I can't think she's written this correctly… over a hundred of our people!'

'How many?!' Mr Garrud exclaimed.

'There isn't room in Holloway prison!' Edith sounded aghast.

'Most will be let out on bail,' Mr Garrud said.

'Has your mother been arrested before?' Isabel asked.

'I don't think so.' Lettice looked wide-eyed around the table.

'Don't you know?' Isabel sounded confused.

'She doesn't tell me anything. I only know about Whizzpoo because I eavesdrop.'

'I've been a member of the Women's Franchise League since I was ten,' Isabel boasted.

'Does it say why they were arrested?' Mr Garrud asked.

'What you do and why you're arrested don't always have much in common,' Edith said.

'That's not true,' Lettice said hotly, defending her father's honour. 'The police are good people.'

'Those police earlier today were good were they? Beating women up and handing them to the crowds?' Edith asked.

Lettice's opened her mouth but no words came out.

'Says here Yukio wants to meet me at eight. It's probably another match he wants to set up. I shan't be back late.' Mr Garrud folded his letter and got up from the table.

'Say hello to Mr Tani from me. If you do come home late, I'll be fast asleep… We have an early start.' Edith nodded to Lettice. 'We'll head to Bow Street court tomorrow. I'll write a few cards tonight and see if we can find out what's going on. At least Mrs Pankhurst will be happy; if this doesn't make the papers nothing will.'

第八章

HACHI

Edith was correct.

The protest made the paper.

Every paper boy they passed the next morning was holding up a front-page picture of a woman on the ground with policemen bent over her looking angry.

'Asquith calls election!' one boy yelled. 'One hundred and fifteen women arrested! Suffragettes attack the Commons! Police injured!'

Lies, thought Lettice, as they marched past another newspaper stand. She was trying to keep up with Edith, who seemed far more used to walking than her.

Lettice was a little sore from yesterday. As she had put her dress on that morning she'd gasped at the bruises on her arms where the policeman had grabbed her, and on her elbow and hip, where she had landed in the dustcart. She also had a small graze on her knee where she'd fallen roller skating. Her muscles weren't used to the exercise and she was stiff all over.

It was rush hour and, even on a Saturday, walking was faster than the bus or a cab. It seemed urgent that they get to Bow Street as soon as possible. Edith had received a telegram that morning, as well as two more postcards from Mrs Matthews.

'What news?' Isabel had asked as she handed round a plate of steaming kippers.

Lettice took one, and stared at it. The whole house smelled of fish; even her tea tasted of it. She picked up her fork and stabbed the kipper a few times, hoping that moving it about the plate would make it look eaten.

'Most of the prisoners were released from Holloway on bail. Any injured women were kept overnight. They've started taking carriages of prisoners to Bow Street,' Edith said, rereading the postcard. 'They have one hundred and fifteen women all having to show up to court at the same time! It's going to be chaos.'

There was a crowd of people outside the court. Some were obviously suffragettes, holding banners and giving out leaflets. Others were forming a queue; presumably these women were the ones who had been charged and were out on bail. There were men taking photos, and groups of fathers with children looking up at the building, seemingly undecided about going inside.

Lettice noticed groups of younger women heading into the grand opera house across the street. They looked too fashionable and elegant to be suffragists: dancers maybe, or a choir. It was so weird to see everyone else carrying on as normal, taxis going past, men with briefcases...

Lettice couldn't see her mother anywhere. She stood on tiptoe, looking around the crowd, holding on to Edith's coat for balance. Edith didn't seem to mind – she was absorbed in conversation with some WSPU members.

'They aren't going to press charges,' one woman in a sash said breathlessly. 'The first ten or so have all been released, so here's hoping the good news continues.'

'Good news?!' A northern accent cut through the mild chatter of the women in line and a woman in a tatty hat with red bushy hair hobbled over to them. As she spoke, Lettice saw that not only was she not wearing gloves – a sign of madness itself – she also had a missing finger. 'Mr Churchill is only releasing us to avoid bad press. No charges, no court dates, no witness testimony in the papers… no hunger strikes.'

'We don't want one hundred and fifteen criminal records! It makes us look bad.'

'We aren't criminals. We are political activists, and anyone arrested is a political prisoner.' The red-haired woman wheeled round to Edith and Lettice, her eyes bulging. 'How are we supposed to get people on our side if they let us go?'

'People will see we aren't dangerous if the police let us go.' The woman in a sash looked angrily at the red-haired lady. Lettice noticed that her accent had become more proper, and clipped.

'Annie is quite right,' Edith interrupted, with a nod to the red-headed woman. '*We* are the victims. If they let us go instead of saying sorry to us, they'll expect *us* to say thank you to them.' Annie pointed at Edith and touched her nose as if to say she was correct.

Lettice was sceptical… She really didn't want Mama put in prison. Her father would be a laughing stock: a policeman with a criminal wife? It couldn't happen.

'Pity you weren't charged, Miss Kenney,' the woman with a sash said to the red-haired lady, seeming to read Lettice's mind. 'You're not facing prosecution.'

'I've been arrested plenty!' Annie snarled right back at her. 'I've had them hold me down and force a tube up my nose and right down into my stomach. What have you ever done?'

'I made scones for...' the woman began, but the stare Annie gave her made her voice disappear.

'There has to be an enquiry. We're documenting everything.' Another woman joined the group with a notebook and a pencil that she hit the pad with repeatedly. 'Black eyes, bleeding noses, bruises, sprains and dislocations. There are photos. The police can't get away with this.'

'No one cares about your documentation,' Annie snarled. 'Have you read the papers? They say *we* started it. That *we* hurt *them*!'

'They won't like that.' Edith grinned. 'Everyone thinking they can't handle a few women.'

'Of course the general public thinks that's what we need,' Annie said through gritted teeth. 'Sense beaten into us.'

The lady with the notebook spoke up again. 'Mrs Billinghurst being tossed out of her wheeled chair... being so cruel to a woman who can't walk. The public can't possibly think that was justified.'

'The press won't report it. They won't even care what we say. We should have fought back,' Annie said bitterly. 'Next time we will.'

Edith changed the subject. 'Has anyone been released already?'

'Yes… we've given them medals. I think you should only get those if you're convicted,' Annie sulked.

'Do you know their names?' Edith asked.

Lettice's mother had not been released. It was horrible, not seeing her. Not knowing when she would see her. She didn't know if she was okay. She didn't know if she was angry with her.

It started to drip with rain and Edith took Lettice across the road to the Royal Opera House where a tearoom was open. They could watch the people come and go from the courthouse while staying warm and dry. The group of ballerinas Lettice had seen earlier were in the lobby, excitedly chatting. Lettice watched closely as they practised balancing and spinning in their street clothes.

Edith stopped and stared wistfully at them. 'Look at their balance. Perfect.'

Lettice was more interested in their fine coats and delicate faces… they weren't all pretty, but they moved as if they were only half remembering not to float away.

'Discipline, athleticism, balance… If only they enjoyed hurting people, they'd make superb *jitsuka*,' Edith said with a deep sigh.

They found a table in the cafe by a large window. The rain had worsened. Edith took off her hat and coat and hung them on a wall hook. They ordered a pot of Earl Grey tea to share.

'My favourite.' Edith smiled at the waiter, who nodded and placed the pot between them.

'Who was that red-headed lady?' asked Lettice once the waiter was out of earshot.

'You don't recognise Annie Kenney?' Edith sounded stunned. 'Does your mother really never talk about the WSPU to you?'

Lettice shook her head as Edith poured the tea. Lettice heaped spoonful after spoonful of sugar into her cup.

'Annie is one of…' Edith sighed. 'Do you want any tea in that sugar?'

'Mama says it gives you spots,' Lettice whispered. 'But I like it.'

'You should take better care of yourself,' Edith said. 'Sugar might make you feel more awake now, but later you'll be sluggish.'

Lettice slurped her tea and smiled at her new friend.

'Annie wants to attack the police because she thinks men only take notice of men, so we should act like them. Deeds not words. It is very hard to get people to pay attention to problems they don't want to deal with, like giving women the vote.'

'Mrs Garrud,' Lettice whispered. 'Why don't they give us the vote?'

'For all sorts of nonsense. They say we're stupid, we have our separate roles, that governing is for men only...' Edith leaned forward in her seat, her bosom pressed against the table, which was too high for her. 'But the real reason is obvious. The men in Parliament are elected by men. If they let us vote too, we might vote for someone else. Who knows who might win? Everything becomes unstable. It's like changing the design of a ladder when you're halfway up it.'

'So it isn't that they think we're stupid?'

'Oh, they think that too,' Edith said. 'But they think everyone is stupid. Being stupid is probably a good thing for a voter to be, as you can tell them who to vote for more easily.'

Lettice frowned. 'So women don't get the vote because...?'

'The politicians are scared of change.' Edith smiled. 'If you could vote, who would you vote for?'

Lettice blinked and looked surprised. She'd never even considered it. 'None of them.'

'Exactly my point.'

At that moment there was a great movement of people outside. Women were coming out of Bow Street court and being fussed over by the ladies outside.

'Come on!' Edith threw some coins on the table and jumped up to unhook her hat from the hanger. They rushed outside. 'Can you see her anywhere?'

Lettice scoured the crowd, jostled in between passing pedestrians. Then she spotted her mother, being led by the elbow down the steps.

'There!' She pointed and was about to run out into the road before Edith caught her. A large horse stomped by pulling a wagon of barrels.

'Watch it, sweetheart!' shouted the driver from his seat high above them. Lettice could see the distant frame of her mother being helped down the steps. It was hard to make her out what with the passing traffic and chattering people.

When they crossed over, Lettice sprinted to her mother and without pause threw her arms round her. Something was wrong; her mother didn't hug her back.

'Careful, child. Mrs Pegg had a nasty fall yesterday,' said a lady in a fur coat.

Lettice looked up at her mother's ashen face. It didn't exactly smile, but her eyes seemed to relax a little when she saw her. 'Lettice.'

'She's been released with no charge...' the women next to her was saying, but Lettice only took in how small her mother looked. She seemed older somehow.

'I can take them home,' Edith said. 'This one can point me.'

'Is there anyone to attend to her there?' asked another woman.

'I would assume so...' Edith said. 'Lettice mentioned a maid. And I imagine Florry's husband will be looking for them.'

The mention of Lettice's father caused her mother to make a sudden movement.

'Shh,' said the woman. 'Everything is okay.'

'Lettice.' Her mother looked at her pleadingly. 'I need my bag.'

'Where is it?' Edith asked.

'I don't know!' Tears swam in Florry's eyes. 'The police took it!'

'Here –' the tall woman in fur handed Lettice an official-looking document – 'don't lose these papers. One has a list of all her effects. Her bag is at Holloway.'

Lettice, surrounded by strangers, couldn't find her voice. Instead she reached for her mother's hand and squeezed it.

'Your father!' Florence murmured, squeezing her hand back. 'He can't know. He mustn't.'

'It's all right, Mrs Pegg. We'll take you home,' the woman in the fur coat said crisply.

'Letty!' a familiar voice called from across the road. Oh no. It was Mabel.

'Who's that waving at you?' asked Edith.

Lettice couldn't believe it. Not here, not now. Not after she'd been so rude to her on Thursday. The grown-ups didn't seem to care for Lettice's reluctance.

'Why, that's Mrs Browning's girl.'

'I didn't know Tabatha was arrested!'

'Letty!' Mabel called again.

'Go on, girl, say hello.'

Lettice walked over to Mabel, dragging her feet as she moved.

'Letty! What are you doing here?' asked Mabel.

'Lettice. My mother got arrested yesterday.'

'Mine too!' Mabel squeaked

'This doesn't make us friends,' Lettice warned.

'No,' agreed Mabel. 'It would be very tricky to make friends if the rule was your mothers had to be arrested at the same time. Hardly anyone would have friends.'

'Has your mother been released?' Lettice asked, trying to change the subject.

'She's about to go into court – they're going to be hours. I have to stay outside with our butler. We're hoping she'll get locked up,' Mabel said happily. 'That was the plan anyway. It would be a shame to do all that only to come home again.'

Lettice couldn't help herself smiling now; she found her classmate so ridiculous.

'Apparently,' Mabel said with a conspiratorial whisper, 'the police *pushed* and *touched* some of the women.'

'They did more than that!' Lettice couldn't help herself, she took off her glove and rolled up her sleeve. The reaction Mabel gave was incredible. It was a squeak of both horror and admiration at the hand-shaped bruise on Lettice's arm.

'A policeman did that? Is that why you weren't in school yesterday? You were allowed on the march!' Mabel's large brown eyes were so wide Lettice could see her reflection in them.

It was as though all the horrible things that had happened to her had magically transformed into a great adventure, just because of this reaction. Lettice was so pleased to be seen as daring that she whispered in Mabel's ear, 'I did go on the march… but I wasn't "allowed" as such.'

Mabel was nearly dancing with excitement. 'You're my hero! I would never… Is that your mother there with Una?'

'The tall lady with the fur? Yes.'

'My mama's friends with her too.' Mabel grinned. 'And the princess, and all the Pankhursts.'

It wasn't so much the name-dropping as another mention of the word 'friends' that made Lettice cut the conversation short. She didn't want to be Mabel's friend. 'I've got to go up to Holloway to get Mama's things,' she said abruptly.

'She was sent to *prison*?'

Lettice thought it better not to ruin the image by saying her mother was in the infirmary. 'Yes. I'm going there now.'

'Can I come too?'

'Don't you have to stay with your butler?'

'He won't mind. Mama won't be processed for hours.'

Lettice was going to protest further when Edith came over. 'How do you do?' she greeted Mabel.

The girl bobbed a small curtsey. 'How do you do?'

'Mrs Garrud, this is Mabel, she's in my class at school.'

'Pleasure to meet you.' Edith smiled at Mabel and turned to Lettice. 'Do you still have your mother's release papers?'

Lettice showed them to her. 'It says her belongings are ready to collect from Holloway.'

Edith was carefully reading the papers. 'I've been asked by Miss Kenney to get a message to one of the inmates… It will be tricky.'

'I can help!' Mabel squeaked, almost bursting with excitement.

Lettice scowled.

第九章

KYŪ

It didn't look like a prison.

Lettice marched alongside Mabel and behind Edith, taking a shortcut across the mud towards the main gate.

'It looks like a castle that King Arthur would live in,' Mabel whispered. 'It looks like it could withstand a dragon.'

Lettice didn't respond. She was still fuming that Mabel had invited herself along and Edith had let her come. Edith didn't realise that Mabel and Lettice weren't friends and had kept asking them questions about school when they were on the omnibus together.

This had pleased Mabel no end and made her even more annoying than usual.

'Right, I want you to take this note. It's in code so if you're caught, it won't look good but it won't look as bad as it probably is,' Edith said as they neared the gates. A policeman was eyeing them suspiciously. 'You need to make sure an inmate takes the note. They'll see it gets to the right people.'

'Won't the prisoners all be locked up?' Lettice asked.

'Some are given jobs in the prison,' Mabel jumped in. 'My mother helped in the laundry until she started her hunger strike. Then she lost her privileges. We should see a few prisoners walking about.'

'Fascinating,' Lettice said sarcastically. 'How are we supposed to hand it to them?'

'Any way you can. But it's important you aren't caught. That's why it's good Mabel is here,' Edith explained. 'She can cause a distraction while you slip them the note.'

Lettice didn't think this was a great idea, 'I think I'd do better alone.'

'Come on, Letty,' Mabel protested. 'I'd like to help. And you do get nervous speaking with adults…'

Lettice threw her a furious look and turned to address Mrs Garrud. 'Why can't you come with me and leave Mabel outside?'

'They are going to be far more suspicious of a grown woman than two young girls. Besides, I'll be helping cause more distraction from out here.' Edith was eyeing the policeman by the gate. 'Off you go. Go and fetch your mother's handbag.'

This was turning into a nightmare for Lettice. Not only would she have to talk to adults she didn't know. She also had to sneak a note to someone. And she had Mabel in tow, who wasn't exactly renowned for being subtle.

'You want the governor's office, miss.' The jailhouse guard seemed friendly enough. He stood aside and let them go through the heavy door that was cut into the massive archway.

Her grandfather's funeral had been held in a church much like this building. Both rose up around you and made you want to duck down at the same time. She crouched as she stepped into the courtyard.

'Look!' Mabel said excitedly pointing at two grumpy women in uniforms.

They were carrying bedding and were flanked by another guard. He was older and was walking about the courtyard like a rooster, reminding Lettice of Mr Metcalfe. Lettice thought that if she watched him long enough he would peck at the ground.

The governor's office was signposted and Lettice quickly walked that way, ignoring Mabel's hushed suggestions that she should drop the secret note in front of the accompanied prisoners. She curiously scanned the thin slits of windows to see if she could see more prisoners inside. It was perfectly quiet, however, and only the wind and their shoes scuffing the cobblestones made any noise at all.

A female secretary greeted them the moment they entered the doorway labelled 'Governor'. 'Yes?'

It looked like she was about to leave, what with wearing one glove, a coat and a hat. But the chill in the building explained the outfit.

Lettice approached the desk and handed over the papers. She opened her mouth to say something but the words caught in her throat. Mabel however, was confident.

'My friend Letty is here to collect her mother's handbag, please.'

'Of course,' the secretary said. 'Aren't you a good girl, coming to collect it? It will be a few moments. Take a seat,' she said, pulling a lever that sent a bell ringing somewhere in the building.

The secretary gestured for them to sit on stools on the far side of the room. 'We had so many in last night...

we were quite overwhelmed. I don't think anyone got any sleep.'

In the distance a metal gate clanged. Lettice shivered.

'Nippy, isn't it?' Mabel said sweetly.

The secretary smiled. 'The rain soaks into the brick; we never seem to dry out. The place is made of a very hard sponge cake.'

A woman in a prison uniform came in and took a sheet of paper from the desk. Lettice sat up a bit straighter, clutching the small note inside her coat pocket. The prisoner was pale and her uniform didn't look warm. She wore a simple white cap, black dress, rough woven apron – it was not dissimilar to a maid's uniform, but white arrows were chalked on the dress and black arrows on the apron.

'Number four hundred and forty-three, please, and Jane, bring me Stan's sheet on your way back.'

The prisoner nodded and without a glance at Mabel and Lettice, left again.

'When she comes back, you have to give it to her,' whispered Mabel.

'She didn't even look at us… I can't get up and walk over there!'

'You've got to try! Throw it at her!'

'Throw it? That's stupid.'

'Pretend to sneeze while you do it, or I can…'

'What are you two conspiring about?' said the secretary from behind her desk.

'Sorry, we were, um, admiring your wedding ring,' said Mabel.

This was possibly the most stupid lie Lettice had ever heard. It was such a personal thing to comment on. Mabel may as well have said they were talking about her ugly nose. The secretary coughed. Lettice looked down at her feet and blushed red.

'You find it a curiosity seeing a married woman at work?' She toyed with her ring. Her voice had lost its friendly edge. 'I enjoy working here. My husband does too. We see more of each other; he's the governor.'

Oh, this was awful, Lettice thought. Any married woman that needed to work was a bit strange. It suggested that her house was not in order. It was why Lettice's grandmother was so against Lettice's mother getting a paid job with the WSPU. The awkward silence had an odd effect on the woman at the desk. She obviously felt she needed to justify herself. Even to eleven-year-old girls.

'I don't like being at home on my own. I have two surviving children; both are married now… church charities aren't really my thing. I find it boring being at home.'

Lettice smiled and nodded, keeping an eye out for Jane's return. The continued silence wasn't the reassurance the woman was after.

'I like to be busy. And there are challenges here. I was never really cut out to be a housewife… my eldest son used to sew better than I could. Not that it's *any* of your business.'

The door opened and the prisoner returned with a pillowcase and some papers. 'Thank you, Jane. I'll take this.' The secretary put the sheets in a drawer and plonked the pillowcase on the desk. 'This is your mother's.'

Jane stood looking bored as Lettice approached the desk. Her hand was in her pocket, clutching the note. She desperately tried to make eye contact with the prisoner.

Lettice took the pillowcase and whispered, 'Thank you.'

'If you can just take the items,' the secretary said. 'Give me back the pillowcase and sign for them.'

Inside the pillowcase was her mother's empty bag, all scrunched up, and a bunch of other things. Hairpins, a hat pin, address book, pencils, receipts, a smelly salve of some kind, peppermints, a comb, a bracelet, gloves, a handkerchief, some coins, a stamp book, a bent blank postcard, and another notebook that looked unfamiliar. There was no make-up of course. Her mother kept that secretly hidden away in her dressing table at home.

Lettice poured everything out on to the desk. This sudden clatter got the attention of Jane, and Lettice waved at her with her hand below the desk so that the secretary couldn't see. Jane looked confused but at least Lettice had her attention. As Lettice started placing items carefully into her mother's bag with one hand, she continued to wave her other hand at Jane from under the desk, pointing to her coat pocket. Slowly she took the note Edith had given her and palmed it. Then she brought her hand up above the desk, making sure Jane saw her placing the note next to the other belongings.

Mabel noticed what she was doing and yelled suddenly from her seat, 'Look at me!'

Both Lettice and the secretary turned round to look at Mabel waving her hands in the air.

'I'm in a prison!' Mabel grinned.

It wasn't the most subtle of distractions but it worked. When Lettice turned back to finish putting the final items into her mother's bag, she saw the note had vanished. Jane though, had stopped looking at her. Lettice handed the empty pillowcase back to the secretary, who dismissed them with a shake of the head.

Out in the courtyard, Lettice berated Mabel.

' "Look at me?" Was that the best you could do?' she said crossly.

'I panicked,' Mabel said. 'I couldn't think of what to say. But it worked! She took the note. Mission accomplished!'

'We aren't out of here yet,' Lettice said her heart thumping as they trotted towards the exit. 'If they search her and find the note, they'll know exactly who gave it to her. "Look at me!" You're so stupid, Mabel.'

Before Mabel could answer they heard distant singing. Guards were running along the bottom of the far wall. A whistle blew. The girls didn't look, they locked arms and headed as fast as they dared towards the gate and to freedom. Lettice had to drag Mabel away from saying goodbye to the guard on the gates, and they carried on marching until they were a hundred yards from the entrance.

The drizzle was fine, like a cloud. Lettice looked about for Edith but there was no sign of her.

'You wait over by that seat,' Mabel said. 'I'll find her.'

Lettice watched Mabel skip back towards the prison. She waited on the bench beneath a large tree, her already dirty coat absorbing the small puddles. Pigeons gathered round her hopefully but they were disappointed. She opened her mother's bag. It was one of those large shoulder ones that could fit a newspaper, a loaf of bread and several large onions in without much trouble.

Lettice rooted through it and unearthed the unfamiliar notebook. Her suspicions were correct. It was a diary.

Lettice's heart ached with longing. She stared at the red cover. On it was emblazoned the word 'journal' in gold-foil lettering. She didn't open it, but looked along the edge. She could tell from the way the pages lay that it was nearly half full. Half full of her mother's innermost thoughts... her plans... her dreams.

What she thought of her only child.

It had always worried Lettice that she had no siblings. Was she so bad they didn't want any more? Were there older ones who died and no one would talk about? Lettice knew lots of children whose cousins and brothers and sisters had passed away when they were young. Fevers and accidents. Mainly fevers though.

She could just open the diary and find out.

Lettice looked up at the prison. Dishonest, treacherous people ended up in there. For years. Was this the beginning of her criminal career? Was this the first step into the dark from which she might never escape?

Inside, the whistles kept blowing. Maybe someone was escaping. Lettice looked back down at the diary. She imagined her mother's face: so angry with her, so ashamed that she knew all her secrets.

But what were those secrets? It was so tempting just to take a peek at the pages. What would happen if the book just... fell open? It would hardly be her fault if it dropped and she happened to read a page as she innocently picked it up.

Lettice tossed the diary on to the floor. It landed on its edge. None of the pages flopped open. Annoyed, she picked it up, wiping off the traces of puddle water, and put it back in the bag. When she looked down again she noticed two pieces of paper. They must have fallen out as the diary hit the gravel. She picked them up and examined them.

One was a boring receipt from the milliners. The price of a hat her mother had purchased – no wonder she kept it in her diary. If her father found out he'd bubble over like the bathroom geyser. Lettice stuffed it in her pocket.

The other was... a photograph.

It was very old. She recognised her mother in a funny out-of-fashion summer dress, with a tiny hat she wouldn't be seen dead in these days. She smiled when she saw herself as a baby in her mother's arms. Her mother had her familiar toothy smile. 'I may look like a pony but better that than a mule,' was a phrase of hers.

Baby Lettice was also smiling and holding a wooden elephant toy up to her mouth to chew on.

But who was that behind them? A handsome man with a great big moustache. Older than her father, he looked nothing like her grandfather. Odd.

Confused about who the man could be, she looked back to the happiness in her mother's eyes. Turning the photograph over, it had 1901 written on the back. Nothing more. Lettice didn't have any photos of her own, and loved this one because of her mother's expression. Her mother wouldn't notice if it was missing, would she? Lettice could always blame the prison for losing it.

At that moment Edith and Mabel appeared… panting. Thirty yards behind them were two large policemen, trotting to catch up.

'Come on, darling.' Edith scooped up Lettice's hand. 'Let's get you home.'

'Madam!'

'Oh goodness!' Edith said, pretending she hadn't noticed them chasing her. 'Can I help you two constables?'

Her innocent response caused the larger of the two to stutter. 'I… we'd like a word.'

'Yes, officer?' Edith said. She let go of Lettice's and Mabel's hands and confidently set her own hands on her hips.

'Both of us saw you up there, on the prison wall.' He pointed. It was stone and brick and nearly twice his full height, or three times Edith's with her arms stretched up.

'You can't be serious, officer,' she said. 'Me? Up there? Look at the size of me!'

'You were singing. You've upset the prisoners.'

'You'd think a sing-song would cheer them up,' Edith commented.

'Those are dangerous women who do not need to be excited,' one of the constables put in.

'We can't shut them up when they get going,' said the other constable with a bitter scowl.

'That sounds very dangerous,' Edith cooed. 'If I ever find myself on top of a wall, I will certainly remember not to sing.'

Both Mabel and Lettice snickered.

'You should take this seriously,' said the first constable.

'No jury in the land would believe someone my size could get up there, in full view of the jail guards and police. What sort of prison would allow that to happen?'

The officer's moustache twitched. 'Don't do it again, all right?'

Edith paused and relaxed a bit. 'Very well. Come on, you two. Let's leave these boys to their duties.'

Lettice and Mabel interlocked arms with Edith, and they walked away, their noses in the air.

The photo of her mother with the mysterious stranger was tucked safely inside Lettice's coat pocket.

第十章

JŪ

Edith left Lettice on the steps outside her block of flats. 'I expect to see you on Tuesday at the dojo.'

Lettice waved goodbye and climbed the stairs to the flat. She found Tilly on the landing.

'Where have you been? Your pa still ain't home and your ma's looking peculiar,' Tilly fussed. 'Some Panks brung her here and ordered me about.'

'I had to get her bag.'

'Two of 'em come in, asking questions, telling me she needs this and that.' Tilly was outraged that a maid was expected to work. 'Proper posh they was, big 'ats. Then they was going through all the cupboards asking about tea. I made them some, put the china out and all. They were after food as well – biscuits can you believe? I gave them those dry crackers everyone hates. Made it look nice on the plate but they barely touched 'em.'

'Is Mama okay?' Lettice asked.

'They said she got beaten up by a bobby. She's in bed.'

'Concussion?'

'Your pa was in the army wasn't he? War does things to a man.'

'He didn't hit Mama,' Lettice said.

'Well what bobby hit her then?'

Lettice paused and pondered a white lie. Her mother wanted yesterday's events kept secret from her father. She didn't want him finding out from Tilly.

'I think she was knocked over,' Lettice explained. 'I didn't see it happen.'

Tilly wasn't convinced. 'She's in the bedroom. Doesn't want the curtains open or the lamp on.'

'I'll go and see her.'

'Ask her if I can have the rest of the day off!' said Tilly.

Lettice went into the flat and knocked softly on her mother's door. There was no response. She opened the door a crack.

'Mama?' She saw her mother's body lying flat on her side in bed. She went into the room and placed the bag on the low dressing-table stool. 'I got your bag.'

Florry turned over. 'Any news? Will there be a vote?'

'I don't think so.'

Mrs Pegg stared at the ceiling. 'Is your father back?'

'No…'

'He mustn't know. Tell him…' She shut her eyes as she tried to think of a believable lie. 'Stupid brain… I… I can't think.'

'I'll tell him… we got the wrong train and… you were knocked over on your way home,' Lettice suggested, it being half true.

Her mother nodded. 'Good girl. Get Tilly to send a telegram to Brighton – he's probably wondering where we've got to.'

For a moment she seemed to regain some energy, as though she was about to say something.

'Mama?'

But Florry just shut her eyes and turned away. She didn't want a hug. She didn't care what had happened to her daughter. She just lay still in the dark. Lettice reached out into the blackness, and felt nothing but cold air.

Jack Pegg arrived home just as Lettice had taken dinner out of the oven and was dubiously prodding it with a bread knife.

'Smells… interesting,' he smiled.

'I put flowers in it by mistake,' Lettice said. 'I mixed up lavender and rosemary.'

'Looks better than your mother's last effort. Talking of who…' He looked a little peeved, 'Why didn't she cook dinner?'

'Mother had an accident and fell and hurt her head,' Lettice said, to keep the information at a bare minimum. Her mother could make up something, if she wanted to. It wasn't a lie exactly, but Lettice didn't feel good about it.

'She fell?! At Aunt Catherine's? Is she okay?' Mr Pegg's moustache drooped.

'She's in the bedroom, but be quiet; she has a headache.'

The grown-ups had their secret conversations without her.

There was nothing to do so Lettice ladled out a bowlful of hot stew and ate it in her room, hurriedly writing down all the Japanese names Edith had taught her. She also drew a map of Holloway prison and wrote down all the names of women she could remember. It was late by the time she turned off the gas lamp.

Tilly had left the moment Mr Pegg had come home. She had a small room next to the main bedroom, opposite Lettice's room, but spent her free time with her family. Lettice had never met them. It was weird, she thought sleepily, how Tilly saw so much of her life, knew all her family's secrets, and Lettice didn't even know the names of Tilly's brothers. She drifted off to sleep and dreamed of Tilly inheriting a fortune and asking Lettice to photograph her sitting on a prison wall.

第十一章
JŪ ICHI

Church the next day was a lonely affair without Lettice's mother. Mr Pegg had insisted they go along without her.

'You're not to worry,' he'd explained on their way to church. 'When I was in South Africa one chap got hit on the noggin by a bullet that had gone through his friend. It hardly made a scratch on 'is head but he had such bad headaches after it happened. He couldn't remember anything; he could barely march. His mate who the bullet passed through was fit again before he was! A lot of the lads accused him of making it all up, but I knew the bloke – he wasn't the type. Very brave.'

'Did he recover?'

'Yes! Joined the police, same as me. He's in a special division dealing with the gangs. He cracks their secret codes.'

Lettice's mother usually struck up conversations outside the church before they went in. Now they stood there awkwardly. Mrs Pegg had a way of ingratiating herself in any group of people. Mr Pegg struggled. So they didn't say anything other than 'how do you do?' to people as they shuffled into the service.

Her father returned to the pew after receiving his communion. He nudged Lettice and passed her half a communion wafer.

'A bit of God's elbow,' he whispered and she giggled as she put it in her mouth.

At the end of the service the vicar shook their hands as they were leaving.

'Is Mrs Pegg not well?'

'She fell over and hurt her head,' said Mr Pegg.

'I understand,' the vicar said in a conspiratorial whisper. 'Listen, I know it's important to keep your house in order, but I hope you understand that the role of a man is one of sacrifice and duty. By all means enforce but also forgive, yes?'

'I… She fell over… Her friends brought her home.'
Mr Pegg was going pink.

'Oh, I didn't mean to accuse you… Mrs Pegg is a very spirited woman! I would understand if things… well, the people she fraternises with are quite confrontational.'

A queue was forming. Lettice's father tried to get away. 'Yes, Father, I see your point.'

'As a police officer you must see a lot of unrest on the streets… very important that the unrest doesn't seep into your home.'

There were murmurs of agreement from those assembled behind. Mr Pegg was going from pink to red.

'And please don't thank me,' continued the oblivious vicar. 'I've been having private words with all the women of the congregation who might be tempted from the fold by the false promises of the suffragettes. While I agree it is good and true to allow a woman as much freedom as possible, it has to be in the limits of decency.'

'Florry may be a bit of a character but she's not indecent.'

'I'm going by what I read in the newspaper, those attacks on your fellow policemen…'

'You shouldn't believe everything in the papers!' Mr Pegg coughed. 'We arrest lads armed with bats and meat hooks, foreigners with guns… Skirt isn't an issue.'

'Now now, constable, it is Sunday. No talk of violence in God's house.'

'See you next Sunday, Father.' Mr Pegg grabbed Lettice by the arm and steered them both out of the church. As they left he said loudly so everyone could hear, 'It wasn't me. She fell over.'

'Papa,' Lettice said as they walked back towards the flat. 'Do you really have to arrest men armed with meat hooks?'

Her father chuckled. 'It isn't that bad; there are more of us than them. We're trained. They're not. Rare you come across someone who knows what he's doing.'

'How do you train?'

'Oh, they teach us ways of controlling people without having to knock them out.'

'Like arm locks?'

'Meh.' Mr Pegg grinned. 'It's easier to just clobber them. Best way to get a man to take you seriously is give him a bloody nose…' He paused and looked down at her. 'Not sure this is the right topic for us to talk about.'

'Why?'

'I tell you what, let's go to the Arms for dinner. Bring your mother back a pie.'

'Can I have some ale?'

'We'll see.'

Entering a public house was a rare treat for Lettice. On weekdays there was a certain type of women who frequented the pub, and they wore lots of make-up, something proper women would never do. Lettice's mother only had a tincture of rouge she used on her lips and cheeks.

'Otherwise you have to keep biting your lips and they can get awfully chapped,' she had explained. 'But don't go believing that old wives tale that laughter ruins your lips. Laughter is always the most important thing.'

There were quite a few women in the pub today, but this was post church, so many were there with their husbands. The servants had taken the children home. Sunday afternoon was the one time when the public house was a more genteel affair. Lettice followed her father through the haze of cigarette smoke to the bar, squeezing in between the older gentlemen crowded there. She knew they were regulars as they drank out of lead tankards, which the barman kept for them on hooks behind the bar. They also seemed to know everyone.

'Hey, Bob,' said the barman. Because he was a policeman, everyone called Lettice's father Bob. 'This can't be your girl! She's got so tall.'

'Grow up quick they do,' another man said wearily. 'Fortunately, miss, you look nothing like your old man. Little replica of your mother!'

'Lettice! That's enough!' Her father looked stern as Lettice helped herself to a second handful of nuts from the bowl on the bar. Lettice took that as an opportunity to start on the pork scratchings.

'Wifey not here?' asked the barman.

'She's got a chill,' Jack explained. 'She's in bed.'

'Sorry to hear that. If she needs a doctor, we can help raise some coin,' one of the men said.

'That's right, Bob, we've got your back if you need us,' said another.

Her father thanked the men and took Lettice over to a quiet corner.

'Here,' he said and handed her a lemonade bottle and a glass.

Lettice beamed. The opaque liquid frothed as she poured it into the small glass.

'To family,' her father said and reached over the table to clink her glass with his.

She sipped at the sharp sweet liquid as he licked the white beer froth from his moustache. She didn't know what she had done to be spoilt so much. She felt so grown-up and happy. She almost wished her mother were ill more often.

'Here you go, sir,' the bartender said as he came over with two plates of eels and mash.

The plate had a good dollop of mashed potato, and a bowl of what looked like luminous-green soup. Lettice knew that underneath that parsley sauce was tasty delicate fish like no other. Her tummy growled as she waited for her dad to finish with the vinegar.

'Tuck in,' he said.

She didn't hang about, filling her mouth with warm buttery mash.

'Now,' he said, taking a glug of beer, 'are you going to be honest and tell me exactly what happened on Friday?'

Lettice quickly put her fork back in her mouth, giving herself time to think.

She swallowed.

'What do you mean?' She tried to sound innocent, but thoughts blossomed in her head of the naughty things she'd done. Getting the train by herself. Running from the police. Doing jiu jitsu. Sleeping at a stranger's house. Also, Lettice realised with a pang of worry, she'd left her new roller skates there.

'Your mother...' Mr Pegg sighed. 'She didn't accidentally get the wrong train from Aunt Catherine's and magically get transported to London... she was hurt in the riot, wasn't she? At Parliament?'

Lettice looked as innocent as possible. 'There was a riot?'

Her father's expression turned sour. 'Stop protecting her and tell me what happened!'

Lettice suddenly didn't feel hungry any more. She wanted to tell him the truth but she didn't want to get her mother in any more trouble.

'Do you mean the march?' she asked.

'All right. The march...' Her father glared. 'It was bad, was it?'

'I don't know?'

'You jolly well do!' He hit the table, making the cutlery jump. 'I knew it was going to be bad and I wasn't even there.'

Lettice blinked in confusion. 'You knew before it happened...? How?'

'I'm a policeman, Lettice!' Her father sounded exasperated. 'On Thursday my boss, Inspector Gray...'

'Walrus face?'

'The very same. He gets word from the home secretary that there's going to be a protest. Some women want to deliver a petition and we were to stop them entering Parliament… throwing eggs and spitting on people, you know, those ladylike things your mother approves of!'

Lettice giggled.

'So I think, fair enough, no doubt I'll give Florry a wave and we'll chat about it later. But then walrus face says that the home secretary, this Churchill idiot, has banned us from arresting anyone! He doesn't want it getting in the papers that he's responsible for women in prison. They've got in the habit of not eating. Which makes him look bad. So he takes away the only actual power we coppers have… Well, I could see what would happen.'

Lettice, through a mouthful of mashed potato tried to say, 'What would happen?' 'Muh Muh Mmmphn?'

'Those suffragettes are all like your mother. Stubborn as mules. Once they get an idea in their heads they keep going and going. They take all their nagging skills and hammer them into a single task. Enter Parliament. It's like trying to stop a bolting horse. You can't use reason. Arresting them is the only off switch.'

'But lots of them did get arrested on Friday,' Lettice said.

'Yes. Walrus face gave in and got in a lot of bother for it too… but for hours beforehand orders were to pick them up and hurl them back. You keep trying to stop someone doing something for hours without a break… tempers fray. You know how I get without a tea break. Something like this was bound to happen. The moment we were briefed I asked for leave and sent a telegram to your grandmother. Spun a story about wanting to bury the hatchet. I didn't want Florry involved. I heard my colleagues joking about things they'd do to the women: what Winston Churchill outright gave them permission to do to them!'

'Mr Churchill sounds like a bad man.'

'He couldn't lead a dog on a leash.'

'Maybe if women got the vote he could be punished for what he did to Mama.'

'Maybe…' Her father sat back and pointed his fork at her. 'So, Florry *was* injured on the march!'

Lettice went bright red. 'I didn't say that.'

'You just said Churchill was responsible for hurting her. Did you see it happen?'

Lettice paused… she had a dilemma. Her mother's cover was blown. Her father knew about the march, he knew her mother had been there, and if he didn't, he was a policeman and it wouldn't take a great detective to check the arrest records to see if her name was on them.

Lettice knew that you should always tell the truth. Especially to your parents... but she didn't want her mother in any more trouble and she didn't want to confess she had travelled to London all by herself. She had been so bad. What if she'd lost her ticket? Or been kidnapped? No one would have known where she was. It was just as much for her own skin as it was for her mother that she shook her head.

'She told me to wait at a place called Caxton Hall and I did, and she didn't come back.' The lie came out so easily it surprised her.

'And the women there helped you?'

'Yes.' She thought of Edith nearly breaking the policeman's arm.

He sighed. 'I don't know what to do. My sister, your auntie Ethel, keeps warning me that your mother is a liar. Why won't Florry tell me what she's doing? Does she think I'll divorce her? That I'd take you away from her?'

Lettice's tummy bubbled at the thought of being taken away.

'Maybe she just wants you to think well of her... and doesn't want you to find out she is bad every now and then.'

He interrupted her. 'Was she arrested?'

Lettice froze.

'Lettice Pegg, tomorrow I have to go to work. Imagine how embarrassing it will be for me if all the other constables know stuff I don't! Was your mother arrested?'

Lettice looked down at her mashed potato and slowly nodded.

'Hey now, constable, there's no need for tears.'

Lettice sniffed. 'I got Mama in trouble.'

Her father reached over and wiped her cheek with his napkin. 'You haven't got her in trouble. She got herself in trouble, mixing with the wrong sort.'

Lettice felt a pang of guilt. She didn't imagine her father would think much of Mrs Edith Garrud. He'd think *she* was definitely the wrong sort.

'I'm as delusional as the suffragettes. They run after the vote, ignoring all the evidence that they're too irrational for it to happen. And I run after your mother, ignoring all the evidence that she's set in her ways. But right now –' he placed his hands on the table, his eyes all watery, beer foam still on his moustache – 'I know what I'd like and that is to buy us three pork pies to take home for supper.'

'Four!' Lettice corrected. 'One for Tilly.'

'That glutton can buy her own pie. We pay her enough.'

Mr Pegg stood up and went to the bar. Lettice saw he was also taking the opportunity to have another drink and chat with his friends.

'Oh dear, you shouldn't cry.' A drunk man staggered over and stood too close to her table. Lettice reeled back, away from his breath, which smelled of cider. 'You been a bad girl? Your old man giving you what for?' He laughed to himself and moved closer. He needed a bath. 'Why are you weeping, my angel?'

Lettice shuddered at his missing teeth. She knew not to talk to strangers. How was she going to get rid of him? Ignoring him wasn't working.

'You can tell me,' he said. 'Does he beat you? I'll set him straight!'

The drunk turned to go and challenge her father to a fight. This was too much for Lettice. She didn't want her father to punch him like the man at Victoria station. She'd be in trouble again.

'No!' she said.

'Then tell me why you're crying.' The man sounded angry. He wasn't asking any more.

'My mother is ill.' Lettice looked at the table when she said this, trying to avoid his eyes. But the man moved closer so she had to bend sideways, out of his way, as he leaned right over her chair. His breath fell on her cheek.

'My mother is a villain,' he said. 'Can't trust women. Not even pretty ones like you…'

'I'm eleven,' Lettice said and noticing the threat in his voice she quickly added, 'And my father is a policeman.'

'Think you're better than me?' The man was leaning right over her now; his jacket was touching her shoulder. 'Hmm?'

Lettice thought he was going to hit her.

'Look at me!' He said this so loudly she jumped up from her chair, nearly butting heads with him. She was going to her father at the bar. When she got up, however, the man grabbed her by the wrist. His rough paw wrapped itself round her arm. It was a weirdly familiar feeling. Edith's voice popped into her head.

'Sink your weight, pin your elbow to your side, then imagine you are opening a really stubborn jar of jam… What is it, Lettice?'

'Can it be marmalade?'

'Even better! Keeping that elbow pinned, drop low, step back as far as you can and use your hips to open the jar.'

It happened very quickly.

Lettice dropped her weight and it caused the man to bend forward. The chair was in his way, so as she stepped back his arm stretched further out, keeping hold of her. She twisted her hips and opened the imaginary jar. Her wrist slid out between his thumb and forefinger. Before he could work out what had happened she was gone.

Dashing up to the bar, Lettice rejoined her father.

'Hello, trouble,' he said. 'They have the pies with an egg in the middle – shall we get those?'

第十二章

JŪ NI

There was no post on Sundays, so there was quite a pile first post on Monday. Lettice had two notes. The first was one from her grandmother, expressing delight in seeing her and concern over her bad posture. The second was picked up by Mr Pegg, while he drank his breakfast tea.

'That's mysterious,' he said. 'This one is addressed to "L". What does "roller skates, 5 p.m. Tuesday. E." mean?'

'Ohhhh,' Lettice said, her eyes wide. 'I was... er... can I go roller skating on Tuesday?'

'I thought you might have been put off that idea after you fell over in Brighton. Glad to hear you're back on the horse…' Her father looked at the note again, 'Who is E? Your friend Eleanor?'

Lettice ignored the question. 'Can I go?'

Mr Pegg smiled. 'I'm glad you're putting them to good use.'

'Thank you, Papa.'

'Pass the marmalade.' He held out his hand and watched her do a strange movement as she took it from the shelf. 'I can open it myself you know.'

'Sorry, Papa – here it is.'

'And be quiet when you're leaving – your mother has a headache. She's in bed. No piano.'

Lettice didn't see Eleanor or Sam, so she was forced to walk to school with Tilly in the rain. At least she had a brolly. Once at the school gates, though, Lettice had to run inside to avoid getting even more soaked.

She bumped into Mabel in the corridor.

'Letty!' the girl whispered in a hushed tone.

'Lettice,' Lettice corrected her.

'How's your mother?'

'She's fine.' Lettice tried to walk away.

'There's going to be a protest on Tuesday at Downing Street,' Mabel persisted.

'Uh-huh.'

'They want stories about how bad the police were on Friday.' Mabel tried a new tack. 'Trying to keep it in the news.'

'We're late for class; I don't want to get beaten,' Lettice snapped, walking away.

'We've got to spread the word about what happened,' Mabel said, following her up the corridor.

'The papers say the police were in the right...' Lettice said.

'They're lying! Mrs Pankhurst says undercover policemen were in the crowd, hurting the marchers and encouraging other men to do the same.'

'I don't see what this has to do with me...'

'Your mother was injured wasn't she? Florence Pegg?'

'Shh!' Lettice looked around, thankful that the girls around them were paying no attention.

'Her account could be printed with the others in *Votes for Women*.' Mabel opened the corner of her satchel and Lettice saw the newspaper tucked away behind her books. 'There were lots of serious injuries.'

'My mother is no longer a member of Whizzpoo,' Lettice said hotly. 'And neither am I.'

Mabel looked crestfallen. 'You can't give up! You must see how we're treated. The boys upstairs get to learn astronomy, while we sew...'

'I like sewing.'

'Good. You can help me make some rosettes then!' Before Lettice could protest, Mabel had handed her purple, white and green swatches of fabric and some rather nice ribbon. 'I'm useless at it. I wish we could do more maths and science. I stole one of my brother's textbooks. He got an awful beating, but now I know all about Archimedes' Principle. I plan on going to university like my oldest brother.'

She turned and marched into the classroom, leaving Lettice holding the ribbon and looking dumbfounded.

Lettice thought she was going to freeze. At one point her nose dripped on to the slate in front of her she was so cold. The fire was lit, she could see the glow, but the weather was too foul, the walls were too damp and their small bodies weren't generating enough heat to stop her fingers, toes, nose and ears getting more and more numb. Mr Metcalfe was attempting to get them to underline the direct object in sentences he had written on the board. She stared at the sentence in front of her. 'Mary caused her husband to have headaches because she asked too many questions.' She couldn't work out what the direct object was. Her husband? The headaches? The questions?

'Thank God!' Lettice swore under her breath when the bell rang.

Mr Metcalfe asked for dinner money and they rose, like old women, rubbing their hands together in the cold.

'Hey, Eleanor,' Lettice whispered. She offered Eleanor the penny.

'I don't need your charity, thanks,' Eleanor huffed.

'I'm sorry about Friday,' Lettice began, fully prepared to explain everything.

'I nearly missed the show waiting for you,' Eleanor grumbled.

'Sorry…'

'And I know you spent Saturday with Mabel,' Eleanor spat. 'She's been telling everyone. Angela said your parents won't have you mix with us any more. Not good enough, are we?'

'I wanted to come to the music hall, but things happened…' Lettice tried to change the subject. 'What's Angela's fiancé like?'

'Enough chit-chat.' Mr Metcalfe swooshed his cane. Eleanor turned her back on Lettice, handed Mr Metcalfe her penny and ran over to Alice and Angela. The three giggled and left Lettice to pay for her first-class meal and walk to the canteen alone.

Lettice felt hurt. Just because she hadn't shown up for the stupid music hall. She might have known Angela and Alice would no longer speak to her, but Eleanor was supposed to be her friend.

The first-class luncheon was served at the high end of the hall, closest to the staff table. It was distinguished by the fact that it was the only table with a tablecloth. It was also raised on the low stage. Lettice could see her classmates further down the dining hall, laughing and chatting. Occasionally she thought she saw Eleanor glance over from the third-class table.

As the head boy said grace, out of the corner of her eye Lettice saw Mr Metcalfe sneaking a peak at Miss Troxell, rather than bowing his head properly like the other teachers. She understood why: Miss Troxell was very beautiful, with clear skin and perfect rosebud lips. She also seemed kind. Definitely not suited to Mr Metcalfe. She must have been twenty years his junior.

The young boys carrying bowls of soup and thickly cut white bread and dripping came to their table first. The second-class tables didn't get any dripping with their brown bread and the third-class tables, including

Angela, Alice and Eleanor, only got soup. It was lentil soup and looked a bit like the puddle Lettice's mother had been thrown in on Friday.

Lettice's attention was firmly on Eleanor, who was happily chatting to her new friends. A second course of meat stew came out but she only picked at it.

'What do you think they're talking about?' Mabel gently elbowed Lettice in the ribs.

'Who cares?' grunted Joan.

'I care. Ellie is my best friend,' Lettice said defensively.

Joan scoffed. Lettice was just about to say something incredibly rude to her, when Mabel spoke up.

'Eleanor is only talking to those two because you're sitting up here, Lettice,' she said sagely. Lettice knew it was a white lie to protect Lettice's feelings but it did make her feel better.

Joan shrugged. 'There's no point in making best friends. Everyone will be going their separate ways soon enough. I'm being sent to boarding school.'

'I'm going to sit entrance exams for prep school next year, I want to get into Westminster or Harrow,' Mabel put in.

'Those are boys' schools,' Lettice said.

'So? I'll dress like a boy if I have to, they're the best schools.'

'You not eating your spotted dick?' Joan asked Lettice.

'Have it,' said Lettice, pushing her bowl towards her. 'I'm not feeling hungry.'

***

It was strange coming home to a silent flat. Usually there would be tinkling from the piano, or visitors' laughter and voices.

While Tilly went round lighting the gas lamps, Lettice tried to make liver and bacon. The liver stuck to the pan. She'd used butter and it had caught, billowing smoke into the kitchen.

'You should've used the bacon rind like I said,' grumbled Tilly.

'You never said!' Lettice squeaked, outraged.

The noise of their argument had woken Lettice's mother who came to sit in her nightie at the kitchen table. Tilly poured her a good measure of gin. She stared into the glass and looked so miserable it would have broken Lettice's heart had she not been distracted trying to stop the bacon fat spitting in the water she had used to cool the pan.

'Mama,' Lettice said brightly, 'a girl at my school is collecting stories about Friday to put in *Votes for Women*.'

Mrs Pegg looked at the table, ignoring what Lettice was trying to tell her. 'Not now, dear. My head is pounding.'

'That's just it, they want to report injuries like yours,' Lettice tried again.

'I'm going to lie down.'

The scene her father walked in on when he came home was not the stress-free environment Lettice had hoped to provide. He looked around... kissed his daughter on the head and left again.

Tilly and Lettice served up a rather blackened meal for themselves. The bacon was nice but the liver was ash and the gravy had congealed. Mrs Pegg didn't want any food. Her bedroom door remained shut.

'She needs a doctor,' Tilly said.

'They are expensive,' Lettice worried. The men in the pub had said they'd help out, but that would mean going back there alone and actually having to speak to adults she didn't know. There was one adult she did know, who could afford to help. 'Do you think I should ask my grandmother?'

'Why wouldn't you? She's rich enough.'

'They don't get on.' Lettice knew she shouldn't be confiding in Tilly. She wasn't family. She shouldn't be eating with her either. Never mind. 'They had an argument. Mama wouldn't want Grandma to know what happened. She promised her she'd stop going to those marches.'

Tilly looked thoughtful. 'Your gran doesn't need to know how she got hurt, only that she's poorly.'

'Shall I write a letter?'

'Hurry, if you want to catch the post.'

301 Brockway House,
Erasmus Street,
Westminster

Monday 21st November 1910

Dear Grandma,

Thank you for your note which arrived this morning and also for the generous meal and room and looking after my parents and me and myself. I'm already looking forward to spending time with you at Christmas. Also, please thank Sarah for making me a drink in the parlour while she was busy with her other chores.

I'm writing to let you know that my mother has taken ill and is currently in her room unable to come out. We are hoping it is nothing serious but would be reassured if we had money for a doctor, or one could be fetched. She hasn't got no any worse but she really isn't herself.

I worry my father is too embarrassed to approach you for help.

    Written in haste, with love,

    Lettice

'Want me to post it?'

'You don't mind?'

'I'd rather do that than clear this lot up.' Tilly took the letter and left Lettice to scrub the kitchen.

At breakfast the next day, both Lettice and her father had porridge. They were out of bread and marmalade and very nearly out of tea. It was clear to Lettice by the way her father was re-reading the paper that he'd drunk too much beer the night before. Lettice's mother was still in her room with the curtains drawn. However, Tilly was full of pep and, without ceremony, handed Lettice not one but two postcards. Her father reached over and took one from her.

'Hey!'

'Have you got a suitor or something?' He picked up the first card. 'Remember. E.'

'Oh yeah, roller skating! Can I go after school today?' asked Lettice.

Her father sighed. 'I suppose it costs?'

'Not much! Just entry to the dojo…' she quickly corrected her mistake, 'rink.'

'It seems silly to have spent money on them for you not to use them,' her father said, placing some coins on the table. 'There's your dinner money too. At least your mother isn't spending at her usual rate.'

He was silent at that point and looked a bit upset. Lettice wanted to distract him so she picked up the second postcard.

'It's from Grandma,' Lettice said, showing him the card, which had some flowers and a cat on the front.

'Hold tight?' He read the back. 'What's that supposed to mean? What have you said?'

'I…' Lettice sighed. She would have to come clean. 'I asked her to get a doctor for Mama.'

'Lettice Pegg!' her father barked. 'Who made you head of the household?'

'I wanted to help…'

Mr Pegg's eyes widened with worry. 'You didn't tell her how your mother was injured did you?'

'I only said she was sick and to send a doctor.' Lettice glared back at him, her courage returning. 'She DOES need a doctor and YOU haven't got her one.'

'Enough of your answering back!'

'Sorry, Papa,' Lettice muttered resentfully.

'Get to school. Enjoy your roller skating.'

'Yes, Papa.'

School felt even colder than it had the previous day. The heavy rain meant lunch break was restricted to the hall. Eleanor was still not speaking to Lettice. Angela and Alice were playing tricks on unsuspecting younger girls.

'I'll swap you this really large shiny bronze coin for that tiny silver one,' Alice was saying to a girl of about five. The girl was in deep thought about it… She grinned and made the swap, handing over her coin and happily skipping back to her group of friends. Alice grinned at Angela; they'd just made a considerable profit.

'That was mean,' said Lettice.

'No one asked you,' Alice scowled, putting the coin in her pocket.

Lettice's stood her ground. 'You aren't poor. You should give her money back.'

'Or you'll do what?' Alice scoffed

'School is about learning lessons,' Angela chimed in.

'I certainly will learn from it,' Lettice said cooly and went to sew in the corner of the hall.

There was no Tilly at the gates again today. Lettice used the cover of the rain to run to the bus stop. With her hat and her mother's brolly and basket she looked like a housekeeper going to collect last-minute shopping.

She took the Mellish and Boffin omnibus, squeezing into the back seats. The conductor forgot to sell her a ticket – he was dealing with the adolescent boys sat on the exposed top deck in the drizzle, refusing to pay their fare.

Lettice sat in her seat, damp, cold and utterly miserable. It was only a few jerky stops before she alighted and trotted quickly through the crowds to the Golden Square dojo. She jogged into the steamy tattered lobby and, just as she was about to climb the stairs, a familiar male voice greeted her.

'Lettice!' It was Mr Garrud. He was dressed in shorts and a white *gi* jacket. 'Miss Pegg, I'd like to introduce you to Mr Yukio Tani, who will be training with us tonight.'

'Miss.' The Japanese man bowed. He had a kind round face and big black moustache that couldn't hide his friendly smile.

'I'll be training with…' Lettice whispered the word like it was rude, 'gentlemen?'

'We aren't gentleman!' Both men chuckled. 'We're *jiu jitsuka*!'

'You'd better behave yourselves!' Edith Garrud arrived and ushered for them to go upstairs. 'Come on!'

Rather charmingly, both of the men acted like boys, chasing each other up the stairs, taking them two at a time. Lettice had never seen sober men having such a gay, silly time, except at the music hall.

'Good to see you, Lettice Pegg,' Edith said and hugged her.

The sensation was a surprise. Lettice realised she hadn't been hugged in days... she was used to giving her mother a hug before bed. As Edith gave her a little squeeze, Lettice felt a warm happy feeling spreading through her body. He shoulders dropped and the hallway seemed brighter.

'It should be a fun session: we have plenty of space,' Edith said as they entered the dojo.

'Why the low numbers?' asked Mr Garrud.

'Judging from who hasn't turned up... the WSPU are up to something...'

Mr and Mrs Garrud exchanged worried glances.

Edith turned to Lettice. 'There are clothes for you in the changing room. Be on the mat in five minutes!'

Five minutes later, Lettice was beaming. The cotton *gi* top she was wearing felt heavy on her shoulders. There were only a handful of people training. Isabel, Miss Lilburn... Miss Horvat... She followed then to the dojo door. They all bowed at the waist like men and marched in. Lettice bobbed a curtsy and followed.

Inside, Mr Tani and Mr Garrud were on the mat. One man would throw a punch, the other would step aside, gently collecting the wrist in his hands and swiftly twisting it, causing his assailant to tumble on to the mat, stand up, and then defend himself from a punch. It was rather like watching a clockwork toy, the never-ending smooth motion: punch, collect, twist, roll, stand, step, punch, collect, twist, roll… They were both getting rather red and out of breath but kept going. The fatigue seemed to power them on, as the punches came in harder and faster. Mr Tani was quietly instructing Mr Garrud and encouraging him to smile.

After Lettice and the rest of the women had gone through the same breakfalling routine as the previous week, Edith got everyone assembled around her and the lesson began properly. Unlike last time, Mr Garrud was the one talking: explaining each throw while his wife cleanly dispensed of Mr Tani, who attacked her with great gusto. The noise the man made when he hit the mat, which he did at such a speed, quite frightened Lettice. He grinned from ear to ear, his face becoming sweaty and red as he jumped up, turned and with a beaming smile tried to lay hands on Edith again.

'This shoulder throw is called *ippon seoi nage*,' Mr Garrud said, ignoring Mr Tani shaking his head at his Japanese pronunciation. 'It's very useful if the attacker is armed with a police truncheon.'

Edith ran to the side of the mat and handed a real wooden cosh to Mr Tani. They exchanged the weapon with a little bow. Very quickly Mr Tani turned and, taking a step, with his full force, swung the cosh straight down on Edith. Lettice gasped - for a split second she thought Edith would be struck, as he had moved with such force the blow could have killed her. But Lettice needn't have worried, the little woman darted forward to collect his arm, ducked under him, and the force of his attack caused him to trip up vertically over her. His feet seemed to scrape the ceiling and he landed with a thud, right in front of Lettice. Everyone apart from Mr Garrud jumped. Mrs Garrud still had control of the cosh in Mr Tani's hand. In a quick movement she prised it out of his fingers and pretended to hit him as hard as possible in his exposed ribs, letting out a shout.

'*Dai*!'

Everyone jumped again.

'Understood?' Mr Garrud asked the assembled women, who looked blankly back at him.

'Do you understand?' Edith repeated.

'Yes, sensei!' shouted the women, and they all nervously split into pairs to begin practising the throw.

Lettice was more than nervous at the idea of being flung vertically. Isabel was having difficulty in convincing her it would be okay.

'What's this?' Edith came over. Lettice was about to cry. 'I threw you good and proper on Friday, and not on to nice soft mats either. What's the problem?'

'I can't... I can't do it,' Lettice admitted.

'The thing about can't is,' Edith said smiling, 'it can't last forever.'

She watched Isabel try again to throw Lettice, but Lettice was frightened. She had set her weight on her heels, making it impossible for Isabel to take her balance forward.

'Do you trust me, Lettice Pegg?'

Lettice looked into Edith's eyes and nodded.

'Have you ever walked past Selfridges? I want you to pretend that you are a mannequin in the window. Imagine you have a big fur collar on your coat, that you are in the tallest heeled boots... taller than that, up on your toes. Your left arm is clutching a jewel-encrusted bag. Your feathered hat needs showing off, so keep your head upright. That's it. Now, you're made of wood so you're as stiff as a board. And they've positioned you as though you're hailing a cab with your right arm. Can you do that?'

Lettice giggled throughout this and quite forgot about the throw.

'She's wobbling, sensei.'

'You're made of wood, remember!'

Edith played with her arm, trying to move it, and Lettice giggled as she resisted. Then, without warning, Edith pulled gently at her arm from above the elbow. Lettice gasped as she felt herself fall forward on her tiptoes. Her body met Edith's back as the tiny woman turned beneath her and, still stiff as a board, she felt her feet leave the ground and the room spin around her. Her hair, which she had done up in a ponytail, whipped the floor, and her stomach became light and free. She landed on her side by Edith's bare feet. Her eyes wide, her arm still being held by Edith's strong grip.

Lettice tried to feel anything other than wonder at the experience. Being thrown wasn't like it had been on Friday, where she'd had all the distractions of the protest, the policemen and her mother. In the safety of the dojo it felt like a ride on the swingboats at the steam fayre… only better… she wasn't stuck in a chair.

She had flown – all by herself. And even though she had been flung, she felt like she was in control.

'Are you hurt?'

'No, sensei!'

'Why are you crying?' Isabel asked

'I'm…' Lettice thought for a moment. 'I'm happy.

第十三章
JŪ SAN

Lettice made her way home with Miss Lilburn and Miss Horvat. Both women were chatting happily about the various bruises they had sustained and who was most at fault for causing them. They dropped her at the entrance to the flat.

'You coming Thursday?'

'I'll ask my parents.' Lettice grinned.

Lettice was surprised to find her father wasn't home. It was half past seven. Tilly thought he must be at the pub.

'On a Tuesday?' Lettice peered into her mother's darkened bedroom.

'It ain't just your old man who's acting funny,' Tilly admitted. 'Your ma still ain't eating proper. I tried her on soup but she says she ain't got no appetite.'

'There is one food she can never resist,' Lettice said as she went over to the empty larder. 'Shall we get chips?'

They smelled the fish and chip shop before they saw it. Lots of people were out and about, and there was a queue inside. Here housewives, shoe shiners, cabbies, dockers and even gentlemen from the city all rubbed shoulders. Men stood by the counter laughing loudly, drowning out everyone else's conversations.

Something about it made Lettice think of policeman R21: his grip on her arm, the way he just lifted her off her feet, the idea he would strike her ribs, her mother trying to rescue her and finally of being thrown to the ground. Lettice shivered, watching the men closely as they took their food and left.

'You want open or close?' Mr Gasparoni asked.

'Closed, please,' said Tilly.

'Your mama, she okay now? Still poorly?' Lettice liked the way Mr Gasparoni said 'mama'. Lettice pronounced it 'mar mar' whereas his accent made it a happier word. He handed over the parcels of hot food; it amused Lettice to see that hers was wrapped in a newspaper article about the release of the suffrage protesters. Mr Gasparoni didn't wait for an answer. 'She should pay me Friday but she didn't come.'

Tilly called him a rude word.

'Hey!' he said. 'I give her reminder; this a business not charity.'

'You should pay us to eat these chips! No one manages to get them soggier than you,' Tilly retorted.

'I want use proper oil, but my customers are saying, "I pay you later, I pay you later," so I cannot afford the oil. You get beefy fat. You want crisp fry, you pay me on time. You tell your mama to get better, okay?'

When they arrived home they found Mr Pegg sitting in his vest at the kitchen table. He looked totally broken. He had poured himself a drink in a mug, but the open bottle was on the table. When he turned to look at Lettice, she saw he had a black eye. All up his arms were bruises and on his neck and wrists there were scratches.

'Hello, love,' he said despondently, before looking back at his mug.

'Papa! What happened?'

'Chip?' asked Tilly.

Mr Pegg grunted and took a couple. 'Work.'

It was strange. Usually when he came home with an injury he delighted in telling them both how he had got one over on the ruffian.

'Did he escape? The man who did this to you?' Lettice asked softly.

'It… it wasn't a man.' Her father's face dropped. 'It was some awful women. The lads are calling it the Battle of Downing Street. They were so violent. I just don't understand how your mother can want to spend time with those… hags!'

Lettice looked confused. 'Whizzpoo wouldn't attack the police.'

'We tried to move them along and they launched themselves at us. I will not hit women, but by God they don't half make it difficult! I don't know what's changed! When I met your mother she was walking quietly with the other girls, with their banners. They sang beautifully; it was a pleasure to escort them. I was even convinced by them for heaven's sake.'

'They're losing hope,' Lettice said. 'The consolation bill is delayed and Mrs Pankhurst has told them that the ceasefire is over. They think the government don't take them seriously.'

Mr Pegg's eyes narrowed. 'How do you know so much about this?'

Lettice pointed at the article on the fish and chip paper.

'Huh. Your mother keeps muttering about it in her sleep. Pankhurst this, right to vote that…'

Tilly reached over and added more salt to her chips.

'That's one good thing about your grandmother's conditions. It keeps Florry away from the WSPU.' Mr Pegg grunted. 'Lettice, I forbid you to talk to those women. They are insane. You be a little girl for as long as you can.'

'Yes, Papa.' Lettice paused. 'I can still go roller skating though, right?'

He nodded.

And so it was that every Tuesday and Thursday Lettice went 'roller skating'.

第十四章
JŪ YON

Lettice missed the sound of the piano. All her mother wanted to do was rest and sit in the dark. Lettice wanted to tell her about her training. She could now defend herself from a (very slow) knife attack and she had managed to throw Mr Garrud with such momentum that he spun all the way down the mat and crashed into Edith. She wanted to share tales of Miss Lilburn and Miss Horvat, who were both so vicious that they came away with clumps of hair missing and had given each other black eyes, though after each session they were best of chums. Lettice wanted to tell her mother about all of it, but Mrs Pegg would only half-heartedly respond when her daughter touched her hand or kissed her cheek goodnight.

Lettice's grandmother had paid for a doctor to visit, but he advised against Lettice's mother having visitors and so Florry's life was very restricted.

'It's important the invalid is not overly stimulated,' the doctor said. Fat chance of that, Lettice thought. Her mother was like a prisoner in her own home.

Fortunately for everyone, the doctor's visits had not gone unnoticed and Mr Pegg was forced to accept the charity of his neighbours. Women from the church, Mrs Gue from across the hall, Mrs Miranda from upstairs, and Mrs Key from the bottom flat came every day, bringing with them pots of soup, pies, puddings and biscuits. Tilly was quite shaken with all this activity and, after watching Mrs Gue clean up the kitchen, must have felt that her usefulness to the household was dwindling. She therefore made considerable efforts to ensure everything was spick and span and glowered at Lettice every time she dared dirty a cup or move a cushion.

It had been a long time since Mr Pegg had played any games with Lettice. It was clear he was worried about his wife. He kept bringing her things: novels, embroidery kits, magazines (non-political ones), puzzle books, drawing pencils… and they were accepted with kind words but left untouched.

Florry preferred to sit quietly. The longer she stayed in isolation in her room, the sadder she seemed to become. It was like her soul had escaped when the policeman threw her down, but left her body on earth, sitting in a darkened room with nothing to do.

In her bedroom, Lettice looked again at the picture she had taken from her mother's diary: her mother holding her and laughing, baby Lettice beaming back up at her, the strange furniture, the handsome man standing behind them. It seemed like another world. Lettice wished she could see her mother that happy again.

Lettice carefully placed the photo back in the trunk under her bed. She took out her policeman's notebook and added to her sketches of all the locks and throws she had learned that evening while they were still fresh in her mind.

Jiu jitsu lessons soon became a hub of gossip about the goings-on in the suffrage movement. After the Battle of Downing Street the police had started to deliberately intimidate the suffragettes, following them to their meetings and disrupting their events, so some Whizzpoo members found the Golden Square dojo a safe space to swap news and gossip. More women hung out in the lobby on Tuesdays than entered the dojo.

This was frustrating for Edith, as anti-suffrage demonstrators began leaving her nasty notes and the police started to hang about outside.

'It makes me shudder somewhat,' she said, looking out of the large windows at the two men with notepads in the square below. 'We aren't breaking the law, but it makes me feel like we are.'

However, Edith did manage to convince a few of the women to try jiu jitsu. Lettice quite enjoyed having new people in the group. She helped teach them a wrist lock while Edith trained the experienced *jitsuka*.

If Lettice had known she would be expected to speak to a group of people, she would probably have never come to the dojo. Edith didn't give her time to worry about it though. Lettice wasn't very eloquent and did a lot of showing rather than explaining, but the adults around her all took her very seriously and asked her questions as she showed them again how to grip the hand and step forward so the *uke* bent over in pain. Interest in the young instructor followed her outside of the dojo.

'You can't be much older than my youngest,' said a plump woman. 'I should bring her along.'

'I must say, you do remind me of someone…' said a black-haired woman, putting on her gloves.

'She's Mrs Pegg's daughter. Florence, you know…'

'Of course! She was hit on Black Friday wasn't she? How is Florry?'

'She's doing well, thank you,' Lettice lied.

She was relieved when Una, the tall lady with the fur she had met outside Bow Street court, arrived. Una always slunk in at about six thirty as they were putting mats away. Usually just for a chinwag and to share secret plans with Edith.

However, today Una came straight to Lettice first. 'Darling thing, do be an angel and hand these to Florry for me. I think your father is intercepting our letters, the cad! They're being returned unopened with "not known at this address" written on them. He has awful handwriting.'

This shouldn't have shocked Lettice, but it did.

She knew her father was only following the doctor's and her grandmother's orders: 'Do not excite the invalid.' 'No more suffragette nonsense if you want your inheritance.' They did need the inheritance. Once her mother was better she would still want all those little luxuries she'd grown up with. The soaps and furs and trips to tearooms with her chums. The problem was it seemed

185

that all Lettice's mother's friends were suffragettes. To be cut off from your friends and not even be allowed to read their letters. It felt very wrong to Lettice.

On the other hand, the letters Una had given her were from women who, only a few weeks ago, had attacked her father and given him a black eye. Wasn't it bad enough she was already lying to him about going to jiu jitsu?

Lettice couldn't decide what to do with the letters, so thanked Una and hid them in her coat pocket. Later they were added to the trunk under her bed, along with the photo and her policeman's notebook.

She didn't sleep well that night. It felt like the contents of the trunk were bulging up and poking her in the back.

I'm like the princess and the pea, she thought. And in the early hours she extracted the letters from the trunk and made the decision that if her mother wanted them, they were hers. She could always choose not to open them.

***

Lettice waited for her father to leave for work before placing Una's letters by her sleeping mother's pillow. She kissed her on the head and ran to school.

She was late but she didn't get in trouble.

Mr Metcalfe was standing in the classroom with another man. They were both talking loudly, oblivious to the children surrounding them, or Lettice sneaking in. The man was well turned out, but Lettice noticed from his accent that he was not, as her grandmother would say, 'a man of means'. His attire however said he was well-to-do. Or at least self-made.

'I thank the Lord I have boys,' he was saying, looking at the classroom of girls and sneering. 'Eleven is such a funny age. Not kiddies any more but useless until they marry.'

'What these girls will end up doing is anyone's guess,' said Mr Metcalfe.

'I thought this was a good school.'

'Best in the area does not equate to good.' Mr Metcalfe sniffed. 'I don't see any of this lot going on to public school.'

'It's different for the girls.'

'Indeed, any girl who steps foot in a public school full of adolescent boys will be devoured in seconds.'

The two men chuckled.

Lettice frowned as she sat at her desk. She'd never been to a public school and she imagined it similar to Holloway prison. She imagined entering the gates and a boy (similar to the one who had laughed at her when she was alone in Brighton station) grabbing her arm. She pictured herself dropping her weight, moving through into an arm lock and snapping his elbow. As another boy reached over her, she slammed her elbows into his ribs, wriggled free from under his armpit and kicked his foot away... Another one did the same move and his weight was set so she couldn't repeat the movement. Instead she crouched low, and with a twist she cast him over her shoulder.

Multiple attacks was something Edith had them doing last week.

'Everyone is going to form a circle around you and they are going to attack you,' Edith had said. 'With a fist, a foot, a grab, or a weapon. Your only job is to put them on the floor.'

It had been a lot of fun.

'Good effort, Lettice. You have anger inside that little heart of yours.' Edith had smiled as Lettice stood panting in the circle, her arms still raised to protect herself, her hair stuck to her forehead. 'But anger isn't good for jitsu. Also, you are holding your breath. You have to breathe deeply and slowly. Emotions are healthy, but you can't let them govern you.'

'Pegg. Pegg. PEGG!'

Lettice blinked her eyes open. She'd been daydreaming. Mr Metcalfe's voice sounded angry. He swooshed his cane in front of her face. She wasn't sure what she'd missed, but evidently he wasn't going to beat anyone with his guest in the room.

'See what I mean? Girls! They're hopeless.' Mr Metcalfe coughed and raised his voice to address the room. 'After we salute the king, I want to introduce you to Mr Stevens from His Majesty's government.'

If anyone hoped Mr Stevens would be a welcome break from Mr Metcalfe's teaching they were soon disappointed. He recited his spiel like a fly buzzing against a window.

'The census is taking place in April. It's important that you explain to your parents how to fill in the form *and* the legal requirement to do it correctly.'

Blank faces looked back at him. Evidently not one girl in the room knew what a census was, but everyone was too scared of Mr Metcalfe to interrupt.

'In the week leading up to the second of April, a census-taker will visit and give each one of you these census forms. You *must* accurately record *everything*, and write *clearly* in each box.'

'What's a centus?' Eleanor whispered.

'I thought it was a man with the body of a horse,' Lettice whispered back.

Eleanor didn't laugh. 'I was asking Joan.'

Joan looked confused and said, 'It's where the government count everyone. Like a register.'

'No talking!' Mr Metcalfe interrupted Mr Stevens with a loud stomp of his foot.

Mr Stevens proceeded to explain how to fill in the form. Halfway through, Angela shot her hand up.

'Yes?' Mr Stevens said, looking surprised.

'Could you show us an example? Like, how would Mr Metcalfe fill his out?'

Mr Metcalfe coughed at this.

'I say, that might be a fun way of them learning. Why not?' said Mr Stevens.

Mr Metcalfe agreed. Begrudgingly.

'Name. It is *very* important you write your *full* given name,' Mr Stevens began.

Mr Metcalfe's eyes narrowed. 'Mr Metcalfe.'

'Sir!' said Angela in a pleading voice. 'That's not your *full* name.'

Mr Metcalfe coughed again. 'Mr Francis Hillary Metcalfe.'

'Hillary?!' Alice guffawed and the room chuckled.

'Date of birth?'

'Seventh of the sixth, seventy.'

'He's forty!' Lettice whispered to Eleanor.

Eleanor ignored her. The class murmured.

'Occupation? Schoolmaster, that's an easy one.' Mr Stevens wrote it out on the form.

Mr Metcalfe was fuming, but his anger doubled when Mr Stevens asked his address.

'Number eight, Ponsonby Place,' Mr Metcalfe said through gritted teeth, his face red with rage.

'I say, I do like the houses down that street. You must be doing well,' said Mr Stevens.

'Room four.'

'Oh, you're a lodger…'

More stifled giggles. A lodger in a single room was not the impression Mr Metcalfe gave of himself.

'Girls!' Mr Stevens's voice rose over the giggling. 'It's important you get this right – see here? The head of the household goes here with their family beneath them, then servants. Lastly you put guests and lodgers. Now, what is your wife's name?'

'I'm not married.'

'Widower?'

'No.'

'If Mr Metcalfe were married, he'd put his wife's name beneath him, and any children in age order below

191

her. It is of course very simple if you are alone in the world, like Mr Metcalfe.'

'Thank you, Mr Stevens,' Mr Metcalfe grunted.

第十六章
JŪ GO

Lettice came home after jitsu that Thursday to hear the sound of a piano. She had more letters from Una for her mother, but left them in her coat pocket in case her father was at home.

She walked in, carefully hung up her coat, and peeked round the living-room door. There was her mother, looking better than she'd seen her in weeks, the colour restored to her cheeks. She was wearing her husband's dressing gown, humming away as she played.

Lettice smiled to herself.

In the kitchen, Tilly was scrubbing the frying pan and Lettice's father was polishing his police boots next to a plate of sausages. He pushed it towards her.

'Help yourself.'

'She seems to be getting better.' Lettice smiled again, before picking up a warm sausage and eating it like a carrot.

'We all are. I'm being considered for promotion, my shifts have changed a little, but…' Her father knocked on the table, 'touch wood I'll make Sergeant by Easter.'

Lettice nodded her approval.

'Aaaaand…' her father said happily, 'I get Friday nights off now – no more marching down Bishopsgate in the small hours. So we can go to the music hall! See a pantomime.'

'Really?'

'Really.'

Mr Pegg beamed, then idly picked up a sausage, forgetting what he was doing, and used it to polish his boot.

Lettice finished her own sausage, and went to see her mother. She ran over to the piano and hugged her. It was so good to feel her warmth, her arms. She hadn't been hugged since Edith had done it weeks ago.

'Glad you're feeling better, Mama,' Lettice said into her mother's shoulder.

'Thank you, darling... and thank you for... you know what.'

Lettice did know what: the letters from Una that she had brought home on Tuesday.

'I have another for you in my coat,' she whispered.

'There's a good girl!'

***

Christmas was fast approaching. School was colder and instead of hymns they sang carols. Late December was a jolly time of year, despite the cold.

Mr Metcalfe wore little gloves until the room heated up and added something warming from a flask to his mug of tea. This put him in a much better mood than normal. The afternoons, when the girls were supposed to be learning domestic skills, turned into Christmas decoration making. Angela, Eleanor and Alice would sit together and pretend to make salt-dough decorations to bake later. Really they just whispered and giggled and talked about where they had been, and where they planned to go.

Lettice was happily making her father a Christmas present. She was halfway through embroidering little holly patterns on a handkerchief when Mabel interrupted.

'We need at least twenty-five yards of paper chains,' she said brightly. 'I want to take them to Whizzpoo HQ and cheer the place up.'

She plonked a heap of newspaper down in front of Lettice.

'Cut these into strips.'

'Where did you get all these newspapers?'

'The fires, duh.'

Every morning boys would come in early and light all the school heaters. They would also make firelighters by folding up sheets of newspaper and tying them in knots. Some would make extra and sell them after school. There wouldn't be any extra today; Mabel had stolen the lot.

'Hurry up, we need loads!'

'I'm not your maid. What will you be doing while I'm doing this?'

'I'm going to colour these sheets in purple and these ones in green,' she said, proudly holding up some wax crayons. 'Then we'll make a pattern. We don't have any white paper so the newspaper will have to do... I think we should do three white for every one green and purple in the chain... colouring in will take forever.'

'What if I don't want to?' Lettice grumbled.

Mabel looked outraged. 'This isn't for me, Letty! This is for us! Our liberation. Mrs Pankhurst said…'

'I've not ever been to the headquarters, Mabel! My mother hasn't been going recently either. She's given up. I don't care if they need decorating.'

'But you went to the protest,' Mabel insisted. 'And I know your mother is still getting letters because she writes to my mother AND she told me you're the go-between.'

Lettice's jaw hung open. 'You haven't told anyone, have you?'

Mabel looked offended. 'Of course not! I keep secrets. But I am curious. How come you go to the meetings if your mother doesn't?'

Lettice grew red. 'I'm not going to Whizzpoo meetings. Una comes to the dojo and she gives me the letters there.'

'What's a dojo?'

Lettice realised she'd said too much. Mabel was going to be like a dog after a bone now, pestering her for information. And in truth, Lettice was desperate to confide in someone – she wanted to show off about jiu jitsu so badly, how she was learning all the Japanese names for the throws and making sketches of them in her policeman's notebook. She could do a forward roll from standing and was soon going to be able to dive over people and breakfall as well as Isabel. She had been doing all these incredible things and had had no one to tell.

Mabel leaned over the pile of newspapers and repeated, a little louder this time, 'What's a dojo?'

'All right, all right!' Lettice said in a hushed whisper. 'Be quiet and I'll tell you all about it.'

She put down her embroidery and began slicing up the paper. She explained how she had followed her mother, narrowly escaped arrest and been taken to her first jiu jitsu lesson. Mabel was doing a very good job of keeping quiet as she soaked up Lettice's whispered tale. Lettice could sense the girl's excitement by watching her arm move faster and faster as she coloured in vast sheets of newspaper. Her tiny gasps only just audible over the noise of the crayon moving back and forth. When Lettice talked about Mr Tani, Mabel could contain herself no longer.

'A man hits you?!' she squeaked. 'You fight men?'

Several girls looked over.

'Shh!' whispered Lettice. 'He tries to hit me, but I'm taught to move so I can throw him. He does it so I can practise.'

'You're so brave!' Mabel said, utterly shocked. 'And Miss Dugdale does this jiu jitsu too?'

'No, Una turns up after the sessions, and I hide the letters in my roller skates.'

'Roller skates?'

'I tell Father I go roller skating,' Lettice explained. 'He made me promise I wouldn't do any suffragette stuff, and a lot of the women I train with are Whizzpoo people.'

'Talking of which, have you seen the latest copy of *Votes For Women* –' Mabel mouthed the last three words in a hushed tone which, if anything, made anyone eavesdropping more able to understand her – 'Kitty Marshall got arrested.'

'Oh yeah.' Lettice giggled. 'She threw a potato at Winston Churchill, cos he looks like one.'

Mabel giggled so loudly some girls looked over. 'Oh, he does! He does! A potato with ginger hair! My mother despises him and so do I!'

Lettice smiled. Mabel's disapproval made her feel justified in her contempt for Winston Churchill. It was he, after all, who had told the police not to arrest the suffragettes on Black Friday. It was his fault the protest had turned violent. Because of him Lettice's mother had got injured. She liked the fact that Mabel confirmed her feelings instead of correcting them.

'Is he going to be at the nativity play?'

Lettice felt her stomach leap and her eyes widened. 'Why would he be?'

'There's usually an MP or two who comes down for the nativity isn't there? It makes a nice story for the newspapers and our church is the closest one to Parliament. He was there last year, I think.'

On the last Friday before Christmas they would march in a crocodile down to the church and perform a navity play for the parents and congregation. Lettice always played an angel. All the girls were angels except the one who got to be Mary. That was given to the prettiest girl in the school, which for the last three years running had been Angela. It was a peculiar casting choice, Lettice thought. A blonde Mary. Angela hardly looked like she was from Bethlehem. Really Mabel looked the one most likely to have come from the Middle East, or they should have given it to Miriam as she really was Jewish. But Miriam was short with curly hair and a wart on her cheek.

The boys played shepherds, the three kings, innkeepers, Joseph, King Herod, his soldiers, and Gabriel. They even got to play both ends of the donkey.

They got to dress up and wear beards and sing the solo parts to the songs. The girls just stood in a line in white smocks and tried not to fall asleep along with the congregation.

Mabel was right, last year there had been a group of important grown-ups having their photos taken with some of the children. Her mother had made a point of talking to some of the wives, while Mr Pegg embarrassed her by pretending to arrest the children. All the important grown-ups posed on the church steps. Angela and all the blonde girls (except Joan as she could never keep still) were placed sweetly either side. She recalled Sam drawing moustaches on the picture when it was printed in the paper.

'If Winston Churchill *is* there…' Lettice's mind leaped to the sort of revenge she had fantasized about, 'we need to humiliate him.'

Mabel looked quite taken aback. 'How do you mean?'

'We could always throw potatoes…' Lettice murmured, 'or rocks.'

'I don't want to be arrested!' Mabel said nervously. 'I've been reading about what they do to women who are arrested.'

'That's only if you go on hunger strike.' Lettice dismissed her worry and then thought about what had happened to her as a result of the decisions by Winston Churchill.

'I know… we can throw manure! It's easy to get hold of *and* more likely to stick to his fat head.' Her nose wrinkled at the memory of the stench.

'We'll get in awful trouble.'

'You don't have to do it,' Lettice said, her jaw set. 'But I will.'

***

Returning home after school that day was particularly hard for Lettice. Eleanor and Sam were walking together as usual, and Sam had tried to be friendly. Lettice had responded, but Eleanor cold-shouldered her, telling off her brother for making them late. Lettice walked alone in the crowd of children. It felt rotten to have no friends. She considered waiting with Mabel for her nanny to collect her, but despite getting on quite well with her now, she wasn't quite prepared to be seen leaving school with her.

Back home, Lettice was greeted by Tilly, who was collecting the post from the pigeonhole in the lobby.

'You've got a posh card here,' Tilly said, holding up an envelope.

'What are all those?' Lettice looked at the massive pile of letters.

'Christmas cards, duh!' Tilly pulled a face and started climbing the stairs to the flat.

'You know there's a service staircase at the back of the building? For servants?'

'Yeah,' Tilly said, 'but it's really cold and narrow. Here, take these.'

Lettice had a bundle of envelopes plonked in her arms. A couple fell to the ground and Tilly picked them up while she searched for her key. Lettice shook her head and followed the maid into the flat.

'Grandma will be visiting soon. For Christmas,' Lettice called after her, while putting the letters on a side table.

'Yup, I heard.'

'She's got a full house staff,' explained Lettice. 'She's used to certain standards.'

'She'll also be sleeping in your bedroom,' Tilly said happily. 'You gonna bunk with me like last year?'

Lettice had forgotten that.

Originally, they'd planned to spend Christmas at her grandparents' house last year, but after an argument on Christmas Eve her parents had come back to the flat. Peter, Lettice's uncle, had also stayed with them, and slept in Lettice's bedroom. So Lettice shared Tilly's room.

Tilly was even greener back then, straight from the workhouse. She was full of stories about the best methods to steal and smuggle food back from the kitchens. After two nights the girls had quite a haul: a jar of raw mincemeat, a tin of crackers, some sugared almonds and gingerbread. They had waited until Mr Pegg had finally got out of his comfy chair and gone to bed before lighting a candle and sharing ghost stories.

On Christmas Day, while the grown-ups went to church, Lettice had stayed behind with Tilly and helped her prepare the feast. Tilly could read but wasn't confident, and Lettice took great delight in reading *A Christmas Carol* to her while the goose was slowly cooking. She particularly enjoyed Tilly's reactions:

'Read that bit again!'

'He's a right rogue, reminds me of Mrs Dean from the workhouse.'

'Yer mean it was *his* grave? Blimey, that's horrible! Imagine finding your own tombstone!'

When the others had got back, the flat had been steaming, the goose was resting, vegetables were cooking and the Christmas pudding was waiting to be set alight.

Tilly had hugged Lettice goodbye and gone to her parents' house with a great big sack of treats for her family. When she returned at six o'clock they'd all sat back down and eaten the scraps together.

Lettice realised Tilly was the closest thing to a big sister she was ever likely to have. She was worried her grandmother would be angered by her lack of work ethic. Her grandmother could easily demand that Tilly be sacked. Lettice resolved she would do all she could to stop her family from being ripped apart.

Even if it meant cleaning windows.

'Is your uncle coming too?' Tilly asked.

'He's abroad…' Lettice said vaguely, looking at the envelope addressed to her. She recognised Edith's handwriting.

'But your gran will be here on Christmas Eve?'

'The day before,' Lettice mumbled.

'Christmas Eve Eve.' Tilly giggled. 'I'll set the cot out in my room and make sure the sheets are done for then,' she said happily. 'It'll be fun.'

'Yeah…' Lettice read her invitation.

Punch on Boxing Day!
Mrs Garrud requests the pleasure of your
fighting company to celebrate the festive season
and New Year.
26th December 1910 at the Gardenia, 6
Catherine Street.

In the bottom right-hand corner were further details: *6.30 pm. Fruit punch plus vegetarian supper. Dress: casual.* And on the left was Mrs Garrud's home address, where she had written *répondez s'il vous plaît*.

'I need to reply to this,' Lettice said.

'Is it from a boy?' Tilly asked.

'No!' Lettice was appalled at the idea. 'It's my friends from… roller skating.'

Lettice went into her bedroom and slid her trunk out from under the bed, searching for her letter-writing stationery. She wrote a brief note to Edith, thanking her and saying she would see her tomorrow at the dojo.

Returning the box of stationery to her trunk, she paused. In the trunk, along with the old doll, souvenirs, her lucky elephant, a box of buttons, African jewellery, seashells and other treasures… was the police notebook she had been updating with throw techniques and their Japanese names. It was next to the picture of her mother laughing, which Lettice had 'borrowed' from her mother's diary. Underneath that were several issues of *Votes For Women*, which she had felt obliged to purchase and sneak home after jiu jitsu.

Votes For Women was the WSPU's weekly newspaper and contained some quite incendiary articles. On the cover of one was the statue of Boudicca standing in her chariot with a spear in hand. It was full of articles with headlines like 'The Sword and the Spirit' or 'Who Is to Blame?' and open letters to the prime minister.

She also had some leaflets that she'd promised to distribute at school, but she knew if Mr Metcalfe caught her with them she'd end up explaining it to his cane.

However, the person she was most concerned about discovering them was her grandmother.

She was just the sort of person to rifle through Lettice's things.

All the suffrage items would be hard to explain away, particularly the newspapers. They had dates on, and were bought after her mother had promised not to be a suffragette any more. But Mrs Pegg wouldn't be the only one in trouble. What if Lettice was asked where she got the photo of her mother? She couldn't admit to her grandmother that Florry had been in prison...

and it would look to her mother like Lettice had read her diary.

There was only one thing for it.

Lettice put all the evidence in an old pillowcase... she would have to find a place to hide it before her grandmother came to stay.

第十七章
JŪ ROKU

It was still a week until the nativity play, and while Mabel wasn't keen on throwing manure at Winston Churchill herself, she certainly took her role as assistant very seriously. Lettice was very pleased to have a co-conspirator. At last she felt she could actually do something rather than just watch things fall apart around her.

Mabel and Lettice had been spending more time together in the playground. Lettice had thought she would be embarrassed, but realised she actually didn't care. Angela and Alice could gossip all they want; she had real-life work to do, and someone she could trust to help her do it. She didn't even mind spending time in the school's back yard, waiting for Mabel's nanny to walk them home.

'I've worked out a bucket you can use,' said Mabel. 'Also, we can use the manure from the taxi rank. It won't be as fresh, but that means you won't be able to smell it. We can put some of the snow confetti on top so it looks like a prop.'

Lettice picked up a ball of the semi-dry manure and aimed for the bottle on the wall. She flung it with all her might, but it didn't land anywhere near the wall.

'How far away is the choir from the congregation?' she asked, weighing another ball of dung in her hand.

'At least ten yards,' Mabel said with a worried expression. 'You're going to have to get better at throwing. My brother's a good bowler, but he's away at university.'

Lettice paused. 'You have a lot of brothers, don't you?'

'Four,' Mabel said. 'I'm the youngest and the only girl. Mother said she always wanted a girl.'

'How much younger are you?'

'Nine years!' Mabel said. 'My father was abroad a lot for work and Mama stayed here. Then when my brothers were all old enough for boarding school, she joined him. When Papa got his job in London they came back with me.'

'Must be difficult for you.' Lettice was tiptoeing around the question she really wanted to ask her. If Mabel's mother wanted a girl, did she want it enough to adopt one? 'I mean, it must be strange for you being so much younger… and the only girl.'

'Yeah.' Mabel looked awkward and tried to change the subject. 'I think it's the way you're tensing your arm; just let it go.'

A thought crossed Lettice's mind. What was it Mrs Garrud always said? *I don't care how strong a man's arm is, it's never going to be stronger than my hips. Use your hips.*

Lettice squeezed the ball of manure. This time she turned her body, letting her arm fly away from her and twisting her hips. She relaxed her arm and let go of the ball… it went flying past the bottle and the wall, and into the road beyond.

'Oi!' A shout came from the street.

'Brilliant, Letty!' Mabel smiled. 'How did you do that?!'

'It's something I learned at jiu jitsu,' Lettice said coyly. She paused and really thought about what she was about to offer. 'You should come with me. It's every Tuesday and Thursday. You get a bit bruised, but it's worth it.'

'It sounds so scary, though.'

'It's a good sort of scary,' said Lettice. 'I just wish I could have my own *gi*; it's this special cotton jacket that everyone wears. I borrow an old one and it has a ripped sleeve. It makes me look tatty – and Isabel and Edith and Mr Tani… they all look so smart. Like an army. But everyone is really friendly, and you're treated like a grown-up…'

Mabel held her hands up. 'Thanks, Letty. But I'm happy with both feet on the ground. I don't even do jump rope.'

'You're canny though,' Lettice said. 'You need to be clever for jiu jitsu, because you have to quickly work out what to do.'

'Oh, my goodness! You think I'm clever!'

Lettice looked confused. 'You are clever.'

'You're being nice to me!' Mabel beamed.

Lettice rolled her eyes. 'Stop being silly and help me work on my aim.'

***

Mr Pegg was true to his word and took Lettice and her mother to watch *Aladdin* at the music hall that Friday night.

Lettice wore her poshest frock, and tied up her hair with a velvet ribbon.

The place was sparkling from the moment they arrived. There were plush red carpets and a throng of cold but excited people clutching their programmes. The ushers escorted them to their seats. Seats that Lettice nearly toppled out of on several occasions. She squeaked when she spotted Mr Tani, being used as a punch bag by Wishy Washy. He did elaborate breakfalls to the delight of the audience and he appeared again later, dressed as one of Abananzar's guards.

It was a terrific show. Lettice hadn't laughed so hard in ages.

They took a cab home, everyone humming the songs and chatting about the elaborate costumes, and how even if those weren't real jewels that set would have cost a fair sum. All the way up the stairs to their flat they giggled and on reaching the top, Tilly opened the door for them.

'There's a bobby here for Jack,' she said.

'Mr Pegg,' Florry corrected her. 'Come on, Tilly, we've been through this.'

Lettice's father went into the living room. Lettice followed, clutching her programme to add to her collection.

'Jack.'

It was walrus face… Inspector Gray. He stood awkwardly with a false smile tucked under his bushy moustache.

'Did the girl offer you a drink?' Mr Pegg asked, gesturing for him to sit down.

'Er no…' Inspector Gray sat, stood up and sat again.

'Tilly!' Mr Pegg barked and then turned to his boss. 'Would you like one?'

'Please, something stiff, and pour yourself one while you're at it.'

Lettice sat in the corner. The men clinked glasses and lit pipes. It was like Lettice had become invisible. She figured she probably wasn't supposed to be eavesdropping, but now adult business was going on, the men treated her as if she were a dog. Something with ears but no capability to understand. She sat quietly looking at her programme, listening intently.

'It's the Latvian gang.'

'The anarchist lot?'

'Bentley found them tonight. In Houndsditch. I've just come…'

'My old route!' Mr Pegg smiled. 'You mean to say they were under my nose the whole time? I say, Inspector, are you all right?'

Inspector Gray sat forward in his chair; he looked like he was going to be sick. 'He's dead, Jack. Shot. Bryant and Woodham got hit too, but last I heard, still breathing.'

'Blimey!' Mr Pegg stood up clutching his head in his hands. 'They killed one of ours?!'

'Three of ours… Bentley was first; he'd forced the door… but they got Choat too… and Tucker. All quite dead.'

Lettice's blood ran cold. If her father had been doing his usual round tonight… Her heart hammered in her ears.

Inspector Gray downed his drink and stood up. 'I need you in tomorrow, Jack. First thing. You will obviously make Sergeant well before Easter.'

'Of course, sir.'

'These bloomin' guns,' Inspector Gray said as he handed his glass back to Mr Pegg.

'I'll have my wife take a pot roast to…' mumbled Lettice's father, still in shock. Inspector Gray had already put on his hat.

'First thing tomorrow, Pegg!'

The front door slammed.

第十八章

JŪ NANA

The dojo was particularly cold at this time of year. Lettice had taken to wearing two vests underneath Edith's spare *gi* top. The more jiu jitsu she did, the less she considered her size and relative lack of strength as a weakness… It meant she was fast, and getting faster. She was also better at balancing. She could get very close to Miss Lilburn and jab her in the ribs with a well-placed knuckle, instead of trying to block an attack.

A great trick Mr Garrud had taught them was to sweep away their opponent's feet, just as their opponent was about to place them. It took hours to learn, but needed no strength at all: just timing.

'If you can feel them advancing, it is much easier,' Mr Garrud had said. 'Let them take hold of you. If you shut your eyes you can feel their steps. Then when you know they are just about to put their toe down, sweep their foot away... Ow!' Edith had kicked him in the ankle.

'That works too,' she said.

And Lettice's new-found speed had made her quite a confident thief.

With her roller skates round her neck, along with her woollen scarf, she had spotted a pile of Miss Lilburn's flyers in the changing room. She was curious, so had grabbed a handful, placing them in her hand muffler as Miss Lilburn's back was turned. She could have just asked for one, but for some reason she had instinctively grabbed a few.

Now the flyers were in the pillowcase along with the leaflets, ribbons, *Votes For Women* newspapers, and her mother's photograph.

'What's with the pillowcase?' Mabel asked as Lettice passed through the school gates.

'It's Whizzpoo stuff. I need to hide it while my grandmother is visiting.'

'Why?'

'Because my mother promised her that she wouldn't get involved in Whizzpoo any more.'

Mabel looked confused as they entered the hall. 'Doesn't your grandmother want the vote?'

'No,' said Lettice. She wandered over to the broom cupboard and checked, but it was locked.

'Have you tried to convince her?'

'Mama tried,' said Lettice while looking under the stage area, before having a look behind the curtains. 'She says we have our separate balls... spheres... She doesn't want to wear trousers. I dunno.'

'Well, I don't see why, just because she's got her head in the sand...' began Mabel.

'It's complicated.' Lettice sighed. 'It has something to do with when my grandfather died. He left her in charge of his will. And she won't give Mama any money until she stops being a suffragette.'

'Doesn't your father work?'

'I don't think you get much money from being a policeman,' Lettice said, looking up at the ceiling for a shelf or something. 'My mother wanted to work but then she got sick... so we have to do what Grandma wants. And she wants my father to "show ambition".' Lettice gestured like her grandmother, her accent becoming plummier as she pointed with a finger in the air. 'And she wants me to go to finishing school.'

'No!' Mabel said in a hushed voice. 'They don't teach you anything there other than to play the harp and laugh!'

'And when you're sixteen they make you go to a big ball with loads of men who don't speak any English, and then you're married off to whichever one picks you. It's really scary. I don't want to marry a prince. I want to stay here and do jiu jitsu,' Lettice said as she pushed her jaw forward. 'So Grandma *cannot* find this bag.'

'Can't you just throw it in a dustcart? If it's only old newspapers…'

'It has some things I like,' Lettice said, thinking of the photograph. 'You know, sentimental stuff. And the ribbons for your rosettes.'

'Oh…' Mabel thought for a moment. 'She's not staying long, is she?'

'It's usually only a few nights.'

'Then hide it in with the summer sports equipment. There are loads of duffle bags filled with cricket and tennis stuff. And the shed will be open at lunchtime for the dining chairs to be put away.'

'Great idea!'

'I couldn't marry a prince,' Mabel said as they climbed the stairs to the second floor. 'They're all inbred. It's better to be a mongrel.'

'I'm a mongrel,' Lettice agreed. 'Mama is posh and my father is, well… his mother used to work in a jam factory. When she died, he joined the army.'

'How did your parents meet?'

'Papa said it was at a suffrage march, but that can't be right, because he must have known her before the war in South Africa.' She started trying to work out the dates.

Mabel looked over and saw Lettice doing numbers in her head, a deep look of confusion etched on to her face. She paused and looked at her friend.

'I don't think it matters.' Mabel smiled. 'I'm happy to be a mongrel with you.'

Both girls giggled and started to howl like dogs.

第十九章
JŪ HACHI

The day of the nativity arrived.

Lettice and Mabel put their plan into action.

The first bit was hardest: trying to get the confetti snow for their bucket. This involved Lettice distracting Eleanor's brother Sam, whose job it was to pour the snow confetti over the nativity scene when they all sang 'In the Bleak Midwinter'. Sam was charged with the task because he was the most responsible boy in the year. This was rather like saying he was the muddiest potato or the kindest teacher. His year was known for their mischief, and nearly all of them were regularly beaten.

'We've got two buckets,' Sam said proudly. 'One would do, but I reckon the more snow the better.'

'Does it snow much in Bethlehem?' Lettice asked.

'Whadya mean?'

'Well, it's in the Middle East. It's hot there isn't it?'

Sam shook his head. 'Nah, Bethlehem is a made-up place – like Heaven.'

'I don't see why they can't let a girl do the buckets,' Mabel said crossly. 'It isn't as though they're heavy, and once they're in the pulley it won't feel like any weight at all.'

She then proceeded to explain about rope tension, the direction of force, and her plans to be a famous engineer. Lettice used this moment to grab one of the buckets and a couple of handfuls of confetti. She wished she'd grabbed more, but she didn't have time. Hopefully it would be enough to spread a thin layer over the horse manure, which they would collect later.

It wasn't until Lettice was back in the classroom that she remembered she'd picked up the flyers at the dojo. They were in her pillowcase in the sports equipment shed. The shed was unlocked at lunchtime, so it would be easy to swipe them, as long as no one saw. She was in the shed with her arm in the pillowcase when a group of older boys came in. She hid behind the gym horse and eavesdropped, feeling like a police detective.

'You got them, Hugh?'

'We need matches.'

One boy decided to start punching the gym mats that Lettice was hiding behind. This sent the spider that was inches from her nose into a dance… She tried to ignore it, as it regained its hold on the shed wall.

'Quit it, Charlie, someone will hear.'

'Hurry up with them matches.'

They sat down to smoke their cigarettes and began talking about the various girls who had caught their eye. It surprised Lettice to learn how horrible they were about Angela. They called her dog-ugly and vain at the same time. Evidently she hadn't shown much interest in them. They were especially cruel about Joan and used a lot of nasty words describing all the girls; the worst were directed at Mabel.

Lettice crouched low, getting more and more angry, but knowing she couldn't risk them finding her and her suffragette hoard.

It was only after the boys finished their conversation, stubbing out the fag ends on the floorboards, that Lettice realised that not once had they mentioned her; that she was so plain she didn't even qualify for ribbing. This made her more determined to be noticed.

She was late back from lunch break, which got her a warning from Mr Metcalfe.

Now they had a bucket, some real confetti, and some extra Lettice had made by ripping up the leaflets. All they needed was the manure.

Mr Metcalfe had been keeping an eye on the troublemakers. This included Lettice for being late. So it was Mabel who had bravely asked to use the facilities and instead ran out of the school to the nearest taxi rank and picked up as much horse poo as she could.

When she came back in the classroom, having left the bucket outside, Mr Metcalfe said loudly, 'How long does it take one girl to use the…'

But the faint smell of manure that followed Mabel back into the classroom made him pause. 'If you're not well, you should stay at home. Sit.'

After the bell rang to signal the end of afternoon lessons, they went to find the bucket.

'It is a bit wetter than the stuff I've been practising with…' Lettice said.

'I think the horses are sick. It's the weather,' Mabel explained.

'It smells too.'

'It will be fine; put some paper over the top.'

Lettice put the ripped-up suffrage leaflets inside, and then covered that layer with the small handfuls she'd snatched of the real fake snow. From the outside, it looked exactly like the other bucket.

The entire school gathered in the hall and the slightly sweet smell of manure was mixed with the sour-milky, cheesy-footed, one-bath-a-week grubby odour of boys and girls, squawking with excitement and dressed in their best church clothes. Lettice's year all had to wear white to be angels, so there was also a distinct whiff of mothballs.

They trekked down to the church in the drizzle, Lettice and Mabel carrying the bucket between them. It was already dark, and once they arrived they were ordered about by the teachers. It was exactly the sort of chaotic scene Lettice had hoped for. Teachers and children all rushing around, trying to get the church ready before they let the congregation in.

Mabel was sent to the vestry and Lettice to the porch to put away their coats and get ready. There was quite a commotion as the children in costumes were ushered around, the scenery was moved from the chancel next to the pulpit, and benches for the choirs were repeatedly adjusted. The church was full of candles and, instead of flower decorations, wreaths of holly and ivy were hung on the pillars. Hay was being scattered around the manger and small candles were lit along the aisles and nave. It would be hard not to feel Christmassy in a place like this.

Miss Troxell and another teacher were organising the girls into their choir. Mabel and Lettice only met up again when they were told to stand on the benches in the back row of the choir, facing the congregation. Lettice tried to work out if she would be able to throw as far as the front pews from where she was standing. It would be hard. She didn't have much room to move either, all the children were packed in so tightly.

Mr Metcalfe stood in front of them. He was the conductor, and prompter for some of the younger children. He was dressed in a formal three-piece suit and tails and was swishing his conductor's baton threateningly, as though it were his cane. Standing on the back row of the choir, Lettice had a falling sensation in the pit of her stomach. She elbowed Mabel in the ribs.

'Ow!'

'Where's the bucket?'

'You had it!'

'I thought…' Lettice realised she had set it down when she took her coat off. Of all the stupid things.

She could try and get it now... there was still time. But just as she thought this, something else popped into her head. 'Oh no...'

Mabel looked relieved. 'All the parents are coming in. It's too late now.'

Lettice saw her father and grandmother with her pale mother take their seats near the middle of the church. There was no sign of Winston Churchill. However, there was a man with a big gold chain and some other important-looking people in fancy clothing in the front row.

'It's good really,' Mabel continued. 'I doubt you could hit the front from here. And Winston Churchill isn't there anyway! No, I'm honestly relieved. We would have got in a lot of trouble.'

'No, Mabel... we are not okay. Look!'

Lettice pointed at the winch and pulley that hung high above them. Instead of one bucket of confetti, there were two buckets dangling high above the very centre of the nativity scene.

'No...' Mabel's eyes were really wide. 'They can't have.'

'Why didn't they realise one bucket was heavier than the other?' Lettice whispered out the side of her mouth.

'They are boys; they're born stupid.'

'We have to tell Sam not to empty them.'

'He'll get in trouble.'

'He'll be in a lot more trouble when they tip manure all over the baby Jesus!'

Neither girl knew what to do as the vicar began the ceremony. They watched, helpless, as Mr Metcalfe cued up the narrator, poking him sharply with his conductor's baton.

'Over one thousand nine hundred years ago, God sent the Angel Gabriel to Nazareth, a town in Galilee, to a virgin named Mary who was pledged to be married to a carpenter named Joseph.'

The boy playing Gabriel proceeded to strut about in front of the pulpit. Angela as Mary cowered and looked as 'afeared' as she could, while still managing an air of smugness that made Lettice want to roll her eyes. If she had been pretty like Angela with blonde hair… she could have been Mary. It just wasn't fair. Then she remembered what was about to happen to Mary… and a dark part of her chuckled.

She looked out at the sea of adult faces and back up to the buckets.

She was still hoping, in vain, that the extra weight in the bucket might make it harder to empty, that the mechanism would fail. The manure in that bucket was quite liquid… she tried to gauge the splatter range and looked again at the man with the gold chain. His wife, in blue velvet, sat beside him.

Oh dear.

The strains of 'In the Bleak Midwinter' started up.

The rope began to go taut.

Sam was getting rid of the slack before he made it snow.

Mr Metcalfe was right under the bucket, acting as though he were in front of a grand orchestra. He enthusiastically waved his arms about, glaring at the younger children for singing too loudly and glancing over to where Miss Troxell was sitting in the wings.

The fateful lines left the choir's lips.

'Snow had fallen, snow on snow… snow… o-n snow…'

The buckets emptied.

Mabel had read a lot of physics books that she'd stolen from her brother. All of them stated quite clearly that gravity acted on all objects equally, so they fell at the same speed.

This however, wasn't true of horse manure and confetti.

The manure dropped in one solid mass, hitting Mr Metcalfe directly on the top of his head. The impact caused the manure to splatter outwards, coating the actors and the doll playing the baby Jesus. It also speckled the front row of the congregation as well as the pulpit with its more liquid contents.

The confetti had a larger surface area to mass ratio, so fluttered down from the ceiling at a much slower speed. Mimicking perfectly the weather condition it was attempting to replicate.

Amid the uproar of horrified parishioners and delighted children, Angela's swearing, and applause from some of the boys, the final piece of confetti gently descended softly towards the body of the unconscious Mr Metcalfe. It landed gently on his forehead. As it did, the slight damp of the manure caused the fibres of the paper to relax a little and it unfurled to read 'Votes For Women' in clear, unapologetic print.

第二十章
JŪ KYŪ

Grandma was furious.

She was shaking with rage.

She entered the flat and immediately headed for the drinks cabinet.

'Disgusting,' she exclaimed.

The rest of the performance had been cancelled. The important people had not hung around for photos. They didn't even take a collection.

'We don't know it was suffragettes,' Mr Pegg said, placing the cork back in the brandy bottle.

'Of course it was!' Grandma snapped. 'They made their statement perfectly clear. And I think we both know who put them up to it.'

Lettice felt all the blood drain from her face. She met her grandmother's sharp gaze and thought that the whole world was about to come crashing down. No Christmas. No jiu jitsu. She'd be sent *abroad* to finishing school and forgotten.

However, Lettice's fear was misplaced, because it wasn't her that the old woman was accusing, at least not directly. She was looking at Lettice's mother.

'You put Lettice up to this, didn't you?'

Mrs Pegg said nothing. She knew better than to argue with her mother. 'Lettice, go to bed.'

But Lettice didn't dare move.

'Don't you deny it!' The older woman looked at her daughter shrewdly. 'I knew you were up to something. Look!' She pointed at the Christmas cards, spilling her drink as she snatched one up, opened it and pointed at the signature. 'Do you know who DNW is, Jack?'

Mr Pegg blinked. 'I assumed it was Daniela and Nathanael Wrightson.'

'DNW Stands for "Deeds Not Words". It's a Pankhurst call to arms!'

'Oh, Mother, you're a conspiracy theorist!'

'Am I? It isn't the only one I've found.' Lettice's grandmother opened another card and handed it to Mr Pegg. He dropped the first one by his feet. Lettice picked it up and looked at it. Inside it looked very ordinary.

Dear
Florry and Jack,
Sorry to hear of Florence's illness.
Can't wait to send you news of the vicar's
Visit to Chelsea! Have you seen Selfridges shop
Window? Those new coats are completely
Smashing. We are going there on
Tuesday. We could send a boy to
Bring you some goods. Just ask. Awful weather – hail-
Stones in December despite the cold.
And I do hope it dries up – the rain
Hammers down constantly. Much better to be in
bed! Love,
Etc.
Merry Christmas!
DNW
P.S. Congratulations on the promotion.

Lettice's grandmother was still furiously jabbing her finger at the cards.

'Read the first word on each line… Honestly, the child could come up with a better code.'

Lettice read the first words of the card she was holding.

'Dear Florry, Sorry Can't Visit Window Smashing Tuesday Bring Stones And Hammers Etc. DNW.'

Mr Pegg's face was stricken with disappointment.

'I cannot help who writes to me,' said Florence softly.

Grandmother raised her eyebrows. 'You're going to pretend you knew nothing about tonight's antics? Dropping a bucket of filth on that poor man. On the baby Jesus!'

'It had nothing to do with either of us,' Lettice's mother insisted.

'What about the *Votes For Women* leaflets that just happened to drop with the manure? Was it a coincidence?' Florry was silent. 'Should I ask the child?'

'Be my guest; she'll tell the truth.'

Lettice froze; she didn't know what to do.

She was the one responsible, but her grandmother was acting like her mother had put her up to it. Should she lie? Say she had no idea? She hated lies. She would have to tell the truth. She would let everyone know her mother was innocent.

'I... I only wanted to throw it at Winston Churchill,' Lettice blurted out, her eyes full of tears. 'For all the trouble he's caused.'

The adults looked completely taken aback.

'The girl is talking nonsense!' Grandmother shook her head

'Why did you think Winston Churchill would be at the nativity?' asked her mother.

Mr Pegg looked down at his daughter. 'You could have done some real damage,' he said. 'I thought you wanted to be a police officer. You can't be a police officer and do things like this.'

Lettice's tears of sorrow quickly turned into anger. It was like her father was taking Winston Churchill's side.

'When will you stop pretending?! I can't be a police officer, you idiot! I'm a GIRL. I can't do anything!'

Her father took his hands off Lettice's shoulders like she was suddenly repulsive to him.

She knew instantly what she had done.

Never again would he ask her to line up next to the coats. Never again could they pretend together. She'd just told him she wasn't a child any more. That she was too old to play his make-believe games.

Without a word Mr Pegg turned on his heel and walked out of the room.

'Papa!' Lettice yelled after him.

'You see the influence you've had on her?' Grandmother was still scolding Lettice's mother, who wore a stunned expression.

Mrs Pegg looked genuinely shocked.

'I had no idea…' she said, quite honestly.

'Nonsense. I made it quite clear when you and Jack visited that in return for an increased allowance you were to stop this suffrage nonsense and he was to try and better himself. In fact he's managed this superbly well… a task I didn't expect him to achieve with such gusto considering his lowly birth…'

This was too much for Lettice to hear.

'Papa's friend died!' she yelled. 'They were gunned down on his old patrol route while he took us to the pantomime! He didn't want the promotion. He was really upset!'

She heard the front door slam. 'Papa!'

Lettice ran into the hall, staring at the closed front door. She could hear her father's footsteps growing fainter… thudding down the stairs to the lobby.

When Lettice returned to the living room, her mother was looking upset, while her grandmother was pacing around. She ignored Lettice entirely and focused all her fury on telling Florry off. Lettice didn't listen. She went to the window and watched to see which direction her father was going in. To her surprise, he didn't head towards the pub but hailed a cab. Just before he got in he looked up at the flat. She saw him recognise her face pressed against the window, blocking the light of the room with her hand so she could see out. She instantly waved down to him but he looked away and got in the carriage.

'... bringing shame on your father's name.' Grandmother stopped talking.

'I don't have my father's name. I have Jack's name.'

'That poor man had no idea what he was letting himself in for, marrying you. You lied to him, you lied to me, and you turned your daughter into a toerag!'

Both women were red with fury.

'I didn't know about the bucket of manure!'

'She's telling the truth!' Lettice said.

'You've taught her to lie very well, too! I think I need to spend the next few weeks looking round for a finishing school that will take her. She can't go back to that school now.'

'What?!' Lettice protested, but neither woman even looked at her. They were so used to acting as though she didn't exist, that even when they were talking about her, they ignored her.

'She can go back,' Lettice's mother said. 'They don't know who the culprit is.'

'Oh, so she doesn't apologise and confess?' Grandmother sounded outraged. 'Of all the immoral... '

'If she confesses she'll be expelled. Try finding a finishing school that will take a pupil who has been expelled.' Lettice's mother stood up and looked her own mother in the eye. The effort didn't work... she was obviously still a bit woozy from her medicine and sat back down straight away.

'I don't want to go to finishing school!' Lettice said.

'Be quiet!'

'She is being contrary. She liked the thought of it only a few weeks ago.'

Lettice was fuming. She never said she had liked the idea of finishing school. And things had changed since they discussed it anyway. 'I have friends now. I don't want to go abroad!'

'Maybe you should have thought of that before you sabotaged the nativity play!'

'I hate you!'

'Go to your room!'

Lettice strode past them both, slamming the living-room door. Of course at the moment, her room was also Tilly's room. And Tilly was in it, sitting on the bed, darning a hole in Mr Pegg's trousers, her besocked feet resting on Lettice's pillow.

'All kicking off in there, isn't it?'

Lettice dropped down on to her cot, her eyes full of tears. 'Papa's gone and everyone is fighting and it's all my fault.'

'They've fought before...' Tilly said trying to comfort her.

'They're going to send me abroad,' Lettice snivelled, the arms of her cardigan absorbing her tears.

Tilly watched Lettice sob and prodded her with her toe. Lettice looked up over her knees at the older girl, her face lit by the faint gas lamp that hung on the far wall and the lights of moving motor cars outside. The rain pattered softly on the glass, and Tilly spoke very softly and slowly.

'When I was in the workhouse these two sisters had a fight over this boy... or a pie... Anyway, they hit and spat and pulled each other's hair and they was split up.' Her hands worked as she spoke, and she continued to look out of the window into the street below. 'In the workhouse they usually keep families apart. We wasn't allowed to talk to our brothers. But you got to work along with yer ma or sister. Being on yer own is no fun, so I felt sorry for the girl who stayed in our dorm. Not because her eye was cut from the fight. I never seen no one tremble so much. She cried all night, saying such nasty things. Hitting her mattress. We couldn't say nothing to her. I reckoned she would've attacked us too. Next day, if anyone mentioned her sister she spat on the floor. But… only a week later, they put them back together and you ain't never seen such a big hug they gave each other. Like they were clinging to life itself.'

Lettice blinked. 'Why did you tell me that?'

Tilly sighed. 'You know how when you stitch up a worn pair of trousers… or the arm of a jacket… or a rip of some kind in a fine fabric?'

Lettice blinked again.

'Well, sometimes the stitch is stronger than the original fabric… sometimes it's stronger where it was once broken than the areas around it.'

Lettice sniffed. 'They didn't even notice him going! I didn't give him his Christmas present.'

'What are they scrapping about?' asked Tilly

Lettice told her all about the nativity play: Mabel's reluctance to get involved, her teacher and his pompous baton pointing, Angela's bad acting, the bucket going missing in the church and the final splattering of everyone in the front row... including the baby Jesus. Tilly's face was delighted.

'You're a sly one! Weren't you scared of getting caught?'

Lettice realised that the consequences had never really crossed her mind. 'I hate that man. He's why Mama's been sick. She was thrown on the ground by a policeman...'

'That makes a lot more sense. She tried to tell me she fell off an 'orse. She hadn't been riding no 'orses,' Tilly said.

'She was trying to stop the policeman from hitting me...' Lettice said, expecting Tilly to ask why a man would hit a defenceless woman. But this didn't seem remarkable to Tilly.

Just then there was a tap on their door. It creaked open. It was Grandma.

'Can I speak to Lettice alone?'

Tilly huffed, put down her darning and slipped on her shoes. Lettice's grandmother held open the door and waited.

'There is plenty of washing-up to be done,' she said, glaring at the maid.

Tilly grunted and went into the kitchen.

'Your mother has gone to bed. I fear she is still not quite well.' Grandma stayed in the doorway, silhouetted against the light in the hall. 'You both need to take a long hard think about these women you insist on loitering with. They are not of a good class…'

'Yes they are!' Lettice protested but a stern look shut her up.

'They have caused your mother to be very ill indeed. I'm going to instruct that your maid, Matilda is it…?'

Lettice nodded.

'She is to make a report each day of the comings and goings. All correspondence will be forwarded to my address.'

'She'll need help with the spelling…'

'You in particular, Lettice Pegg, are not permitted to interfere in any way. Under no circumstances are either you or your mother to fraternise with ANY suffragettes. Including that Indian girl at your school.'

'Mabel is my friend!'

'Races should not mix, not as equals anyway. She may be a perfectly pleasant child, but it isn't appropriate,' Grandma snapped.

'Why?!' Lettice demanded.

Her question was ignored, 'I'm sending a doctor who will check on your mother regularly. She is to

have no visitors other than the ones I have approved –
respectable neighbours, doctors, women from the
church. Matilda will inform me if she is going against
any of my rules. Your mother is an invalid, and those
awful women will only make it worse. They have
infected her brain much more than the fall.

'You are to come straight home from school, every
day. Until I find you a place at a decent school, you're
to keep well out of trouble. If you do not, you will come
and stay with me.'

'Can…' Lettice stopped herself.

'What is it, child?'

'Can I still go roller skating? I go with a good family,
they are called the Garruds,' she said nervously.

Her grandmother paused. 'Where do they live?'

Lettice knew better than to answer 'Islington'.

'Knightsbridge,' she lied.

'If it keeps you out of trouble, fine. But if you so
much as think the word 'vote', you will be on a train to
Brighton within the hour and I'll put you on a boat to
France myself.'

Lettice nodded.

Grandmother slammed the door.

第二十一章

NI JŪ

Grandmother left first thing in the morning. She didn't leave any presents and didn't take the ones they had wrapped for her.

She had arranged for a doctor to attend to Mrs Pegg. The thin man arrived promptly, wordlessly handed Lettice his hat and, clutching his black leather bag to his chest, barged past her and walked straight into her mother's bedroom unannounced.

Evidently he was in a hurry.

Lettice stood in the doorway, watching him check her mother's pulse and make his observations. He ignored Mrs Pegg's murmured questions and instructed her to hold out her tongue. Using a pipette he dropped some medicine into her mouth, placing a small bottle by her pillow with instructions for her to take it when she felt the need. After that Lettice's mother fell asleep. The doctor nodded, clicked his heels and strode past Lettice out of the room and whisked himself out of the flat, only stopping to collect his hat.

'Merry Christmas,' he said and closed the door firmly behind him.

Lettice's father still hadn't come home. Tilly had dutifully gone to the shops, and unable to cancel the orders, Lettice had to stay at home to let in the delivery boys. Every hour or so another would arrive, bringing ingredients and gifts that no one would enjoy. Lettice wondered if she should ask her mother if they were going to go to the midnight carols. Then again, she thought mentioning the church would be a bad idea.

If Lettice thought Christmas Eve was bad, Christmas Day was worse. Tilly had gone to see her family and neglected to tell Lettice how to cook the goose. Lettice resorted to making scrambled eggs, which she ate alone with some beef tea that her mother had refused to touch. She sat in the kitchen, next to the raw goose, writing in her police notebook about how to do wrist lock four, *kote dori*, and drawing little men with x markings to indicate where best to strike them.

She heard a knock at the door. As she opened it, Mabel fell through it with her arms wide open.

'Letty!' She gave her the biggest bear hug. 'Merry Christmas!'

Lettice breathed out. 'You shouldn't do that; I nearly threw you on the floor!'

'I got you a present.'

The stern face of Mabel's butler appeared in the doorway behind her and reluctantly handed Lettice a large parcel wrapped in brown paper.

It was large and heavy. It could be a coat, or a rug… Lettice invited them in but the butler coughed.

'Sorry, we have to rush off – I'm not supposed to be here,' Mabel whispered. 'We're on our way to the orphanage to help Mama. Daniel and I are going to dress as Christmas elves. I love Christmas Day; everyone is so full of joy!'

Daniel looked more like he was full of insipid milk and holly leaves.

'I'm sorry I didn't get you anything!' Lettice hugged her friend. 'But this has really has made my day!'

'I'll see you at school next week.'

'See you then!'

Lettice shut the door and took the parcel into her bedroom. On the label it said:

'To The Unstoppable Letty Pegg, A Costume Befitting a Fighter. Merry Christmas. Mabel.'

Unstoppable. Not pretty, not kind. Unstoppable. Lettice smiled. She unwrapped it carefully, keeping the brown paper neat. Inside was a bright white cotton *gi* jacket. Lettice buried her face in it, smelling the clean linen. Tucked inside the jacket was her very own sash belt and, under a layer of tissue paper, she found a pair of fighting trousers.

Lettice felt her eyes burn with happiness. She swallowed and immediately tried the jacket on. It felt much lighter than the jacket she usually practised in. It was softer too, and the sleeves were the right length, the shoulders fitted, and the sash when she tied it, kneeling as she would in the dojo, was the correct length to go around her waist, without trailing ends. She no longer felt swamped in fabric; she was able to move more freely, and began practising an *empi kata* across her bedroom, enjoying the movement of her arms, turning and doing a diving roll towards her bed and narrowly avoiding crashing into the dresser.

It was the best gift she'd ever received. She slid out the trunk from under her bed. She saw that her grandmother had indeed gone through her possessions; nothing was in its proper place... but Lettice didn't care. She carefully took off and folded her jitsu uniform and, kneeling in ceremony, placed it perfectly in the centre of the trunk.

The sun set and Lettice took her mother some toast and leftover soup.

'Hello, darling.' Florry rolled over.

'How are you feeling?'

'Rotten.' Her mother sat up in bed and Lettice plopped the tray on her lap. 'What's this?'

'It was supposed to be your Christmas present,' Lettice said, watching her take a small parcel from the tray and open it.

'A hanky.' Florry grinned. 'With some embroidery. "Deeds not words". Good thing your grandmother didn't see that. You're very clever though; it's a neat stitch.'

'I'm sorry, Mama,' Lettice said, her eyes welling up with tears. 'I didn't mean to get you in trouble.'

'Don't be daft.' Mrs Pegg smiled at her daughter. 'I'm proud as punch. Coming up with that all by yourself! I'm just surprised you're suddenly so political – you never showed an interest before. What has bought this change of heart about?'

Lettice looked down at her feet. She owed her mother the truth.

'When you were arrested, a woman rescued me from the police. Her name is Edith Garrud…'

Mrs Pegg thought for a moment, 'Garrud… not that tiny little Welsh woman? She does some sort of kung fu doesn't she?'

Lettice blinked. 'Yeah, jiu jitsu. I've been going to her classes. I told Papa I was going roller skating.'

'That explains how you've been getting those letters from Una,' Florence said, putting two and two together. 'I must admit I couldn't see her roller skating… But really, darling. You shouldn't lie to your father.'

'You lie all the time!'

Lettice's mother winced; clearly her headache was back. 'No need to raise your voice.'

Lettice sighed. 'I didn't want to lie, but I knew he wouldn't let me go.'

'He certainly won't let you go now, if he finds out about it. He'll see it as another way of our keeping things from him.'

'I don't know where he is.'

'There's no need to get worked up. He'll come back once he's cooled down. Men always do. Here,' she said, handing Lettice a book, 'read this to me while I eat. It's part of your Christmas present.'

'Reading to you?'

'The book!'

Lettice cracked open the book and began reading to her mother about a little English girl in India whose parents had died. By the time the story had got as far as Yorkshire, both of them had succumbed to their tiredness. When Tilly got in, she found both of them fast asleep on the bed.

第二十二章
NI JŪ ICHI

Her mother spent Boxing Day in bed. Lettice, however, had a party to go to. She turned up at the Gardenia right on time. Even though she didn't need to make an excuse, she still wore her roller skates around her neck. They had become part of her jiu jitsu persona.

Seeing everyone and being welcomed by Edith made her feel a lot better. Mr Tani wore a dinner jacket while Miss Lilburn had dressed up in green velvet. She was asking him all about the pantomime and what the stars were really like backstage. They all sat eating egg sandwiches and drinking mugs of leek and potato soup.

As it was the Christmas dojo outing, the entire club had turned out.

'First of all,' said Edith, standing up, 'a big thank you to the Women's Franchise League and WSPU… '

'Whizzpoo!' the table cheered.

'… for all their help in organising funding for the new dojo. Come the summer we may have some new digs! Secondly, as some of you know, I've been working on a new play and we are going to have to teach a couple of novice performers to beat each other up for an audience… '

She said this somewhat bitterly. Her great full-length production had been cut from two hours to just one sketch.

'Can we audition?' Miss Horvat asked hopefully.

'No! The Actresses' Franchise League have put their noses in…'

As she said this, three women entered the restaurant. They were looking around and headed for the dojo table, coming up behind Mrs Garrud as she continued to complain about the wrong decisions that had caused her epic saga to be cut to one short scene.

'They're bossier than the Panks at Whizzpoo,' Edith grinned, 'But at least they're more handsome.'

'We can't all be as dainty as you,' said a plummy voice behind her.

Edith jumped and put her hands up in a fighting stance.

'Oh!' She seemed to recognise the face instantly and lowered her guard.

The small Indian woman was wearing modest furs and her large brown eyes looked as sorrowful as those of her companion. Lettice recognised the tall woman now, though her usually pretty face was puffy from crying. It was Una. She was dressed all in white and slinked round the table, trying to hold her head up against the emotion she was obviously feeling.

'Mrs Garrud, so good to see you,' Una said. Her voice quivered a little.

'Miss Dugdale!' Edith squeaked. 'Princess Sophia! And?'

'I'm just Boots,' said Boots in a familiar cockney drawl. 'And the mutt is Joe.'

Boots was carrying some bags, and had a large white dog with her. Princess Sophia looked somewhat irritated that Boots had spoken.

'Lovely to meet you, Boots. Do join us won't you?'

'Actually, Mrs Garrud,' the princess said quietly, 'we do not wish to interrupt your celebration. I feel most inappropriate sharing the sad news.'

Everyone leaned in.

'You must know dear Mrs Clarke. May?'

'Mrs Pankhurst's sister?'

'Yes, that's her. She was arrested in the Battle of Downing Street the Tuesday after Black Friday; they accused her of breaking a window. She was badly treated, as I'm sure you're all aware.'

The Battle of Downing Street... that was the time Lettice's father had returned home with a black eye and they had fish and chips at the table.

'She passed away today. She was released on Christmas Eve but her treatment in prison... she couldn't recover.'

Gasps. Cutlery clattered as it fell back on to the table. Mugs of soup slammed down. Miss Lilburn stood up in shock.

'No!'

'She was incredibly brave. She refused to eat unless she was recognised as a political prisoner. She underwent the horror of being force fed,' Princess Sophia said above all the noise. 'I can promise you her passing will not be in vain.'

Isabel leaned into Lettice, who was looking confused. 'What's that face for?'

'I dunno,' Lettice whispered. She didn't feel much sympathy for May Clarke. 'Making yourself sick is stupid.'

She was thinking of her mother, who, when they went to the pantomime was in fine fettle, but now, just because she was upset about Grandmother and Mr Pegg storming out, had spent the following days lying down, refusing to talk. She didn't have a fever or a cough, or anything outwardly wrong with her.

'I think it's brave,' Isabel said in a whisper. 'If we're prepared to die for our rights, the men might take us seriously.'

'The only way you can make a man take you seriously is to give him a bloody nose,' Lettice said, quoting her father.

Miss Lilburn slammed her fist on to the table. 'It is so unjust the way the authorities let this stuff happen and the public don't give a monkeys!'

'Even when we die they don't care! How on earth can we make them listen? Without a vote we can't change anything.'

'We need to embarrass them! Make their lives difficult.'

'Yeah, make a really big show of it!'

'Maybe,' Lettice said, her mouth full of cress and egg, 'instead of making a fuss we should hide.'

'What do you mean?'

Lettice swallowed. 'If you want something, you should do the opposite and then you get it.'

'Not sure that works...' Edith cocked her head.

'I wanted a pair of roller skates all summer,' Lettice said. 'The moment I stopped asking for them, I got given a pair.'

There was a murmur of recognition but also scepticism in the group.

'You want us to do the opposite of a protest?' Asked Isabel.

'Yeah,' Lettice said.

Una thought for a moment. 'The girl's got a point. If all the women disappeared overnight it would create a massive news story.'

'Where would we go?'

'We can't ask working women to risk their livelihoods. They have to work. We'd never agree on a time to do it.'

'There is one night when we're all expected to be counted...' Princess Sophia blinked slowly and, once everyone was paying attention, in her clipped voice said, 'The night of the census.'

There was a lot of interest at this. Conversations broke out up and down the table.

'It's a brilliant idea!'

'That's illegal isn't it? We have to be counted… '

'Isn't the point of being counted that the government can use the data to help people?'

'I'm going to put my cat's name down. She's as much of a person as I am in the government's eyes… we both have the same voting rights.'

'We need to find something to do instead.'

'Where do we go?'

'Could we hide in Parliament?' asked Isabel.

'We can't all fit in Parliament,' Una grumbled

'Can't we just march?'

'All night? It'll be chilly and likely raining. It will only be April after all. We need somewhere sheltered.'

Una, who had been sitting quite quietly, had her eye on Lettice. 'Why does that child always have a pair of roller skates around her neck?'

Edith shrugged. 'She just does.'

'I tell my father I'm roller skating when I go to jitsu practice,' Lettice said.

'Where does he think you roller skate? In the streets?'

'Aldwych rink, I think.' Lettice shrugged. 'I've never been very specific.'

'Lying to your parents is wrong,' Una said sternly.

'They lie to me often enough,' Lettice retorted.

Una raised her eyebrows at Lettice's cheek. 'How big is Aldwych? Perhaps we could all do with a spot of roller skating once the ice has melted.'

第二十三章
NI JŪ NI

Mrs Pegg's health was getting worse. Doctor Raynes' handwriting was as spindly as his body. He had written a long note for Lettice to send to her grandmother. He told both Lettice and Tilly that Mrs Pegg's headaches were reducing and she needed to go for walks. He said the sadness was less to do with the injury and more to do with her spirits. He was quite right. She hadn't played a note on the piano since Christmas and, with no friends coming to visit or reason to leave her bedroom, she was becoming isolated once again.

Lettice watched as Tilly went through Florence's mail, putting all the post directed to her in a larger envelope to be inspected by Lettice's grandmother. However, Tilly could not stop Lettice from bringing home notes and messages from the dojo. These scraps of information were not the same as having real friends. Mrs Pegg was missing out on so many events and the plans for the census boycott. Lettice was in half a mind to throw the notes away; they only seemed to make Florry more miserable.

Tilly didn't like being a prison guard much either.

'I feel awful, Lettice. Your gran is giving me two shillings a week to do this,' she said, when Lettice came back from school one day and found her writing a long list of events for Grandma to read through. 'It's a lot. But I don't like it, I really don't. I like your ma and she's so sad all on her own.'

Lettice nodded in agreement.

'Loads of people have been bothering me. I did what your gran said and told them to hop it. But your ma gets me to tell the church people and the neighbours to hop it too, so other than the doctor, and you and me of course… she's been on her own. It's like she's punishing herself. She'll only eat plain food: won't touch the biscuits. Do you reckon we should ask your gran to get her a telephone? I've heard good things about them.'

'I doubt Grandma would allow that,' sighed Lettice, fingering a stack of calling cards. 'Have these been here since Monday?'

'Uh-huh. And some of them came twice,' Tilly said.

'Princess…' Lettice looked at the neat white calling card and took it with both hands.

'Hmm?' Tilly came over, and used her slightly diminished feather duster to point at it. 'Oh yeah, she was asking after your ma. She weren't no real princess though.'

'Her calling card says "Hampton Court Palace"!'

'Nah… look, it says "Faraday House, Hampton Court Palace". Not the actual palace. Besides, she can't be a princess.' Tilly gave Lettice a knowing look. 'She was foreign.'

Lettice looked at her incredulously. 'Other countries have royalty.'

'Yeah, but she sounded English. And looked foreign. You know, like those lascar fellas at the docks.'

'She's Princess Sophia Singh,' Lettice said, exasperated. 'She's the goddaughter of Queen Victoria!'

'The pub?'

'The actual queen. Sophia is very well-to-do.'

'Can you be well-to-do and Indian?'

'Of course you can!' Lettice said. 'She was here?'

261

'Yeah, that's twice now. First time was when she brought your ma back from when she had percussion, while you were off getting her bag.'

'You never said it was Princess Sophia that…'

'She's the one who complained about the crackers,' Tilly said happily.

'I'm going to write to her.'

'Why? She's definitely a suffragette. She isn't allowed to write to your ma.' Tilly sighed. 'And if she visits again I have to turn her away. Unless…'

'She a member of the church, or a neighbour, or Doctor Raynes,' Lettice finished off her sentence for her. 'Can you not tell Grandma? Mama could do with some friends.'

Tilly shook her head. 'I can't risk the sack. I can't go back to the workhouse. Sorry, Lettice. I won't lie for no one.'

第二十四章
NI JŪ SAN

Lettice hadn't heard back from the princess. She'd checked the post that evening and abandoned her porridge the day after to double check the pigeonholes. She was becoming quite desperate. Her mother had missed her bath. She was drinking more gin. Lettice was tempted to write to her grandmother, but she was still angry with her and didn't want to speak to her. She distracted herself by practising jiu jitsu movements in her bedroom and drawing jiu jitsu locks and throws in her policeman's notebook. It was getting rather full. Days turned into weeks and her mother showed no improvement and her father still hadn't come home.

She needed him to make her mother see sense. She couldn't ignore her husband. He needed to order her to look after herself.

When she was younger Lettice had scraped her knee and her mother kept rapping her knuckles with a fan every time she went to pick at the scab. 'If you leave it alone, it will heal faster.' It was itchy, and satisfying to lift off, but her mother had been right; she still had a slightly darker patch of skin on that knee. She knew she should leave things alone. Things heal with time. But nothing seemed to be getting better and Lettice wanted to do something, to pick at the scab.

'Do you think…' Lettice said to her mother, who was sitting up in bed staring out at the street below. 'Do you think I should try and find Papa?'

'Lettice… how many times? You need to leave him be. If you leave him be, he will come back.'

Lettice thought it had been too long already. 'He has been gone for nearly a month, Mama. I don't think he's going to come back.'

'He's been busy. You saw his picture in the paper?'

Lettice grimaced. The siege of Sidney Street had been in all the papers: her father's face looking down the street with the evil home secretary, Winston Churchill, cowering behind him. Lettice had run to show her mother but all she said was, 'I wish the WSPU could get publicity like that.'

Mrs Pegg had even handed Tilly the paper to use for firelighters. Lettice had rescued the article from the flames and hid it next to her new *gi* in the trunk under her bed. She looked at the picture every now and then, just as she had with the photo of her mother that was now forgotten in the summer sports equipment at school.

Lettice's heart skipped a beat when Tilly said she had post that evening. Was it from Sophia? No. She was disappointed to see it was a note from her grandmother. No mention of her mother's condition. No questions asking after anyone in the family. Just a list of various schools and their locations, from Italy to Scotland. Asking Lettice her preference. Lettice scoffed. This was the first time her grandmother had wanted to hear her preference on anything. The truth was Lettice didn't want to go to any of them. She wanted to stay in London, have happy parents, be friends with Mabel and do jiu jitsu.

***

'You've got to stop hard blocking,' Edith yelled. 'Do it again!'

Lettice was getting more and more frustrated. Her legs were tired, her hands hurt; it wasn't fair.

'Now you're stepping too close. Again.'

Lettice breathed and watched as Mr Tani launched himself forwards, swinging at her head with his cosh. She darted in, stepping deep, reaching for his arm, stepping her other leg back behind her and whipping her hips round so that she accelerated his movement. Instead of blocking and fighting him, she was trying to use his own momentum to get him to trip on her leg and fly over her shoulder on to the mat in front of her. But no. She hadn't stepped deep enough, and she was too close to him so the fully grown man ended up like a sack on her back.

It was his laugh that made the red mist come down. Lettice shoved him off her back and marched right up to where Edith was kneeling.

'I can't do it! He's not hitting me properly. He's too heavy!' Lettice yelled, inches from Edith's face. 'This is stupid!'

'Out. Now. *Rei* off.' Edith was not angry. She said the words in a calm whisper. It was actually scary. She pointed at the door. 'Isabel, take over. While I'm gone, do balance and *kuzushi kata*.'

'Yes, sensei,' Isabel said from the far corner of the mat.

Lettice stomped out, only doing the smallest of head nods to bow out of the room. She was in tears of frustration. Edith followed her.

'You cannot behave like that on the mat,' Edith snapped.

Lettice was ready to yell at her for teaching her something wrong, or blame Mr Tani, but instead she looked down at her feet. She nodded.

'What's going on?'

Lettice shrugged. She was ashamed of what was happening. Normal families didn't behave like this.

'You've got all this anger inside you,' Edith said. 'I saw it on the day we first met. It is quite something. But you have to learn to channel it better. You cannot let every frustration weaken you. When you are out of control, you are weak. You are still a girl. You cannot hit a man to make him feel it. But you can trick him. You can use his force and double it. No man's fists hit harder than the ground. But you have to stay neutral. Confident but calm.'

'Are you expelling me?'

'No, no.' Edith chuckled. 'I know it is frustrating, but you were frustrated before you got on the mat.

Leave that outside. Take how you are feeling and throw it away. If your *uke* represents your anger or fear, head to him directly, avoiding his punches, scoop him up and fling him away. You can cast off anything if you can throw Mr Tani. So. Slowly. We are going to go back in. This time he will be armed with a metal chain.'

Lettice's eyes widened. 'But…'

'He is going to try and whip you in the face with it. He will run at you, swinging it. Your job is to get to his shoulder before he has a chance to make contact. It is the same throw. You won't have time to think about it. If you hard block his arm like you were doing, the chain will swing round and hit you in the head. If you step too close the chain will also hit you. If you can move calmly, step to his shoulder, take his balance while stepping back behind you, then whip your hips round and face the wall, you will have him at your feet, the chain will be under your arm and you will be in control. You have to commit to it though. If you hesitate, you *will* get hurt.'

Lettice gulped and followed her sensei back into the dojo.

'*Yame*!' Isabel called. Everyone faced the doors and bowed to Edith.

'Everyone sit round the edge! Mr Tani, get the chain. Lettice, you're up.'

Mr Tani and Lettice stood at opposite ends of the mat. They bowed to Edith, then to each other. Then Mr Tani started to run for Lettice, his usual cheerful face locked in concentration, his mouth tiny, eyes fixed on her head as he drew back his arm and swung the chain.

Lettice didn't pause. She stepped slightly wider than she thought wise and caught his arm by his shoulder. She could feel its weight and the weight of the whipping chain as it began to circle. Her toes clung to the mat. She stepped back and in time with the movement of the chain she spun her hips round, dropping her weight into a lunge and breathing out. She found herself facing the exact same direction she had started. Mr Tani landed with a massive thud in front of her. His arm with the chain was tucked under Lettice's arm as he continued to slide to a halt. His eyes were wide looking back up at her, a massive grin on his face.

'*DAI*!' She mimed hitting his nose with the heel of her palm, placing it in the exact spot where her father had punched the man at the station. She got up from her lunge, taking the chain from his hand by squeezing his fist. Mr Tani played dead on the mat while Lettice walked slowly and placed the chain at Edith's feet.

Only when she turned back to bow to Mr Tani did she hear the applause of the club, and see the beaming grin of her sensei.

***

Getting expelled was also something Lettice avoided at school. She and Mabel had got away with the nativity incident. At the beginning of term, Mr Metcalfe had threatened the entire school to try and make them come clean. As the one who had pulled the rope, Sam had been beaten for the crime. Lettice felt bad about it but Mr Metcalfe realised Sam wasn't the one responsible. As Sam couldn't even spell suffrage, let alone tell you what it was, he was an unlikely conspirator.

Mr Metcalfe was seething about the entire thing. His mood had grown worse as he had to continue to teach the girls. Classes had been so dull with him, Mabel was going mad: asking if they could learn more Latin, or physics or anything other than etiquette lessons. A taxing afternoon of folding serviette squares into fleurs-de-lis was not exactly what she had in mind.

It was exactly the sort of lesson Lettice's grandmother would approve of: nothing dangerous, nothing interesting, and all about presenting yourself as sophisticated. Folding napkins seemed utterly pointless to Lettice too. Why dress up something that would just have beef stew smeared on it later anyway?

'Tomorrow,' Mr Metcalfe said, swishing his cane and knocking Miriam's napkin onto the floor, 'I have an important meeting. So you will be in the infants' classroom with Miss Troxell.'

'He treats us like infants anyway,' Eleanor said as she got up. She smiled at Lettice.

Lettice didn't return the smile; she looked confused. Angela and Alice were arm in arm, walking out the door of the classroom. It seemed they had lost interest in Eleanor.

Lettice joined Mabel in the playground while they waited for Tilly and Mabel's butler to collect them.

'I see Eleanor's no longer welcome in court,' Lettice said, watching Eleanor shuffle over to her brother.

Mabel looked sad. 'I suppose you'll want to be her friend again.'

'I'm not sure,' said Lettice. 'I think she was only my friend because I gave her lunch money.'

'Are *we* friends?' Mabel asked in a nervous voice.

Lettice blinked. 'Of course we're friends, you idiot! We are *best* friends.'

Mabel grinned at this. 'Really? I don't think I've had a best friend before.'

'Nor have I,' Lettice said and felt slightly silly. 'Mabel, you know my parents had a big row at Christmas?'

'They've made up tho now, right?'

Lettice looked at her hands. 'They will do, once Papa comes home...'

'What do you mean?' Mabel looked outraged. 'You didn't say he left. You only said your mother was sad again and Tilly was spying on the post.'

Lettice shrugged. 'It's not a big deal.'

Mabel punched her friend in the arm. 'Letty! It's a *huge* deal! Why did he leave?'

Lettice looked down at her feet. 'It was my fault. He found out about the nativity play and thought my mother had put us up to it... And he... well, he doesn't like liars.'

Mabel looked outraged. 'He can't just leave! You shouldn't abandon children. Hasn't your mother tried to get him to come back?'

Lettice shook her head. 'She says he'll come back when he realises he misses us.'

Mabel shook her head. 'We need to get him back home. Right away!'

Lettice didn't really understand why Mabel had such strong feelings about it, but suspected it might have something to do with her own parents. And rather than pry, she resolved to just be happy someone agreed with her.

'Where's he staying?' Mabel asked.

'I'm not sure. Most likely with his sister in Waterloo.'

'Waterloo isn't far,' said Mabel. 'We could go right now.'

'We don't really get along that well...' Lettice mumbled. 'She doesn't like my mother – calls her a party girl.'

'A peace pipe,' Mabel said brightly. 'You should bring her a gift; that always works. Come on, the bakery's still open.'

第二十五章

NI JŪ YON

The door to the small terraced house creaked open. A woman who looked just like Lettice's father, but with a smaller moustache, dressed in a white smock and housecoat, stood on her front step looking down at the two schoolgirls with disdain.

'Hello, Auntie.'

There was a call from inside the house. 'Maaaaaa!'

'Get your ugly mush out of that!' Lettice's auntie shouted over her shoulder then, addressing Lettice, nodded her head at Mabel. 'Who's the Indian?'

Mabel stopped smiling.

'This is Mabel, Auntie. She's my best friend... and she's not...'

'If we are playing pretend, then yes, I'm your auntie, and she's as white as snow.'

'We brought you some biscuits,' Lettice said. It had been Mabel's idea: a gift to ease tension.

Lettice's aunt looked at the tin but didn't touch it. 'You can't come in. I've got a lodger and he's very particular.'

'That's okay. I just wanted to ask – have you seen my father recently?'

'You mean Jack? I ain't seen him since Boxing Day.'

'He isn't staying with you?'

'Has he finally come to his senses and left that posh tart?'

Lettice grew red in the face. 'That's my mother you're talking about!'

'You can be sure of that at least.'

Lettice didn't know what that meant. 'What has she ever done to you?'

'She treats us like a charity case, got me in trouble at work with her daft marching and turns my brother into Little Lord Fauntleroy...'

Mabel grabbed Lettice by the wrist to stop her slapping the woman in the doorway.

'What's the matter? Cat got your tongue?'

'She's shocked that you can read!' Mabel glared. 'Come on, Letty, it's clear you were right.' She dropped the biscuit tin on the floor and both girls marched away.

'Why doesn't she want you to call her Auntie?'

Lettice shrugged. She was now really worried about her father. He wasn't at home… he wasn't saying with family…

'Shall we go to the police station and try to find him there?'

Lettice shook her head. It wasn't a bad idea of Mabel's… but she felt anxious about going to the police station. Deep down she was worried she'd meet R21, the policeman from the march. It wasn't that she thought he would arrest her, hit her or even recognise her. It was just she didn't want to run into him. She didn't want to hear his laugh or see his face again. She was, she realised, scared of him. Like her mother was scared of daddy-long-legs. It was something primal within her. She had her heels set back. She wasn't ready to be thrown.

'Another time perhaps. I've got to get to the dojo.'

***

Lettice was very glad she'd gone to jitsu that night. All the tension she was feeling was put to good use. She punched Miss Lilburn as hard as she could and enjoyed the feeling as her balance was taken and her legs swept away. Every time she hit the mat she wanted another go at feeling weightless. Training with Miss Horvat was also amusing. She was tall but determined to throw Lettice vertically, which meant she had to crouch right down. She winked at Lettice and asked when she was going to grow into a proper sized human. Alas she did so in earshot of Edith, who took the comment personally and made her do push-ups as punishment.

School the next day was bizarre as they were being taught in the same class as the infants. These girls were half Lettice's age and had no concept of personal space. They put their fingers in her hair and poked the bruises on her arms. She found it hard to pay attention to Miss Troxell. The poor teacher had the impossible task of trying to teach a class with more than seventy pupils in it. Some as young as four and some as old as twelve. Unlike Mr Metcalfe she didn't use the cane or the dunce's cap.

'I tell you what,' Miss Troxell said after lunch, 'this afternoon we are going to practise the most important job of any woman.'

Mabel slumped in her chair and whispered to Lettice, 'I can feel myself getting more stupid.'

'Who knows what that is?' asked Miss Troxell.

All the infants put up their hands. Miss Troxell called on them in turn and each offered her thoughts on what she imagined the most important job that their future selves would face was.

'Is it baking, miss?'

'Is it the mangle?'

'Is it cleaning?'

'Is it fetching cooking water?'

This was so depressing, thought Lettice.

'Is it looking after your family?'

'Close,' Miss Troxell said. 'Where do you get a family from?'

'Is it Jesus, miss?'

'In order to have children what do you need?'

'Gin,' said a small girl at the front. 'That's what my mother says.'

'You need a husband,' Miss Troxell said.

Suddenly the lesson became a lot more interesting to the older girls.

'And it is very important that we get the right one. What do we look for in a husband?'

'A Christian,' one girl said.

'Yes. What else?'

Miriam rolled her eyes.

'He comes from a good family.'

'What else?'

'Tall?'

'He has prospects,' Miss Troxell said. 'And how do we get him?'

The class stared blankly at her.

'We look pretty?'

'Yes. But also we show him we like him without letting him think we do.'

'That doesn't even make any sense,' Mabel scoffed.

'Men are hunters; they like to play a game and win their prize. We are the prize. Pretty prizes for good men.'

Mabel swore under her breath. Lettice giggled.

'But no one wants a prize that is being given away for free. Next week is Valentine's Day, which is the perfect time to send a special someone a card. But sending a card is hard. Ideally it should show how little you care for him. The fact that you send him anything at all will let him know you're thinking of him. So you should send him a card saying you're not interested. Even if you're hoping he will court you.'

It seemed to Lettice that being an adult essentially meant lying all the time. Even to someone you wanted to spend the rest of your life with.

'Can't you just buy cards, miss?' Angela asked.

'It's more fun to draw something and write a poem, remembering to disguise your handwriting. Don't forget that if you think he knows who it's from, it's better that he thinks he must win you over, so let him think he's unappealing to you. They call them vinegar valentines… '

'This is too confusing,' Lettice said, staring at her blank piece of paper.

'We don't actually have to send these do we?' asked a small ginger girl.

'I know who I'm going to marry anyway,' said another tiny girl. 'I made him promise me when we were four. I had to hold his head underwater.'

'How are boys supposed to know if you like them or not if you only tell them you don't like them?'

'What have you written?' Mabel asked Lettice.

'Your looking glass calls you an ass, and what it says is true, you ugly swine no valentine, could make me marry you,' Lettice recited.

'You're a genius, Letty,' Mabel said. 'Can you do mine?'

'Don't cheat,' the ginger girl whispered. 'You can't copy off her.'

'I've nothing else to do,' said Lettice. She looked up out of the window at the blue sky. She smiled to herself. 'I'll do one for Miss Troxell.'

'You can't give a valentine to another girl,' the ginger girl said.

'I meant for her to give to her valentine.' Lettice grinned and put pencil to paper.

Ten minutes before the final bell Mr Metcalfe marched into the room. Lettice quickly hid the card she had made for Miss Troxell to give him under the desk so he wouldn't find it.

It was a stupid move. He immediately saw what she had done.

'What's that?' he asked. 'Cabbage!'

'What's going on?' Miss Troxell left the teaching desk and came over.

'Pegg here is hiding something under the desk.'

'Don't be shy,' Miss Troxell said sweetly and turned to Mr Metcalfe. 'We've been making vinegar valentine's cards.'

'Have you now?'

'She probably doesn't want you spying on the contents of her heart.' Miss Troxell smiled.

Lettice wondered if, while Mr Metcalfe was gawping at her, she had time to scrunch up the card in her hand, pretend to cough, put it in her mouth and swallow it.

'You see, I made one,' Miss Troxell said. She showed him a card with a pink rose on it and read the words aloud so that the entire class turned to watch her. 'I'll never say never but your love is fair weather, I need a man to say, "together forever".'

That was awful, thought Lettice.

'That's wonderful.' Mr Metcalfe beamed at her. 'Pegg! Show me.'

Lettice shook her head.

'I've noticed she's nervous about speaking in front of adults,' Miss Troxell said. 'Don't worry, my dear, I'll read it.'

Mabel dug Lettice in the ribs as her eyes followed the impatient swishing of Mr Metcalfe's cane.

'Hand it to your teacher, girl!' he snapped.

Miss Troxell's face fell as she saw the cartoon of the strutting bald rooster that Lettice had scribbled. She read the words underneath.

'You're having a laugh, Mr Metcalfe. Your love may be passionate red, but you're twice my age, are paid a low wage, and there's nothing on top of your head.'

The entire class burst out laughing. The infants were uncontrollable. The only people who didn't crack a smile were Miss Troxell, Mr Metcalfe and Lettice.

第二十六章
NI JŪ GO

It's a strange thing, fear. Once you face it, it dwindles. The more you build it up, trying to avoid it, the worse it gets. Perhaps it was because Lettice had faced so much fear in jiu jitsu that by the time the other children had left the classroom she didn't feel scared any more. She had been hurt plenty. A few strikes of the cane and staring into the angry red face of Mr Metcalfe was all she had to do. She wasn't worried about getting in trouble. It was like when Mr Tani had run at her with the chain. She only had to keep her cool and let whatever happened happen.

'Insolent, disruptive, vulgar... am I missing any adjectives, Cabbage?' Mr Metcalfe swept round her.

Lettice calmly stood still, eyes looking in front, just as Edith had taught her.

'I already caught you thieving once didn't I? You are to have no school dinners for a week and you are to spend your time in the dining hall facing the wall with the dunce's cap on your head.'

Lettice didn't let his words sink in. Now was not the time to be outraged. There was no way of reasoning with Metcalfe while he was so angry anyway. Hopefully he was just blustering; so angry he'd forget what he'd said. She was in the dojo. She must leave her emotions outside. She needed to keep cool.

'Hold out your hands,' Mr Metcalfe barked. Lettice didn't move until he screamed in her ear. She raised her hands up slowly and held them out.

It hurt. She couldn't pretend it didn't. His fourth strike was particularly hard. She didn't look at her hands while he beat her. Her eyes were foggy with tears, but she didn't cry. She didn't try to block out the pain either; she actively noticed it. Thinking about it made it more like an experiment. Yes, that hurts, but where exactly, it felt hot and sharp... there was a dull ache in there too. But mainly it stung. It felt like she was

284

holding something. Now it felt cold, wet and spiky. She was flinching, but forced herself to keep her hands out. She thought for a moment how much more painful this was than falling over on her roller skates in Brighton and how much of a fuss she had made then. How much younger she seemed, only a few months ago.

Her lack of outward reaction put Mr Metcalfe off, and he seemed to hold off the final hit. She saw later why; he had broken the skin on the fourth hit, and he probably didn't want to flick blood everywhere.

He was still threatening her after he told her to leave. There was a ringing in her ears. Her hands throbbed. She held them up to her, like she did when defending herself. This reduced the throbbing. When she got to the classroom door she turned to the red-faced, shaking man and said calmly, 'Please, sir, can you open the door?'

Beetroot-red, more in shame than anger, he opened the door for her and Lettice slipped out.

'Thank you,' she said automatically.

The vein in the side of Metcalfe's head pulsed uncontrollably at her perfect manners.

Outside the door, a group of little faces were waiting, eyes like saucers.

'She's bleeding! Get a hanky,' Alice said.

'That was the best moment of my life, Lettice!' Angela said. 'You are a hero.'

'Yes!' squeaked Joan.

'I've never laughed so hard, ever.' Miriam grinned. 'You gave one of the brats hiccoughs.'

'Does it hurt?' asked Eleanor.

'Of course it hurts,' snapped Mabel. 'Help me tie these.'

'You all right, Lettice?' Alice asked.

'I've been better,' said Lettice. She looked at her bloody bandaged hands. 'Oh no.'

'What?'

'I'll have to miss jitsu tonight.'

***

Missing jitsu was disappointing but Lettice realised it left her with an opportunity. She wasn't expected back home until late. So if she was going to try and find her father, she had the perfect window. She knew where she had to go. The police station. She risked bumping into policeman R21, but Lettice was still full of adrenaline after Metcalfe had disciplined her. She felt she could do anything. As long as it didn't involve gripping something.

It was strange what she remembered about R21 and what she didn't. His rough hand around her arm, engulfing it fully, his thick blue coat with the button missing, his laughter as he threw her mother by her neck, his continued laughter as he brought his police baton down on her. Still, at least she didn't have to face him alone.

'Letty?' Mabel waved her hand in front of Lettice's eyes. 'Shall we go?'

Lettice nodded.

The police station was only a short walk from school. It was very near Westminster and Lettice's flat. They walked up the steps, which were guarded by a young constable who touched his hat to them and opened the door into a lobby. This was empty aside from a few benches and a large heavy desk, behind which sat another policeman with a neat brown beard. He had a young friendly face and a surprisingly plummy accent.

'Hello? Two young ladies? What's all this then?' Lettice noticed that his questions were directed at her, not Mabel, and he looked surprised but not affronted when the girl with the darker skin spoke up.

'We are hoping to contact PC Pegg...' Mabel began.

'Sergeant Pegg,' Lettice corrected.

The policeman raised his eyebrows. 'Jack's on duty, doing the beat. You want me to leave a message for him?'

Just as he said this there was a commotion at the door. In strode Lettice's father in full uniform and blue cape, manhandling a scruffy gentleman towards the desk. Lettice noticed first that her father was using an armlock called *gedan ude garami*, before she spotted that the man had his trousers around his ankles. The younger officer followed from outside, helping Mr Pegg control his catch.

'Ooph!' said the man as Lettice's father pushed him up against the desk.

'Drunk and disorderly,' Mr Pegg said to the policeman behind the desk.

'I'm not disodderly,' the man gurgled, his face pressed against the wood.

'Mr Hamer, so lovely to have you back with us,' the policeman behind the desk said, as he moved his logbook out of the way. He sighed and watched as the stocky man finally gave up wriggling and allowed himself to be pinned down by Mr Pegg.

Mr Pegg hadn't noticed his daughter waiting there. Mr Hamer, however, noticed the girls and took the opportunity to make friends.

'Good evening, miss and miss... misses,' he hiccoughed. 'Please excuse my state of attire but the pigs didn't give me time to...'

Mr Pegg decided to shut him up by tightening the lock on his arm and pushing his face further into the desk. 'OW!'

'Good timing, Jack,' the policeman behind the desk said, pointing with his pen at the two girls who'd backed away against the wall. 'These two were just looking for you.'

'Lettice!' Mr Pegg did a double take. 'Tom, get this man's trousers on, will you?'

The young constable who'd been trying to help Mr Pegg control Mr Hamer's free arm let go and attempted to pull up his stained trousers. This was made harder as Mr Hamer wanted to show the girls his dancing prowess.

'I used to be in music hall,' he said, his face still pressed against the desk while his legs wiggled and jigged about. The younger constable narrowly avoided getting kicked in the face.

'D'ya know this one? I sits among the cabbages and leaks…' he sang.

'What are you doing here?' Mr Pegg shouted over the din.

'I came to find you,' Lettice shouted back. 'When are you coming home?'

'Did your mother put you up to this?'

'You know these girls, sir?' asked the policeman behind the desk.

To Lettice's confusion Mr Pegg paused. She could see he was thinking about denying that he knew them, denying his own daughter. It was clear he was highly embarrassed by her being there.

'Is this your little girl?' asked Mr Hamer, his face still up against the desk. 'She's got a purple scarf on. I hate purple.'

'Shut up,' Mr Pegg replied. 'That is my daughter and she knows better than to interrupt me at work.'

Lettice didn't take the hint. 'When are you coming home?'

'Oooh, problems with the trouble and strife?' Mr Hamer giggled. 'Ow! Me shoulder!'

'The same time I come home every Wednesday. Now go away!' Mr Pegg said angrily.

'But Papa!' Lettice was being led out by Mabel, who recognised the futility of the situation.

'DO AS I SAY!' Mr Pegg snapped. Even Mr Hamer stopped dancing. Mabel dragged Lettice out by the arm. Lettice's face was furious.

'And you can tell your mother not to use you as a pawn in her little games!' he called after her.

第二十七章

NI JŪ ROKU

It was Saturday and Lettice had spent the morning watching Tilly clean the windows with vinegar.

'The smell's making me want fish and chips.'

Tilly grinned. 'We could get some tonight, though I'll still have to go out to do the shopping; it's Sunday tomorrow.'

Just then there was a knock at the door. A young woman stood there rather awkwardly. She was wearing a rather ill-fitting nurse's uniform.

'Ahem. I'm here to announce Guru Bamba Jind Kaur to visit Mrs Florence Pegg,' she said rather shyly. Lettice felt she had met her before but couldn't place her.

Tilly looked perplexed. 'Are you from the church?'

'Er…' the nurse looked blank.

'No!' said a voice from below. 'We are associates of Doctor Raynes.'

There was a pause and a great amount of tinkling as a woman dressed in brightly coloured thick robes with elaborate jewellery bustled up the stairs and pushed past the nurse and Tilly into the flat.

She looked like a living breathing habadasher's shop window. Her eyes were heavily made up and there was a large red spot painted on her forehead.

'I am Bamba. Doctor Bamba Jind Kaur,' she said dramatically, her bracelets and anklets tinkling. She sauntered into the living room. 'I am here to see your patient, Mrs Pegg.'

Lettice felt like giggling. She was almost positive this must be Princess Sophia in disguise, but the make-up and the elaborate costume was so beyond her imagination, and the Indian woman's accent so rich-sounding, that Lettice couldn't be entirely sure.

Tilly hesitated. 'I'm not supposed to allow strangers…' she began.

'I assure you, I am not strange.' The guru handed over a calling card. It was printed on bright pink paper. Tilly took it, dumbfounded. 'Where is the invalid?'

'She is in the bedroom down the hall,' Lettice grinned.

'Nurse! Accompany me!' the guru clapped her hands and headed into the flat.

Tilly turned to Lettice, her vinegar rag still in one hand and the pink card in the other. 'Do you…?'

'No idea.' Lettice shrugged. 'Grandma said that Mama was supposed to see doctors.'

'Can women even be doctors?' Tilly asked perplexed.

They hovered in the hallway outside the room for a few minutes before being ushered away by the nurse, who Lettice suddenly recognised as Boots.

'The prin—' The nurse stopped herself. 'The doctor must have silence for her treatments.'

'What is she doing to her?' Tilly asked, even more concerned.

'Alternative therapies,' said Boots, looking worried.

Lettice and Tilly took it in turn to peek through the keyhole.

Inside they saw Mrs Pegg in her nightclothes, bending forward at the waist, with the guru trying to get her to step back into a sort of strange crawling position.

Lettice saw the window was open and a wind chime had been hung there.

'Grown-ups are weird,' she said.

Tilly nodded. 'You going to be okay? I need to go to the shops.'

Once Tilly had gone, Boots gave the all-clear and the guru emerged from the bedroom and flinched a little when she saw Lettice.

'Sorry. I'm not very good with children.'

'Nor am I!' Lettice agreed, not really realising that Sophia was apologising to her, rather than making a general statement. 'Would you like some tea?'

'Yes, that's kind. I'll take some in for your mother too.'

Lettice pointed at the kitchen table, which had on it, in various arrangements, three different types of biscuit. 'I thought you might like the gingernut ones, because they're spicy.'

'I prefer the shortbread.'

Lettice blinked. 'It is you, isn't it, Princess Sophia?'

'Is it?' Sophia winked and helped herself to a biscuit.

'Where are you princess of?' Lettice made small talk while she waited for the kettle on the stove.

'My father had an empire in the Punjab. He was tricked by the British into giving up his lands. He has a lot of children. But I am the only one who had Queen Victoria as a godmother.'

'So you are Indian?'

'I was born and raised in England. One of my grandparents was German. Another was African. I'm a bit of a mongrel, unlike my dogs.'

'I have a friend who's like you,' Lettice admitted. 'Her parents are white but we all think she's Indian. She looks it but she doesn't ever talk about it.'

Sophia paused and looked at Lettice. 'Maybe our deeds not our looks should define us.'

'So it doesn't matter?'

'Oh, it matters… to society. It matters very much. I am in a unique spot of being both royal and seen as inferior.' She looked sadly out of the window as Lettice placed the teapot on a tray to be taken through. 'Tell me, if you knew exactly who your friend's real parents were, would it change your opinion of her? Would it make her less or more of a person?'

'No…' Lettice said, handing her the tray.

'So maybe you should tell her that.' Princess Sophia took the tray and left.

***

Lettice was in a much better mood over the next few weeks. Her left hand had a large purple cut that healed very slowly. It was a nuisance, as she bled through her favourite gloves, but she made a point of raising her left hand in class whenever Metcalfe asked a question. He looked embarrassed at the scar he'd left and never called on her to answer. Mabel gave her an ointment that her mother had mixed up herself. It was a soothing balm and had a very sweet smell.

Lettice hadn't gone as far as Sophia suggested, but she and Mabel were inseparable in the playground. In contrast, Angela and Alice seemed to have had a falling-out and Eleanor was stuck spending her time passing notes between them and being accused of taking sides. Lettice and Mabel would walk the long way home past the police station to see if they could catch a glimpse of Mr Pegg. He still hadn't come home.

Mrs Pegg, however, was improving. The piano had been tuned and Princess Sophia, or rather Doctor Bamba, would use it to guide not just Mrs Pegg but an entire gaggle of women in doing stretches and breathing exercises every Thursday and Saturday morning. After they were done with their strange stretching they would all cluster around the kitchen table, drinking tea and talking in unconvincing 'code', which seemed to fool Tilly enough not to raise her suspicions.

Aside from her father not coming home, and the threat of finishing school still hanging over her, Lettice was as happy as she had ever been.

That was, until the worst day of her life.

第二十八章
NI JŪ NANA

It started badly. It was the last Friday of March and Lettice was opening an envelope at the kitchen table. She had just woken up and was aching from jiu jitsu the previous night. She knew the note was from her grandmother by the familiar stationery and elegant handwriting.

Reading the letter, Lettice felt her stomach drop. She looked up at Tilly, horrified.

'You told her?'

'Hmm?' Tilly was busy folding bedsheets.

Lettice waved the letter at her. 'You told her about the princess… about the Indian doctor coming to visit?!'

Tilly looked puzzled. 'I have to tell her everything.'

'She said Mama could see doctors!' Lettice was angry.

Tilly looked even more puzzled. 'I tell her when Doctor Raynes comes too…'

Lettice was fuming. She wanted to blame Tilly for her own misunderstanding. She didn't think Tilly had to inform her grandmother about visitors she approved of. She didn't realise Tilly was instructed to write everything down. *All* the coming and goings. She had thought her mother could get away with seeing friends if they disguised them.

'Grandma's coming to visit,' Lettice said woefully. 'This weekend. And she says we are not to let the guru back in until she has met her properly.'

'Oh.' Tilly put down her bedsheet and touched Lettice on the arm. 'It'll be okay.'

'It will not,' Lettice snapped.

She stormed off to school. Mabel, as usual, was oblivious to her friend's mood. She chatted about a thing called Boyle's law and water in pipes and pistons or something. Every Friday they had general assembly. So before morning register they hung up their coats and filed into the school hall. They sat cross-legged on the floor, one boy already in trouble, standing upright with his nose against the wall for trampling in mud. The teachers took their positions on the stage, sitting formally behind the lectern where the headmaster stood. After a few prayers and a few notices the headmaster turned to the row of teachers and invited Mr Metcalfe to speak.

To Lettice's horror, Mr Metcalfe looked gleeful, which usually meant someone was in trouble.

'Thank you, Headmaster. I have a special announcement,' he said. 'I think, however, Miss Barlow would be better to explain what occurred.'

Miss Barlow commanded a lot of respect, even though she had a slight beard. She taught the younger boys and was nicknamed the fairy dogmother, though no one dared call her this to her face.

'As you all know we are preparing for a summer of sporting events. Badminton and folk dancing for the young ladies and tennis, field hockey, cricket, wrestling, rowing and gymnastics for the boys. I was retrieving some cricketing equipment last night…'

It was the second time Lettice felt her stomach drop in one morning.

'And found this.'

It was Lettice's pillowcase with all the secret Whizzpoo newspapers and flyers she'd hidden before

Christmas. After the nativity play she'd totally forgotten about it.

'What is particularly noticeable,' jumped in Mr Metcalfe, 'is that these are the exact same flyers that were used in the nativity incident.'

'The exact same,' agreed Miss Barlow with a straight face. 'Just like the ones that got stuck to the horse manure that fell on Mr Metcalfe's head.'

There were stifled giggles across the hall.

'Silence!' yelled Mr Metcalfe. The boy standing with his nose to the wall was juddering in silent guffaws.

Mr Metcalfe continued, head held high. 'The culprits left other clues.'

The photo! Lettice gulped. Mr Metcalfe held up the photo of her as a baby, her mother laughing, and that handsome man, all posing together. He'd better not rip it, she thought.

'Here we have a picture of a happy family,' Mr Metcalfe snarled. 'I do not recognise the parents but it says quite clearly 1901 and the child here must be no more than two years old…'

Silly Mr Metcalfe, thought Lettice, thinking that the man in the photo was her father.

'Which would make the child in this photo eleven or twelve years of age.'

All the heads turned and looked at the top end of the school.

'I intend first thing on Monday morning to go to the local newspaper and have this photograph printed in the classifieds for all of London to see. When the culprit *is* identified, I will not only expel them immediately but I will make sure that their parents pay for the placement of the advertisement. It will cost more than five pounds.'

A few of the younger children gasped. They were all from families who could only afford third-class dinners.

'If *anyone* knows who did it, they are to make themselves known to me. If you are sitting in this hall, guilt eating away at you, you can save your family some money by confessing now before I contact the newspaper.'

He looked around the hall. No one made a noise.

'Very well. I expect our assembly next week will be short at least one pupil.'

He took out his wallet and carefully placed the photograph of Lettice and her mother inside, folded it back up and put it carefully in his jacket pocket. Patting it, he announced that the assembly was over.

'What are you going to do?' asked Mabel. 'Is it your family in the picture? Why didn't he recognise them?'

'I don't know; my mother is laughing so she's a bit blurry. Her mouth is open.'

'And your father?'

'It's not him. It's some other man.'

'Your real father?'

As Mabel said the words, Lettice didn't really hear them. She had started to say that people would definitely recognise her mother if the photo were printed because she was a member of so many societies and so well connected... Mabel's words made her pause.

'What do you mean, "real father"?'

'You know,' Mabel said, looking worried now, 'the man your mother was with when she had you.'

'No...' Lettice shook her head. Perhaps Mabel was confused. It was Mabel who was adopted, not Lettice. The only odd thing about Lettice's parents was that they were of different classes. But her mother was still her mother and her father was still her father. She didn't know who the man in the photo was. 'Mama was with my father...'

'They met at a Whizzpoo march, you said,' Mabel reasoned softly. 'Letty, the WSPU didn't exist before you were born.'

Lettice felt a little hot. 'No, that's not right...'

But it was right. Everything started to make sense. Was that why Grandma hated Mr Pegg so much? Not just that he wasn't posh but that he was the only man her mother could get? Was this why her father hadn't come home? She remembered her last words to him before he left the house at Christmas. 'When will you stop pretending…' Did he think she knew he wasn't her 'real' father? Did he think she had rejected him? Is that why her aunt refused to let Lettice call her 'Auntie'?

Why did adults lie all the time? Were they really that scared about the world knowing? What had happened to her 'real' father?

She thought about what it would do to her mother if everyone knew she'd had a baby out of wedlock. How it could ruin her standing in society. How marrying her father… her step-father… must have saved her from so much embarrassment. Lettice could see now that there was nothing she could have done to make her mother proud of her. It didn't matter how many friends she made or how well she did at school. Her mother would have been embarrassed to admit she had a child, unless that child had a father. And Jack Pegg *was* her father. He was stupid to think she thought anything different.

But if that picture was printed in the paper, everyone would know that he wasn't her 'real' father… that her mother wasn't respectable. What if that other man saw it… who knew what trouble might be started. Lettice also realised that if her mother appeared in the paper, laughing with her illegitimate child… it was going to make Grandmother livid.

If that photo was printed, Lettice was going to be expelled *and* found out to be an accidental suffragette *and* to come from a disreputable family. It would kill her grandmother. Her father wouldn't come back from the shame. Her mother would be locked in her bedroom forever… and disinherited. Lettice would be sent abroad and never spoken of again…

She couldn't allow that to happen.

'I have to confess,' she said. 'If that picture gets printed in the paper… it would destroy my parents.'

'But you'll be expelled!' Mabel said, sounding horrified.

'At least it will mean I won't have to go to finishing school. I doubt they'll take a mongrel child with "expelled for dumping manure on the teacher" written in their school record.'

Mabel stopped her friend and held her shoulders, trying to shake sense into her. 'If you're expelled you'll have to work. Become a maid or get a factory job! We were going to go to university together!'

'I'm not clever like you…'

'You're really clever!' Mabel was in tears. 'It's not right for you to confess on your own. I helped!'

'It was my idea!' Lettice was annoyed but also thankful that Mabel was so determined to be on her side.

'If you confess, I confess,' Mabel said stubbornly.

Lettice tried to cool down her emotions. She turned her back on Mabel and shut her eyes. She thought of the dojo and she thought of Mr Tani attacking her. She thought, what is the simplest way to get him on the floor… she breathed deep.

'Letty?' Mabel tentatively touched her shoulder

Lettice spun round and grabbed her friend by her arms. Her eyes were bright and slightly insane.

'Mabel, neither of us is going to confess. My parents are not going to be embarrassed. We are not going to be expelled. That photo is not going to be printed. Before Monday morning, I'm going to steal it back!'

第二十九章
NI JŪ HACHI

Lettice knew there was no way to get to Mr Metcalfe's wallet during lessons. They were made to sit in rows, he was always at the front and, unless caning someone, always at arm's length.

Unless caning someone. Oh dear.

If she was going to get close enough to get his wallet she had to risk another beating.

The girls settled down to another tedious afternoon lesson. Lettice however wasn't planning on learning anything. Her aim was to get hold of Mr Metcalfe's wallet.

He'd set them a test on geography. Describe three British ports and their main exports and imports. While the class scribbled silently, Lettice took her pencil and pushed it off her desk. It landed with a clatter. Mr Metcalfe looked up like a cat at a window. She waited for a reaction, but when none came she sighed and went to get the pencil. She wrote the word 'Plymouth' and dropped her pencil again.

'Are your fingers cold? Because I know a sure way to get blood into them,' he said as he held up his cane.

'Sorry, sir.' Lettice picked up the pencil and almost immediately after sitting down, dropped it again.

'Right!' Mr Metcalfe marched over to her. 'Stand up.'

Lettice stood up, but she set her distance, holding her hands out, arms nearly full length in front of her, for him to cane. He stopped in front of her, already stooping to get closer to her level. As he prepared to hit her she drew her hands ever so slightly towards her. Without taking a step, he bent forward a little more. His jacket fell open, and she could see the bulge in his inner pocket, a little further and she could see the wallet inside. She knew how close she had to hold her hands, how off balance he would let himself get before taking a step. It was the same amount of balance she would need to throw him. She wasn't going to throw him though. She was going to let him hit her.

Whack.

The stinging was tremendous, but it was only stinging. He hadn't hit her nearly as hard as when he'd listened to her valentine's poem. His lack of vigour wasn't sympathy. Just before the cane made contact, something had hit him on his right ear. From the front of the classroom, Mabel had targeted her spitball perfectly. She looked curiously back at Mr Metcalfe, who twisted round, touching his damp ear, scanning the twelve or so children, trying to find the guilty face. As he turned away, Lettice's stinging fingers plucked the wallet from his pocket and quickly put her hands behind her back.

Mr Metcalfe coughed and, looking annoyed that no culprit could be easily identified, gave up and took a step towards his desk.

She had his wallet; it was in her hand. Her heart racing, Lettice double-checked her prize as she went to sit down. But her hand still stung from the beating. She dropped the wallet. The clatter made Mr Metcalfe look over.

'Stupid thing.' He walked back, picked up the wallet and replaced it in his jacket.

Lettice wanted to scream. However, if jiu jitsu had taught her anything, it was never to give up.

Grandmother arrived on Friday evening. Fortunately she didn't notice the red cane strike on her granddaughter's palms. She didn't ask about the whereabouts of Mr Pegg either – presumably Tilly had kept her up to date. She presided over the making of dinner, which had made Tilly very nervous, causing her to burn the carrots.

The old woman hardly spoke other than to shout at her daughter, who wasn't eating enough for her liking. Lettice stayed quiet, somewhat pleased that her mother was being forced to get dressed, stay sober and eat normally. Things were icy.

The next day Princess Sophia arrived as usual to take her alternative therapy class in the living room. Tilly and Lettice answered the door, both trying to stop her entering. But Doctor Bamba couldn't be stopped.

Grandmother blocked the hallway with crossed arms. 'Doctor Raynes hasn't mentioned you…'

'The patient has made much progress; we have loosened her *chakras* so that her essence is aligned.' Doctor Bamba swept past the old woman and began to light incense sticks in the living room. 'She can also touch her toes.'

'What good is that to anyone?' Lettice's grandmother snapped.

Princess Sophia whipped round. 'I sense you no longer have a husband...'

Tilly giggled. Lettice didn't get the joke.

'You seem familiar, Doctor...' Lettice's grandmother said.

'My reputation has survived several reincarnations.' Sophia was taking this too far, Lettice thought.

'You're not involved in suffrage?' Lettice's grandmother held her nose as the room filled with a heavy sweet floral musk.

'What's that?' Doctor Bamba said innocently.

'Get out.'

Sophia wasn't used to being addressed like this. She straightened up and glared back at Lettice's grandmother. 'My classes help with...'

'I said, get out.' Lettice's grandmother marched to the door and held it open.

'Typical British Raj,' Sophia said in her English accent. She picked up her bag and stormed out.

Lettice walked calmly back into the living room, collected the silk scarves, finger bells and incense sticks Sophia had scattered and packed them into the trunk under her bed. She quickly left the room; it was

311

full of her grandmother's cases and clothing. She spent the rest of the day with her policeman's notebook in Tilly's room. She needed to come up with a plan fast if she was going to get the photograph back from Mr Metcalfe. But she was stumped.

The next morning Lettice woke up as Tilly was getting dressed.

'You can go back to bed,' Tilly yawned. 'I got to go to the early service then get back here sharpish to prepare lunch.'

The first rays of sunlight on a spring morning were sneaking through the window and hitting the white walls of their bedroom. Lettice flopped back down and, when she finally got up, she found her mother in the kitchen, cracking on with breakfast.

'Are you in trouble with Grandma, Mama?'

'No more than usual.' Mrs Pegg winked. 'I've felt a lot better thanks to my guru.'

Lettice sat down and added as much marmalade as she dared to her porridge.

'Atta girl.'

'I don't know how you can eat so much,' her grandmother said as she walked in. 'Where is that maid of yours?'

'Church,' Lettice said. 'Is she visiting her family afterwards, Mama?'

'She usually does.' Mrs Pegg shrugged. 'Why?'

'So she'll be on her census,' Lettice said, wondering if Tilly's family would be boycotting.

'Yes, yes.' Grandmother sniffed. 'Are you absolutely sure that if I stay here I can't put my Horsham address on? Or even my Brighton one? I mean, I don't want people to think I live here.'

'We did a class at school,' Lettice said absentmindedly. 'You put where you are on the day. Even if that isn't where you usually are.'

Lettice smiled to herself, recalling how embarrassed Mr Metcalfe had been when he had to reveal he was unmarried and a lodger. Wait a second... his address! His home address, where he was now... where the wallet was, with the photo in it. She dropped her spoon.

'Manners, child! Clattering every... Where is she going? WE HAVE CHURCH, YOUNG LADY!'

'I'll meet you there!' Lettice said.

'You will not...'

But Lettice had her hat and coat and was already out of the door.

Unchaperoned, hair half brushed, hat all jaunty, Lettice marched through the streets. London on a

Sunday was very different to other days of the week: all the shops were shut, there were no deliveries, no postmen, and no urgency other than the small figure marching as fast as she could in the direction of Mr Metcalfe's lodgings. Ponsonby Place was not far at all. She picked her way through the people starting to congregate outside church buildings, or walking their dogs through the open gates of garden squares until she came to a street of pleasant town houses.

She rang the bell.

A butler answered the door almost immediately.

'Good morning. Can I help you, miss?' he said, looking confused.

Lettice chose her accent carefully. 'Good morning. I am an acquaintance of Mr Metcalfe. I believe he still lodges here?'

'Ah.' The butler immediately relaxed. 'Of course. He's at church I'm afraid. Can I take a card?'

'Alas, I am late for church myself and was in such a hurry to meet him I quite forgot my purse,' Lettice lied. 'Could you take a message for me?'

The butler looked a little irritated but conceded.

'What is your name, miss?'

'Eliza Troxell. Can you tell him that I'll be in the gardens by the Embankment at dusk?'

314

'I beg your pardon?' The butler looked horrified.

'You know.' Lettice smiled sweetly. 'The ones by Charing Cross.'

'Dusk?'

'Okay, a little after six?'

The butler was bright red at this point. This little harlot was luring a gentlemen into romantic liaisons and she barely looked old enough!

'You're sure it's Mr Metcalfe you want me to relay this to?' he said, slightly disbelieving.

'Oh yes,' Lettice said meekly.

'Couldn't you have written him a telegram?' he said with a disgusted face.

'Because,' she said with her eyes wide and lips pouting, 'if I'd sent him a telegram you wouldn't be able to tell him I did this.'

She winked. Then ran back to meet her mother and grandmother at church.

The butler's mouth hung open.

Lettice hoped it hadn't been too much. She wasn't sure how adults were supposed to flirt. Her only real understanding of it was from what she overheard Isabel and some of the other *jitsuka* saying in the changing rooms.

It was another long day of 'silent Christian contemplation' with Grandma, who sat like a palace guard in the parlour, reading her book of psalms and glaring at Lettice every time she made the slightest movement.

Lunch was roast chicken. This was a rare treat; chicken was expensive and Grandmother oversaw its cooking like a hawk, making poor Tilly quite anxious in the process. Lettice enjoyed watching the maid get told off for being over generous with the salt, for not draining the fat correctly to baste the bird in, for not boiling the cabbage for long enough. It was Tilly's fault that the old woman was here. If she hadn't told her about the special 'doctor' that Lettice had arranged, Grandma would never have found out.

Tilly, as usual, left to see her family before they ate.

'It's a pity she can't stay,' Grandmother said. 'Then we could mark her on the census form. Let everyone know you can afford a servant.'

'No one will see that form,' Mrs Pegg said. 'Only government busybodies.'

'Future generations will,' sniffed the older woman. 'We had the enumerator around on Thursday to the town house. I was in half a mind to throw a lavish party. Recorded forever as a great benefactor. Now future generations will think I'm a penniless widow living with her son-in-law in a slum.'

'You can always go home,' said Lettice curtly.

'Lettice!' Mrs Pegg snapped. 'Apologise.'

'For what?' Lettice said. 'If this flat isn't good enough for Grandma, she should go.'

'I'm paying for this place…'

'No you're not. Grandpa does… it's his money.'

'Lettice, that is enough!' Mrs Pegg sighed. 'I'm sorry, Mother, she is becoming quite a madam.'

Grandmother responded as though Lettice was invisible. 'Her grandfather inherited his money. He spent his days sipping whisky with the good and the great while I bore three of his children, organised his house, threw lavish celebrations, kept his correspondence in order, did his books, raised money for his charities, secured his knighthood, plus many other unpleasant duties a child cannot understand. I sacrificed a lot for that man. I moulded him. Is his money and property not even partly mine?'

'Legally,' Mrs Pegg said, '*you* were his property.'

'We shouldn't fill in the census!' Lettice blurted.

Both women looked at her confused.'Why?'

Lettice paused. She had the words in her head; she had the argument. She just couldn't articulate it. 'Because we don't have a vote.'

'You're eleven years old, darling,' her mother said. 'You wouldn't get to vote even if you were a boy.'

'The poor child is confused. The census has nothing to do with the vote.'

'I know that,' Lettice said, 'but people are clotting it and so should we…'

'Boycotting, not clotting,' Florence corrected.

Lettice was frustrated that either her mother knew exactly what she was talking about and was letting her make a fool of herself or that Sophia hadn't been filling her in on the Whizzpoo activities like she had hoped.

'The penalty is stiff for filling it incorrectly,' Grandmother said.

Lettice resented being talked down to. 'But the principle…'

'It's a very good thing that I've found her a school in France.'

'What?'

'Have you?'

'They will take her in May. In a month she will be out of your hands and you can go about getting that stubborn mule back in the house.'

'If I can get him back…' Mrs Pegg said softly.

'He knows which side his bread is buttered.'

Lettice felt heartbroken. She felt like she was being got rid of. She was in the way of her mother's life. Perhaps she should confess to Mr Metcalfe: tell him that she'd put the poo in the bucket. That it had been an accident... If they expelled her, then maybe the finishing school wouldn't take her. But what would become of her? Would she have to get a job as a servant? Work in a factory? Why couldn't things just go back to the way they were? She was going to miss out on jitsu and for what? So she could balance books on her head and laugh in the correct tone?

'I want to stay in London,' she said.

'Headstrong like your mother.' Grandmother looked at her cooly. 'You will make much better connections in France with significant people rather than scrubbing around in London making friends with factory workers and household servants. You may meet your future husband.'

'But...'

'We are not arguing about it. You will do as we say.'

Lettice closed her eyes for a second. She was being childish. Edith would have told her to focus on the task in hand.

She wanted above all for her mother to be happy. If she went to finishing school, she would be out of the way… giving her mother the space to get her father back home… and making her grandmother happy with the task of finding a rich foreign aristocrat to marry. She couldn't do that if the photo was published in the paper, if the world knew her mother had raised a terrorist and Jack Pegg was not her child's real father. She needed to get that photo back. She needed to give up on childish things like women's rights and jiu jitsu.

She needed to mug Mr Metcalfe.

第三十章

NI JŪ KYŪ

The clock on the mantelpiece chimed five. Lettice had an hour. Her mother and grandmother were sitting knitting in the living room. She snuck into her bedroom. It smelled strongly of her grandmother's perfume. Her furs hung in Lettice's wardrobe. Lettice slid her trunk out from under her bed and immediately got changed into her *gi*. She automatically put her roller skates round her neck and then added every single African beaded necklace she had. She tied Sophia's silk scarves around her head and wrists and put the finger bells on instead of gloves. Every time she moved she jangled a little. Then she looked over to her grandmother's toiletry bag on the dressing table. It smelled even more strongly of her grandmother's perfume, mixed with heavy lavender and menthol. Inside were her tiny jars of tinctures and powders, similar to the ones Lettice's mother cooked up in the kitchen. No obvious make-up however.

Lettice felt slightly silly for imagining her grandmother wore make-up. And guilty for going through her belongings. Until, that was, she saw another bag, a tiny one, hidden underneath a handkerchief. *Yes!* Inside were a small tin of concealer paste, some blusher and what Lettice was after. Red lipstick.

She took the red lipstick and, looking at her bejewelled, scarfed head in the mirror, carefully placed a dot in the middle of her forehead. Smiling, she looked at herself. Pretty unrecognisable… but there was something missing. She paused and then, running over to her trunk again, cracked open her old drawing charcoals.

Back at the mirror she filled in her eyebrows a little and drew a thick black line under each eye. She considered a moustache… but didn't want to over egg the pudding. The exotic, flamboyant, jangling pudding that smelled of incense sticks and promised stories from the Far East. Much more exciting than boring old Lettice.

Lettice hid her bizarre costume under her winter coat, her hat covering her headscarf. Even so the jangling jewellery attracted a few odd looks as she walked through the streets. It was late in the day and the taverns and pubs were full of people as she passed them. The air smelled sweeter than usual as the factories on the south bank of the river had been closed all day. The only noise was the laughter from the pubs, the occasional seagull and the clip clop of horses walking lazily by. Very few motor cars were out. As the pale sky grew slightly darker, and mist from the river slowly crept up into the streets, gas lamps were being lit. Lettice could see her breath illuminated by them, and the occasional rays of the sinking sun as it peaked down side streets.

She glanced over at Trafalgar Square as she marched past. Already some of the Whizzpoo members were gathering. When she joined them later, she would have the photo back. She would find Mabel, Isabel, Edith, Una and Sophia and they would avoid the census. They were going roller skating properly, staying up all night. Her final night of glory before having to deal with reality: her angry grandmother.

When Lettice arrived at the Embankment Gardens there weren't many people about. The ones that were, were headed for Charing Cross or the underground.

There was a slight commotion as a tramp began singing a song near the entrance to the park and some women jumped in shock. Lettice used this distraction to climb over some elderly daffodils and hide herself in a large bush. Old leaves and twigs snapped and fell while little green shoots poked into her, bending slightly as she moved about. The whole thing rustled as she took off her hat and coat. It was cold… the mist was growing thicker. She kept double-checking the silhouettes of people walking about. What if the butler hadn't delivered her message? What if Mr Metcalfe had other plans? What if his feelings for Miss Troxell had changed? What if the butler told him the wrong time?

But wait… there was a familiar figure walking up the hill from the river. He was looking around, checking his pocket watch. He was wearing a thick coat and his best hat, and after a minute or two sat down on a bench near to where Lettice was hiding. Miss Troxell had been the perfect cheese to lure this mouse out of his hidey-hole. There he was, waiting to be captured.

From inside the bush, Lettice started to hum. She passed out the back of it and when she reached the path, she began to sing as loudly as she could. It was a song Mr Tani had taught them. It was something about cherry blossoms falling, and she used it to accompany herself doing a gentle, twirling dance. She tried to copy the way Sophia had moved when she was Doctor Bamba, bending her fingers as far back as they would go and touching the tiny finger bells together to get a chime on the notes.

'*Sakura hira hira, machite ochite,*' she sang, moving down the path towards Mr Metcalfe.

In her jumble of Japanese *gi*, African jewellery, Punjabi make-up and what were actually Chinese scarves, she looked incredibly strange. A few pedestrians jumped out of her way as she spun down the little path towards the bench.

'Mama, is that a boy or a girl?'

'Don't gawp.'

Mr Metcalfe was still looking about hopefully for Miss Troxell.

As Lettice neared his bench, still singing, '*Yureo omoi no take, no darkishi meta…*' she pretended to trip and, with a little leap, she did a diving breakfall ending up at his feet.

'By Jove!' he said, lifting his legs up to avoid a collision.

'Sorry, *sahib,*' Lettice said bowing. The greeting was from the Aladdin pantomime she had seen. She wasn't sure of the accent she had picked; whatever it was, it certainly wasn't accurate. It had twinges of Japanese, Welsh, cockney, Widow Twanky and Doctor Bamba all mashed in together. She bowed deeply to him.

'Not a problem,' he said politely, gingerly putting down his legs and staring at her strange costume.

'I do not wish to intrude,' Lettice said to him, 'but you have a spring aura surrounding you.'

'No thank you.' Mr Metcalfe looked annoyed.

Lettice cocked her head. 'I didn't offer you anything.'

'You're a beggar are you not?' he said curtly. 'I do not want whatever it is you are trying to sell or trick me into giving you.'

'I am a prince,' she said. 'Prince Osoto Gari. I am staying at the Ritz hotel. I do not want your money, Englishman.'

Mr Metcalfe looked embarrassed. 'Oh, well... sorry.'

'I look like a beggar to you?' she said in an insulted tone.

'No... you look different,' he said.

'You look to me, with your spring aura and lovesick eyes, like a little boy,' Lettice said aggressively.

'Are you trying to pick a fight with me?' Mr Metcalfe sputtered. 'How old are you?'

'Younger than forty.'

'How did you know my age?'

Because I pay attention in class, thought Lettice. 'Your essence. I can see your birthday as though it were written on your face.'

'Go on then, when was I born?'

'You're a summer child. Born on the seventh day of the sixth month.'

'I say, that's very impressive. You should do a turn at the music halls. Is that what you do?'

'Another insult.' Lettice spat on the floor. 'I told you I am a prince. This woman you're waiting for better be wearing big boots if your dancing is as clumsy as your manners.'

Mr Metcalfe sat stunned. 'How do you know I'm waiting for a woman? I could be taking a moment here before catching a train.'

'Your aura smells.' Lettice pretended to sniff the air around him. 'Even if this woman turns up, I wouldn't be able to tell if she returns your affection unless…'

Mr Metcalfe's face lit up. It was weird to see his eyes so eager; for a moment she could imagine him as a child. 'Wait, you can tell if she likes me?'

'No,' Lettice said. 'Not unless I meet her. Then I can tell you the day she will marry and the hour she will die.'

Mr Metcalfe looked even more eager. 'Can you wait for her with me? No... that would look strange. No offence.'

'I can tell you more about her if you have something she has made or touched,' Lettice said. 'Do you have a lock of her hair or a letter?'

Mr Metcalfe shook his head.

Lettice wanted to roll her eyes. 'Not a post*card*, or calling *card* or...'

Mr Metcalfe shook his head. Come on, Lettice thought. She knew he had that scrap of valentine's paper in his wallet.

'She has never made you anything? A poem?'

'Oh, wait! Yes!' Mr Metcalfe excitedly took out his wallet.

Lettice's heart pounded, this was it... Mr Metcalfe put the wallet on his knee and opened it up. She could see the corner of the photograph poking out from the inner pocket. He slid a familiar piece of pink card out from under some receipts. 'She made me this!'

He drew out the tiny card with the poem Miss Troxell had written on it. The wallet was still on his knee.

'May I?' Lettice opened up her hands like she was about to receive a weapon on the mat.

He carefully placed it in her hands.

'I will be very careful with it,' she lied. 'I see it means much to you. I wouldn't drop it in this puddle.'

She threw the card towards a large puddle next to the path.

'No!' Mr Metcalfe suddenly stood up, trying to catch it before it hit the muddy water.

The wallet dropped to the floor by the bench. Lettice immediately grabbed it, turned on her heel and ran as fast as she could out of the park. She had it this time – there was no way she was going to let it go.

She heard Mr Metcalfe call out, 'Thief! Stop! Police!' as she raced away. She wasn't scared though. She felt nothing but relief mixed with triumph. That was until, over the clanging of the jewellery on her chest and the scuffling of her boots on the ground, she heard a familiar yet terrifying noise. A policeman's whistle.

She very nearly stopped. The constable's daughter was so used to being a good girl that she nearly surrendered just because they blew a whistle that instructed her to. She couldn't quite believe it. When she had played chase in the playground she was always on the catching team. Well, she hadn't played that in a while as the girls were banned from playing it. Now she was the criminal, fleeing from justice.

As she ran through the park gates, she faced a crowd of people leaving Embankment station, which forced her to turn and run up towards Trafalgar Square. A horse and cart were parked just in front of a gated side lane. Barrels were stood at the back of the cart, blocking the pavement. There was no sign of the workman to whom they belonged; he was probably in the pub. Her instinct was to hide behind them, see if she could lose the policeman, if he was still chasing her. She moved close to the animal and its tired eyes blinked with indifference at the strangely dressed character crouching next to its front hoof.

Lettice looked through the spokes of the cart to see if she were being followed. Legs marched this way and that, workboots, brogues and lace-ups covered by long skirts, Sunday best trousers and... Lettice's heart dropped. She caught sight of a flash of blue trousers. Policeman's trousers. They had slowed and were standing still: obviously their owner was looking around. Lettice froze, wondering if it were better to stay where she was or run for it. The policeman was close. Standing on the other side of the cart. If he didn't spot her, she could just stay here and...

Just as she thought she could hide behind the cart forever, some men spilled out of the nearby pub. As they opened the door one of them looked right at Lettice and pointed and cackled. Evidently the sight of a small creature in a turban couldn't be left unremarked; they called over to her. Lettice paid them no attention, instead she kept sight of the boots from her crouched position. They turned to walk around the cart… she had to run.

Too late!

The policeman moved quickly round the front of the cart and saw her. She looked up, terrified. She recognised him immediately. R21. He blocked the path between the horse and the gate. He was bigger than Lettice remembered. Then again she was crouching down. R21's moustache was stretched in a victorious grin. He lunged at her and instinctively she tucked and did a forward roll between the horse's legs.

'What the…' Lettice heard him exclaim as she immediately sprang up from the other side of the animal and bolted into the crowd. She could hear the men cheer her on as she dashed up the hill.

R21 blew his whistle again. She had to lose him, she had to hide. More policemen would come when they heard that whistle. She was running towards the entrance of Charing Cross station, towards Trafalgar Square. There were always plenty of policemen on patrol there. More than enough to help catch her. She barged past a woman packing up her newsstand, hoping R21 was too bulky to slip through. She dived between couples walking: he would be held up in the crowds and she might yet give him the slip. Just before she reached the top of the hill she took an alleyway on her right.

It was a mistake.

The alleyway was just used for dustbins. Each turn that led off it was a dead end, leading only to the back door of one of the buildings. Lettice sprinted as fast as she could, looking for a route out. The mist had crept into the narrow alley. She was running so fast that she only saw the sheer brick wall a second before she came to the end of the path. To her left there was a line of bins, and steps to the back door of a grand property. She rushed up the steps and banged helplessly on the door. There were lights shining through the windows but no one came. She let out a tiny squeak of despair. And hid behind the nearest bin.

R21 was a big man. He hated running after people. He played football at weekends with some of the lads from the station and always preferred to be in goal for that reason. It was hard for the other team to score because he took up so much space. He'd been walking his beat up from the river past Charing Cross and towards Trafalgar Square when he heard a lady shriek for help.

He sighed and began jogging towards the gardens. He'd just got to the gate when he saw what looked like a cabinet of curiosities from the British Museum jangle past him and sprint up the hill. Seeing Constable Brunt and Sergeant Pegg running down towards the victim (who he realised was not a lady but a squawking gentleman), he blew his whistle and chased the likely culprit.

The suspect was fast, and short, and R21 thought he had lost them until he saw them peel away from the crowds entering Charing Cross station and dart down an alleyway.

He yelled, 'Police! Stop!' but he stopped running. He'd walked this beat for years. He knew the alley well. It was a series of dead ends. He caught his breath while leaning on a railing, watching to make sure his quarry didn't reappear. Then, nonchalantly, he sauntered to the corner. The mist from the river had infiltrated the street. So he listened out for the patter of panicked footsteps and the jingling of jewellery as the suspect ran from alley to alley, in a desperate attempt to find an escape.

Only one way in and out. He would check each alley in turn, and would stop anyone trying to go past him. But there was no one else down here. Only him, and the thief.

第三十一章
SAN JŪ

In Trafalgar Square, Edith looked worried. 'Are you sure she said she'd meet us at half past six?'

'That was always the plan,' Mabel said.

'I don't like the idea of her travelling alone.' Edith shook her head.

'She said she'd convince her mother to come.'

'The speeches are almost over,' Una said. 'We'll be moving to the rink soon.'

'I'm going home,' Edith confessed. 'William and I, we can't afford to pay the fines if they do decide to prosecute.'

'That's understandable,' said Sophia, 'but you could always stay out with us and just say you were at home on the forms. It should be amusing.'

'I'm not sure what I will do yet,' Mabel's mother said.

'We have to wait for Lettice!' Mabel insisted.

'I meant on the census – of course we will wait for your friend.'

'I've already written a little message across mine.' Sophia smiled and petted her dog.

Una blew into her hands and walked over to the group. 'I've just been speaking to some of the organisers; it's getting dark so the plan is to move on. You all look so glum – this is supposed to be a fun event.'

'It's Lettice,' Mabel's mother explained. 'She should have been here nearly an hour ago and she was travelling alone… '

'She's a child. She's probably stuck at home,' Sophia said.

'I tell you what,' Una said, 'I'll grab my horse and go get her. Where does she live again? Those awful red-brick tenements near Pimlico isn't it?'

'I know the way,' Princess Sophia said. 'Boots has the horses over by the art gallery. I'll ride with you. Bring a spare for the girl and her mother. It's time Florry came back to us.'

***

Sergeant Pegg conducted a search of the Embankment Gardens. His constable was taking down Mr Metcalfe's statement. It was all very strange. Witnesses had reported that a singing oriental Welsh acrobat had emerged from the hedges in the middle of the gardens. Curious, he made his way into the thicket. He hadn't expected to find anything, so was pleased to discover a hat and coat neatly folded on the ground. However, his pride at finding a clue dropped faster than the coat he was holding. Inside was a nametag.

'Lettice Pegg'

Jack Pegg dropped the coat. His heart froze. He didn't know what to do. Could it be that Lettice was so out of control she had turned into a mugger? What had those women made her do now? Dare he risk his job and lie to protect her? Or dare he tell the truth and risk his marriage and his daughter?

He covered the coat and hat in some mulch with his boot.

'Nothing in there,' he said to the constable.

'Oh well, Sarge, we have a fair description. Hopefully Tredwell has caught him.'

'Tredwell?' Mr Pegg knew Tredwell all too well. He had to stop him going to town during interviews.

He was useful to get stubborn criminals to talk but they often ended up missing teeth and suffering broken fingers. If he was on his own and captured Lettice… would there be any of his daughter left to punish?

'Which way?'

***

Constable Tredwell grinned. The noise of his quarry had stopped. They were obviously hiding, keeping very still in one of these dark alleys. He whistled as he slowly checked each one. Lettice watched him from the dark shadows of one of the dead ends. There was nowhere to run to. Once he finished checking that alley, he would spot her crouched behind this large bin.

She had recognised him of course. Not only by his size but by the way he strutted. He knew he had won. His chuckle immediately reawoke the day he had thrown her mother to the ground, and how he had picked her up like she was paper.

Lettice shivered. Her necklaces clinked against her roller skates.

'Hello, hello…' The constable turned and peered into the only alley he had left to check. 'Fi fie fo fum… I smell the blood of a hoodlum.'

He swung his police baton and patted it against his gloved hand. Lettice picked up a loose cobblestone.

Pat. Pat. Pat. R21 chuckled again and the noise made Lettice shiver. But she knew about fear now. She knew what she had to do. She stood up and moved out from behind the bin.

'Set your distance for the attack you want…' Edith's voice echoed through her memory. 'Remember, head above shoulders, shoulders above hips. Take as few steps as possible. Take his balance, keep him moving in the same direction as his attack. Don't hit him with your fists, hit him with the floor. You can't hit harder than cobblestones.'

Lettice breathed out. Her calm appearance made him pause.

'Giving yourself up then, eh? Hoping it will save you a beating?'

Lettice raised her hands. She breathed in through her nose. She needed him to run at her. She needed him angry. He was too jaunty and relaxed, too calm. The last thing she wanted was for him to grab her – it was too risky. So she made use of the stone she held in her fist. She imagined he was Winston Churchill in the front row at a nativity play and used her hips to turn and throw the rock at his helmet. Sure enough it did the trick, knocking his helmet so the strap rode up and caught his nose.

She backed down the alley listening to his swearing, trying to get the distance right.

'You cheeky little swine! Right!' He blew his whistle loudly and began to move towards her.

As soon as she saw him move to strike, Lettice darted forward. His attack was unlike anything she had felt in the dojo, even when she threw Mr Tani. When Mr Tani attacked with the intent to really hit, they both still knew what would happen. They both knew that he would end up on the floor in front of her, a big grin on his face. She knew Mr Tani didn't really want to hit her and he expected to fall. When it was Lettice's go to hit someone, she did her mannequin in the shop window pose, allowing her partner to throw her more easily. Subconsciously she would set herself up so that she could land safely. R21 had no idea what was about to happen; all he wanted was to knock her out with one massive blow to her skull.

He had fully committed to his attack. It was lightning-fast but when she met his arm with her cupped hands she barely needed to guide his swing. He was doing most of the work for her, naturally allowing his balance to be taken right over his toes, where it was weakest. She felt his footing go, and his attempt to take a step, but she had placed herself perfectly, her knees slightly bent, her hip stuck out. She felt him tip forward and the flinch of his body as he reached to cling on to something, but it was too late. Lettice committed fully to the throw.

The moment Lettice felt his feet leave the ground, she knew what she was going to do. She instantly dropped to her knee, turning her shoulder into the throw, twisting her hips so that R21 was accelerated on to the cobblestones as fast as Lettice could muster. The policeman let out a squeak. The jewellery Lettice was wearing whacked her in the face as she dropped, her makeshift turban dunked into a puddle by her foot. She didn't throw R21 at the ground – she threw him through the ground. When he hit the road below, his helmet split in two. The whistle in his lips shattered his front teeth. The arm he had reached out with broke as he smashed into the cobbles. He fell like a rag doll; every inch of his large frame hit the cobbles with a colossal whumping crack.

Lettice stood up. She was holding on to his unbroken arm. She took his truncheon out of his hand with twist, dropping it. It fell and bounced off his exposed temple. She felt his arm go limp. He was out like a light.

She walked a couple of steps and looked at the mess of the man she'd conquered. The man who had hurt her mother. The man who had, just because he was following orders, ruined everything. Lying on the floor unconscious in the pale light passing through the windows of the grand buildings, he looked small, childlike even, with the whistle still in his mouth. Rubbing her knee, Lettice bowed to his sprawled body, turned on her heel and ran as fast as she could towards Trafalgar Square and her friends.

第三十二章

SAN JŪ ICHI

Back at Lettice's flat there was a knock at the door. Tilly was sulking and nearly refused to answer it, but the glare of Lettice's grandmother made her get up from her polishing. Stupid job and crazy family. She should have stayed in the workhouse or got a job as a shopgirl. If rents weren't so high…

She was expecting to see a sheepish Lettice. She'd run off for the second time that day. That girl was going to end up married to a no-good docker. It was typical. All these women pretending they were better than Tilly, just because they were born into rich houses and had mothers who never showed any real emotion.

Always obsessed with politeness, formality and folding towels right.

Tilly's mother was much nicer. She might not be able to afford all her children but at least she hugged them. At least she let them play and laugh.

Tilly swung open the door and jumped. Two very well-to-do women handed her their cards.

'Front door was open,' Una said. 'Do announce us.'

Tilly stood and stared at Sophia. 'Aren't you the guru lady?'

Una coughed.

'She looks just like…'

'We do all look alike.' Sophia shook her head and stepped past Tilly into the hallway.

'Lettice?' Mrs Pegg turned the corner in the hall. 'Oh my goodness! Miss Dugdale! Miss Singh! Come through, come through!'

'What darling decorations you have,' Una said before shrieking a little as she bumped into Lettice's grandmother rounding the corner. 'Oh! How do you do?'

'How do you do,' Lettice's grandmother replied.

'Mother, may I introduce to you my good friends, Miss Una Dugdale and Princess Sophia Singh. Ladies, this is my mother, Lady Mary Donahue.'

As her daughter spoke, Grandmother's body changed entirely. Her lips unpursed and her eyes brightened. Addressing the princess she bobbed a curtsey before taking her hand. 'Your Highness, what an honour. I once had the chance to meet your father. He was a very handsome man.'

'He was,' Princess Sophia replied. 'Is your granddaughter here?'

'My what?' Grandmother seemed astonished that these women were here for such an unimportant person.

'She's run away twice today,' Florry said in a worried tone. 'We met her at church earlier but she's been gone over two hours now.'

Sophia and Una looked at each other. 'She was supposed to meet us over an hour ago in Trafalgar Square.'

'For the census protest?'

'You aren't supposed to be communicating or associating with those disgusting women!' Lady Mary spat.

'Women like us?' Una stepped forward. 'Are we not good enough for your family?'

'I didn't mean…' The older woman's cheeks grew pinker. 'You must excuse me, I am well aware of your fine family, Miss Dugdale. Your father Colonel Dugdale is a true gentleman.'

'The WSPU isn't just for mill workers, Lady Mary,' Princess Sophia put in.

'Oh course not, Your Highness,' Grandmother spluttered. 'I didn't mean to imply…'

Sophia looked squarely at her. 'You of all people must realise how preposterous the tax rises are. You pay more tax than a hundred men yet their voices are heard and yours is not. No taxation without representation.'

These words struck a slight chord with Lettice's grandmother, and perhaps because the message came from such a wealthy, important woman, she quite forgot her misgivings. 'No, I see you're right.'

'Good,' said Sophia. 'You can both come along. We've brought horses for you to ride with us.'

'What about Lettice?' Mrs Pegg said, trying to refocus the conversation.

'Well, if she isn't here, she must be somewhere between here and Trafalgar Square.'

'Should we call the police?' said Lettice's grandmother.

Mrs Pegg, Miss Dugdale and Princess Sophia looked at her in disbelief.

'Mother,' Mrs Pegg said, 'you have a lot to learn.'

Tilly shut the door and watched from the living-room window as all four women got on their horses and rode towards Trafalgar Square, their cloaks billowing behind them as they disappeared into the mist.

***

Sergeant Pegg had gone in search of PC Tredwell. He felt sick. It wasn't only the shame of having his daughter arrested that made his guts churn – it was what PC Tredwell was likely to have done to her when he found her. Why on earth had Lettice stolen that man's wallet? Was she involved in a pickpocketing ring? Why had he insisted she go to a normal school? His wife's parents had offered to pay for her to attend a public school. But he had been too proud – it was bad enough they helped pay his rent, so he had refused. Now Lettice attended a local school and it had not only made her slang vulgar but it had exposed her to the criminal classes. He had been too stubborn. This was all his fault.

He had heard a police whistle in the distance and ran up the hill towards Trafalgar Square. Something wasn't right. He'd been expecting to hear further blasts on the whistle to indicate where Tredwell was. Had he arrested her already? Another constable came running down the hill towards him. He came to a halt right by the alleyway that Lettice had run down earlier.

'Where to, guv?'

'You didn't pass Tredwell?'

'Nah, guv,' he said breathlessly. 'The whistles came from down here.'

'I thought they came from up there…' Pegg said.

Both men looked down the alleyway. Had they been paying attention sooner they would have seen a small curiously dressed figure sneak past them moments before. Sergeant Pegg wasn't looking for the assailant, however. He was looking for Lettice and PC Tredwell. So the small person blended into the crowd of people exiting Charing Cross station unnoticed.

Mr Pegg jogged down the alley, checking each dead end. His heart was in his mouth. There was an unconscious figure in the beam of the gas lamp. He immediately assumed that Lettice had been killed by his rough colleague. But it was too large to be Lettice. He couldn't quite believe it – PC Tredwell was unconscious. He looked like a train had hit him.

'Tredwell!'

The man came to after Sergeant Pegg slapped his cheeks.

'Crikey!' he said, attempting to sit up and clutching his left arm in pain.

'What happened?' Mr Pegg looked at the scene. Had... had Lettice done this?

'I followed the young lad down here, sir,' Tredwell said, 'and then met a group of big men. Lots of them. Eight... twelve! I fought them off, but...' he sighed, 'they overwhelmed me.'

Sergeant Pegg hadn't seen a large group of burly men leave the alleyway and it seemed somewhat unlikely that a group as described could get out unnoticed... PC Tredwell was evidently embarrassed that he'd been overcome by such a small unarmed assailant. Pegg couldn't believe it himself.

'Probably the Latvians again,' Mr Pegg said. 'You did well, Tredwell. Stay here and I'll get help.'

He blew his whistle and when the other constable arrived, directed him to help Tredwell as he went off in search of his criminal daughter.

第三十三章
SAN JŪ NI

The procession of women was leaving Trafalgar Square when Lettice finally arrived between the feet of the large black lion. She looked up at its paws and chin. She'd definitely picked the right one – the one looking down Whitehall, closest to the Strand. But she was surrounded by women she didn't know. Some were picking up banners, others hugging their friends goodbye, some were already leaving. They couldn't have left without her? Could they?

'Letty? Is that you?' Mabel's face beamed as she ran towards her friend. 'You look like an idiot!'

Lettice breathed a sigh of relief as Mabel flung her arms round her. She saw Edith and Isabel come over, against the slowly moving tide of women leaving the square.

'Sensei!' she blurted out. 'I did *kata hiza seonagi*. The cosh fell on his head. He's out cold! I did it!'

Edith tried to understand what Lettice was gabbling about. 'You call me Mrs Garrud outside the dojo. Remember?'

Lettice nodded. 'Sorry, sensei… Mrs Garrud.'

'Good. Now that we know that you're safe,' she said, giving Lettice a stern look, 'we will head home. I expect you to boilwash that *gi* before you step foot back in my dojo. You have blood and grime all over it. You have obviously put your training to good use. I'm pleased as punch. I will see you on Tuesday. *Osakini.*'

'*Mata raishu,*' Lettice replied, bowing. She turned to Mabel. 'Is it just us?'

'And Mama.' Mabel pointed at the thin blonde woman with a nervous smile. Given what good friends Mabel and Lettice had become, it was strange that Lettice had never formally met Mabel's mother.

'Mrs Browning, how do you do?' Lettice tried to remember her manners but it was difficult to stay formal when hidden under layers of scarves in a dirty *gi* with charcoal eyeliner streaking down your cheeks.

'I've heard a lot about you.' Mabel's mother smiled and shook Lettice's hand warmly. Lettice noticed she was a good deal older than her own mother, and that the blonde hair that peeked out from under a large smart hat had streaks of silver in it too.

'Una and Sophia went looking for you,' Mabel explained. 'We should wait for them to get back. The others have gone on to the skating rink. Oh, Lettice, we were so worried! Tell me everything that happened!'

Lettice happily obliged.

***

It felt like a lifetime since Florry had been on the back of a horse. It was colder than she remembered and the wind threatened to blow off her hat as she cantered closely behind her mother. It was like a hunt except the quarry wasn't a fox but her own daughter. No bugle or beagles, just Princess Sophia's white dog, who led the way as fast as any greyhound.

The four riders scanned the pavements for signs of Lettice. The beast beneath Florry snorted and accelerated, enjoying his rare chance to stretch his legs... but they turned and slowed their pace as they marched four abreast along Whitehall. It was Sunday evening, and other than a few groups of chattering women heading towards Westminster, the streets were largely empty.

Trotting next to her friends, Florry felt a deep sense of belonging but it was tinged with a furious worry. Where had Lettice gone? Trafalgar Square was only a twenty-minute walk from the flat, if that. She blamed herself. If Jack had been around she was sure Lettice wouldn't have been so much of a handful. She had driven him away and, in turn, her own daughter.

She realised then how much she missed her husband, and it was as she realised this that she heard her mother say, 'Look! It's Jack.'

On the pavement on the other side of the road a lone policeman was jogging back towards Pimlico. Geeing her horse, Florry crossed the central reservation, narrowly avoiding a taxi cab and trotted alongside him.

'Jack!' she yelled, 'Jack!'

***

Jack Pegg's head was full of panic. He needed to find his daughter and make her return the wallet... he just had to find her. Then he would decide what to do. He couldn't arrest her, could he? What had she done to

353

PC Tredwell? Was she perhaps infected with a mutant disease? Was it rabies that had trebled her strength and made her aggressive…? A grown woman, let alone a child, couldn't have broken a man so immense… a man would struggle to defend himself against PC Tredwell. The idea that an eleven-year-old girl could break him… it was impossible. Wasn't it? Had he underestimated women's strength? Their cunning? He was so used to living with women, he missed them now. He missed their stupid gossiping, their sniping at him to help with the domestic chores, their daft politics and gentle hugs…

'Jack!' He looked up. The woman on the horse smiled.

'It's me!'

'Florry! Blimey!' He stopped, out of breath. 'Lettice! We have to find her!'

'She's not at the flat,' Mrs Pegg said. 'We think she's headed for the skating rink.'

'Right,' Mr Pegg wheezed. 'I think I'll commandeer this horse of yours.'

'Oh, will you now?'

Mr Pegg heaved himself on to the back of his wife's horse… It snorted at this, the load increasing considerably. Jack sat behind Florry, taking the reins so that she was cradled in his arms. She took off her hat to help him see. Her hair was only loosely tied, and half of it came undone as she leaned back against him. They didn't look at each other but somehow both knew that they were smiling.

Lettice's grandmother watched from a distance as her daughter melted when her handsome husband kissed the top of her head. Something sentimental stirred in Lady Mary's chest. She shook her head, trying to stop the feeling that made her want to dance, pushing it down into her boots. She geed her horse to follow the princess and Una towards Trafalgar Square. Mr Pegg, feeling whole again, if still incredibly worried, gave his steed a gentle kick and they rode on after the others.

***

'Joe! Here, boy!' Boots had been leaning on the granite stone underneath the large black lion when she saw the dog emerge through the mist. He sprinted up to her. 'Who's a happy lad? You have had a good time... sit then, let's get this lead on yer.'

Lettice knew the others wouldn't be far behind.

'Look! There's Una!' Mabel said, seeing the horse trotting towards them. 'And Sophia!'

Una illegally rode her horse over the square and dismounted in a wonderful jump.

'There she is!'

Princess Sophia followed suit. She too was a skilled horsewoman and the dismount was all the more impressive because of how little she was compared to Una.

'Call off the hunt,' she laughed. 'Are those *my* scarves?'

'Sorry I got them dirty.' Lettice hugged her automatically. She felt Sophia stiffen in shock at such an overly familiar gesture.

The princess however recovered quickly and squeezed her back. 'It's fine – I've got boxes and boxes of the damn things. Every time I do a charity event I get scarves, flowers and bubbly. I should open a shop. You've got blood on you.'

'I'm not hurt…'

Lettice felt a shadow cast over her.

'Where were you?'

It was her grandmother. She was shaking with fury.

'Grandma! I… I can explain.'

'You don't need to explain to me, child,' she snapped. 'Your father is here.'

Lady Mary stepped aside and Lettice looked up at Jack Pegg. He was in his uniform. His eyes were hard to make out under the peak of his helmet. His moustache wasn't smiling. In his hands he held a pair of handcuffs.

'There is a policeman with a broken arm who was left unconscious in an alleyway. Another man is in a park sobbing about a rendezvous which never happened and a thief who stole his wallet. If you were anyone else, Lettice Pegg, these handcuffs would be on you right now and my knee would be in your back.'

'I can explain!' Lettice said. Her voice was wobbling.

'You can lie, we all know that. Messing about in school, joining radical violent movements…'

'That's a bit unfair,' Una whispered, but Sophia told her to be quiet.

'You attacked PC Tredwell,' accused her father.

'He was going to beat me!' Lettice protested. 'I defended myself. He's done it before! He's the one who picked up Mama by the neck and hurt her head.'

'Who helped you?' Mr Pegg looked around the group of women… for a man: someone strong enough to fight PC Tredwell and win.

'No one helped me,' Lettice said. 'I did it myself!'

'Lying again? You wouldn't have a hope in hell of…'

'Want to try?' Lettice was angry. She held up her hands as though she expected him to attack her.

'She's been taking classes in jiu jitsu,' Mrs Pegg confessed. 'I knew about it.'

'Why didn't you stop her?!'

'She seemed happy, like she was finally making friends…' Mrs Pegg looked down at her feet. 'But she'd also get me information about the WSPU… I could stay in touch with everyone.'

'Against my wishes.' Grandmother glared.

'Florry was so unhappy, so cut off,' Una explained.

'This is exactly why I told you to stop seeing those women!' Grandmother pointed at Una and Sophia. 'They're a bad influence.'

'They saved my life! And taught me to save my own,' Lettice said.

'They taught you to steal too?' Mr Pegg asked.

Lettice's mother and grandmother gasped. As did Una and Sophia.

'That was…' Lettice spoke quietly. 'I was going to give it back.'

She took out Mr Metcalfe's wallet. Mr Pegg snatched it from her. He looked livid.

'It looks like the money's still inside,' he said in a voice full of disgust. 'Hopefully I can convince him not to press charges.'

'I have never been more ashamed,' Grandmother said.

'Lettice! How could you? We aren't that hard up for money.' Mrs Pegg had tears in her eyes.

'She didn't take it for the money!' Mabel said. Lettice elbowed her in the ribs. 'Ow! What was that for?'

'Why did she take it then?'

'For the photograph. OW!'

'Photograph?'

'He took it from me. He was going to put it in the paper,' Lettice explained. 'I'm sorry, Mama, it… it fell out of your diary from when I collected your bag.'

'Oh, Lettice…' Mrs Pegg realised immediately what photograph Lettice was talking about.

'I'm sorry I kept it.'

'Let me see.' Mr Pegg held out his hand.

'No, Jack, let her keep it, it's not important.'

'Show me!'

Lettice reluctantly handed over the photograph.

She thought she heard her father's heart break as he looked at it. She knew what he was thinking – that she had kept it because she wanted a picture of her real father. However much Jack Pegg pretended that he was her papa, Lettice's natural curiosity had won, and now she knew the truth.

'I kept it because Mama was smiling,' Lettice explained. 'I didn't know who the man was. I don't care who he is… but I had to get it back off Mr Metcalfe. If people saw it in the paper, I knew what they'd say. That we aren't a real family. But they're wrong. We are.'

Mr Pegg handed the photo back to her.

'Keep it. I'll return this,' he said quietly. 'I'll tell Mr Metcalfe I found it on the street next to PC Tredwell. He'll get credit for stopping the thief.'

'Papa?'

Mr Pegg stopped.

'Yes, Lettice?'

'Will you come home?'

Her father shook his head, 'Not tonight, Lettice.'

Tears filled her eyes. 'I've missed you. Mama's missed you. I want to go home and for it to be like the way it was.'

'None of us are going home tonight.'

Lettice looked confused. 'You're arresting me?'

'No, you daft constable.' A grin started to creep out from under Mr Pegg's moustache. 'We can't go back home because we are protesting against the census, remember? We all have to go and watch you roller skate.'

'I... I still can't roller skate. I've been doing jiu jitsu instead. I never even tried.'

'Excellent. I could do with a laugh!'

The group made their way towards Aldwych skating rink. They skated and laughed, listened to speeches and watched plays. At four in the morning they went for tea in the Gardenia. Lettice sat between her parents sharing a plate of hot crumpets, watching as her grandmother cosied up to Princess Sophia. Mabel, half asleep and dreamy, leaned on her mother's shoulder while Una explained to them both of them how they could devise a way to trick the professors and get Mabel into university.

All was well for that moment. The suffragette, the *jitsuka* and the policeman were at peace. If only for that one night.